Chez Betty

(a novel)

Other books by Kenneth Farmer:

Real Lawyers

Chez Betty

(a novel)

Kenneth Farmer

Three Towers Press
Milwaukee, Wisconsin

Published by Three Towers Press,
an imprint of
HenschelHAUS Publishing, Inc.
www.henschelHAUSbooks.com

ISBN: 978159598-524-8
E-ISBN: 978159598-525-5
Audio: 978159598-600-9
LCCN: 2017935964

Cover photo by the author.
Printed in the United States of America.

To my friends at Chez Betty

Acknowledgments

This work would not have been possible without the tireless efforts and consultation of Parisian avocat Pierre-Xavier Chomiac de Sas, and his wife, Amicie. They were very helpful in educating me on France's criminal justice system, and of course, correcting my French. A special thanks is extended to Pierre's uncle, Alain Peyrot, who introduced me to him and has taught me much about French culture in our many conversations at La Maison Française in Madison, Wisconsin. Also essential in translation were my loyal French friends, Stephane and Tanya Esnault. Finally, I would be remiss if I did not include Thierry, Alexis, and Betty Gigant of Villefranche-Sur-Mer, France. They have not only given me permission to use the name Chez Betty, they have also provided excellent support and guidance in my travels in that area of the world.

1

Alan Newberg pinched his watch between his thumb and forefinger and awaited the exact moment his train from Paris would arrive in Nice. When its wheels turned not an inch farther, causing him to rock back gently in his seat, he noted the precise time: it was 2:55 p.m. Marveling at TGV's punctuality, he smiled and shook his head. Then, with a nervous sigh, he stepped down onto the station platform and commenced the last leg of a journey a nagging inner voice had told him never to begin.

Though he still suffered jet lag from his overnight flight from Chicago, with determination he dragged his canvas roller bag down a set of stairs to a walkway that crossed beneath the tracks. The loud pop of the bag's wheels jumping down each step didn't seem to bother the other passengers, who swarmed around him, jostled his backpack and aggressively chased him like a pack of hungry wolves. They had an agenda, it seemed. He strived to have none.

A crowded escalator took him up to the main part of the station, where he found, amongst a plethora of vending machines, concession stands, and information booths, a navy-blue contraption labeled *La Billetterie Régionale*. The machine presented an endless and confusing array of screens: number of adults and children, starting location, ticket class, and date of travel, to name a few. He negotiated them efficiently, however, until he came to the last one: *aller-simple* or *aller-retour*. After a moment of hesitation, he snapped the button for *aller-simple* and a one-way ticket to his final destination of Villefranche-Sur-Mer popped out.

The ticket was the size of a business card, a seemingly inconsequential piece of paper. It had all the necessary information, but one part stood out, a French phrase with which he was not yet familiar—*à composter.* He asked for an explanation from a train company employee, and the man told him that he would have to validate the pass at one of several odd-looking yellow machines that stood sentry-like at the entrance to the tracks. At first Alan couldn't get the one he chose to work, but after four tries, he heard it click. Without examining what had been printed or otherwise giving the process much more thought, he stuffed the tiny ticket inside the zippered left breast pocket of his tan Eisenhower-style jacket.

From a schedule board displayed on a wall by an overhead projector he noted his train would leave in three minutes. He rushed down one set of stairs and up another to *Voie D*, where he found a boxy-looking chain of cars that seemed antiquated in comparison to the modern aerodynamic bullet train on which he had arrived. Over the public address system he heard three sing-song musical tones followed by a female-automaton voice, France's version of Siri. Although it declared a message in French far too rapid for his complete comprehension, he did understand the last part very well: *attention au départ.* For a split second he wondered if the words were meant for him, but quickly discarded the notion as a figment of his paranoid imagination.

His confidence now reinvigorated, he hoisted his luggage onto the train and installed himself on a flop-down seat near the entrance. Through the still-open sliding doors his eye caught the attention of a woman clutching the hand of a girl of perhaps five years. The woman, whom he assumed was the child's mother, stood helplessly on the platform, while ominously eyeing her valise. So he exited the train and with a gentleman's nod lifted the suitcase inside. She in turn grasped the girl by the armpits and swung her aboard, stating one word: *merci.*

The woman appeared to be in her thirties, a good ten years younger than he. She was French thin and had dark brown hair, several strands of which crossed her face. While using one hand to whisk them aside, she used the other to guide her child to the last remaining seat. Though attractive, the woman had a harried look that suggested no bright star had ever shined upon her, except of course that which must have been provided by her beautiful daughter.

The girl, on the other hand, as yet unblemished by the vicissitudes of life, sported a blissful grin. Her locks, slightly lighter than her mother's, were combed back into a neat ponytail. She wore an orange-ruffle dress and a thin matching sweater. Her feet, covered in white socks and little-girl tennis shoes, could not reach the floor and dangled innocently above it.

Alan felt a wave of infatuation, but did his best to put a lid on it. Even though he had been working on being more spontaneous and less analytical, he did not believe in the unrealistic notion of love at first sight. More than likely the woman would rebuff him anyway, causing the train ride to become embarrassingly uncomfortable. Nonetheless he offered her his seat, and she returned the favor with a curt smile.

Suddenly the doors slammed shut and the train jolted into a smooth glide through a mountainside tunnel. The girl babbled in French at what seemed like breakneck speed. She posed various questions to her mother, to which she responded, *"Non,"* and just like her American counterpart, the child repeatedly protested, *"Mais Maman!"*

Fascinated by this interaction, Alan dug into his basic command of the language that he had obtained by studying instructional manuals and listening to compact discs in his car back home. He had learned the nuances of its grammar, the basic pleasantries and enough vocabulary and phrases to function at hotels and restaurants. But he was far from fluent. Intimidated by the prospect of asking his first question of a native speaker, he sought an easy one to pose, and after several minutes mustered the courage to spit it out: *"Quelle heure est-il, madame?"*

Startled by this abrupt overture, the woman glared at his multifunction watch, which was equipped with every bell and whistle imaginable. She turned her face away in disgust, apparently offended by what she perceived to be a come-on line or a ruse to steal something. But the young girl beamed, proudly displaying her pink-banded Mickey Mouse watch, and responded in a small reedy voice: *"Il est quinze heures quinze, monsieur."*

Alan noted the child's perfect use of the liaison that blended "il" and "est" into one word (ee-lay) as well her precise pronunciation of the phrase *quinze heures quinze* (can-zur-canz). *A quarter past three*, he translated inwardly. Only the most advanced classes in America taught such phonetics, so at first he believed her to be a little genius. Then he realized his perception had been jaded by his frame of reference—she was French, and he was in France.

The train made it to Villefranche-Sur-Mer in just six minutes. As the mother and daughter departed in a different direction, he smiled politely at the girl and thanked her for giving him the time. *"De rien,"* she replied, projecting the letter *r* from the back of her throat. It was nothing, she had said. He sensed otherwise, but knew not why.

* * *

A conductor wearing a dark blue uniform with red trim and a hat having a shiny black visor stuck his head out the train and looked both ways. Having assured himself no passengers were still getting on or off, he whistled once to signal a departure, and a dozen or so cars slowly passed Alan one by one.

The station stood in sharp contrast to the hustle and bustle of Nice-Ville. It had no passengers save a young couple, who sat on a bench in a bus-stop-like shelter on the other side of the tracks. Its classic-looking terminal had peach walls and mint-green doors and offered a glimpse into the past, though a dilapidated warehouse next to it, drenched in tagger art, brought things back into the present. Behind these structures, a steep, rocky hillside, densely packed with ornate villas and pastel-colored apartments, towered above in a scene that only an artist could imagine. As the lonely sound of the locomotive's air horn trumpeted in the distance, he whispered to himself, "I'm in deep cover now."

In the States, Alan had rented an apartment in the small town from a Norwegian named Rolf Swenson, a petroleum engineer who dabbled in real estate. E-mail exchanges established the man's credibility, so he took the risk of wiring him three month's advance rent, or 6,000 euros. That morning Rolf had told him by phone he could pick up the keys at Côte d'Azur Immobilier, a local realty office. Hence, his first task was to find the business, get the apartment and settle in.

He trudged up a hill from the station, and before he got too far, he stopped a woman and asked for directions. She did not speak English, so he showed her a slip of paper with the name and address that he sought, and she pointed down an asphalt walkway no wider than an alley that led into town.

As he moved along the path, he savored a view of the Mediterranean Sea on his left, turquoise blue by virtue of the water's reflection of a cloudless day. A mile-long cape protected a mammoth cove and formed a natural harbor for fishing boats and yachts that dotted it like stars on a clear night sky. On his right, a jagged escarpment, out of which the village had been cut hundreds of years before, provided zero tolerance for errant movement. Eventually the route became bordered on both sides by an unbroken chain of medieval-looking four-story buildings that had weathered wooden front doors, windows flanked by large colorful shutters, and balconies from which sheets and recently washed clothing waved gently in the March breeze.

Several hundred feet down the narrow passage, he noticed a small fountain with a brass lion head at its center. Water trickled from the lion's mouth into a pool in front of it, making a soothing, percolating sound, evocative of introspection. A plaque, hanging from a semi-circular stone wall behind the pool, read Place du Conseil. He knew the words meant place of advice or counsel. Though an extremely rational man, unbelieving in the ethereal, he accepted the invitation of a single bench next to the shrine. Setting down his cumbersome suitcase and backpack, he reflected on what had brought him four thousand miles from home.

In the months before his departure, he had left a twenty-year marriage in spirit, though his wife, Sara Elliot-Newberg, was the one who had filed for divorce. With the legal proceedings still pending, somewhat out of the blue, he decided to go to France. This uncharacteristically impulsive detour caused many who knew him to suggest he had lost his mind. But he believed he had found it, or at least the will to discover it.

As an attorney, he did title searches and conducted real estate transactions at his own company. While this might have been viewed as underemployment, he made good money as a result of low interest rates that induced plenty of refinance opportunities before and after the mortgage crisis. His job was quite suited to his personality—precise, predictable and organized. Mechanic's liens, lis pendens, mortgage releases, federally required loan disclosures, warranty and quit-claim deeds, and detailed closing statements excited him, though most lawyers found such technicality boring. He had never practiced inside a courtroom, and this suited him just fine.

The rest of his life was equally nondescript. He and Sara lived in an upscale multi-story home with a two-and-a-half-car garage in Schaumberg, Illinois, a quite ordinary northwestern suburb of Chicago. She was an accountant at a successful firm and provided steady income when closings were lean. The two had very similarly uninspired constitutions and seemed to get along well for most of their marriage. They both had an affinity for classical music, enjoyed going to the opera, frequented book clubs, played Scrabble and Trivial Pursuit, and incessantly corrected each other's grammar. Their impeccably organized household left nothing to chance; the freezer held alphabetized Lean Cuisines, and their garage housed well organized tools and lawn equipment. Even in winter it had no grease or dirt on its painted floor.

Despite their outward congruence, the couple had no anchor in this rather staid existence unfortunately. Early in their marriage, they had decided not to have children even though both were physically capable of it. Sara had felt kids would disrupt her career and elected to defer this challenge until later, and he was hardly in a position to object given his own professional obligations. By the time the subject came up again, and she heard her clock ticking, they had drifted apart, and their lives had evolved into a tomb wrapped inside an economic relationship. He did his thing and she hers, and no longer did they spend time together.

Meanwhile, he had begun to change, so Sara asked him to see a shrink, ostensibly out of concern for his welfare. The impetus for her request was a series of events she found particularly distasteful. For one thing, he had purchased without her consultation or consent a blue Lexus convertible, a bold deviation from his ten-year-old black Honda Accord that he kept in immaculate condition, always washing it on Saturdays and religiously getting oil changes every 5,000 miles. He had also gotten an earring and altered his hair, growing out his close-cropped helmet into a cool-guy messy look. His white Perry Ellis shirts and conservative suits that he had worn at work morphed into casual Columbia button-downs and blue jeans. At one point he had even told Sara that he wanted to be called Al, but she ignored the request, dismissing it as further evidence of his insanity.

The shock of the divorce petition, filed after Alan had refused to participate in counselling, initially inspired him to suspend his rebellion and retreat into the security of the Ben Franklin-like schedule that had heretofore dominated his life. It consisted of the following:

6:00 Rise
6:15 Thirty-minute jog
6:45 Shower and dress
7:15 Breakfast (always a protein shake)
8:00 Arrive at work
8:15 Title searches and paperwork for closings
12:00 Lunch (a tuna sandwich and a latté)
1:00 Closings

5:00 Depart work
5:30 Arrive home
6:00 Dinner
6:30 Read/Watch TV
10:00 Bed

One day, while he was doing his morning jog in a park near the apartment he had acquired at the beginning of the divorce proceedings, he experienced what felt like an epiphany. He observed in the park something he had not seen the day before: a bush blooming with white and purple flowers. He could not name the kind, but the idea of their unexpected appearance encouraged a resurgence of a personal renaissance the divorce papers had temporarily arrested. Thus he resumed his pursuit, if not hunger, for fulfillment undefined.

To be sure, he could have resisted this life-altering force, but chose not to. At forty-two, his own clock had started ticking, and he had begun to focus on death, to him a permanent nothingness that made eternal darkness look good. The only way to make sense of this inevitability would be to open up his life to places he'd never been, talents he didn't believe he possessed, and discoveries his methodized mind had thus far blocked out. If he succeeded even partially in this endeavor, the sting of life's meaninglessness and death's certainty would not be so bad.

As time progressed, he searched the Internet for outlets for his new beginning. Travel attracted him the most, and in particular, to France. So he studied its language. At first the exacting grammar came as second nature to him, his brain being so well structured. But after a while, he savored its beauty and poetry, which motivated his interest all the more and ratified his changed focus.

During the course of his investigation of the country, he came across Villefranche-sur-Mer, or Villefranche for short. The photos of the classic coastal town mesmerized him, not to mention its beautiful weather. His divorce was dragging on due to backed-up court dockets, and so without informing his wife or seeking her permission to spend marital funds on an extended vacation in the Riviera, he closed his title company and just plain left, shocking all who knew him.

A seagull's loud cackle awoke him from his daydream. He felt as though the bird were laughing at him, or perhaps with him. Place du Conseil had afforded him the opportunity to reflect but not the benefit of its wisdom. He washed his face and hands in the shrine's pool and continued his search for the real estate agency and the keys to the apartment, climbing endless stone stairwells that connected to a spaghetti of streets.

Eventually, he entered a mysterious underground passage marked by a barely visible sign that read La Rue Obscure. The passage extended a considerable distance and curved in such a way as to block a view of its end. Nevertheless, he slowly ambled down the bedrock floor that had been grooved and polished by centuries of human traffic and the relentless attrition of time. He saw nobody and heard only the echo of his footsteps and the occasional dripping of groundwater from above.

For a moment, he wondered if he would find his way out and become forever lost in the passage's dark recesses. But after a while, he came to an intersection, dimly lit in yellow by a lantern-styled fixture hanging from the ceiling. The intersection offered two more passages, one going left and the other forward. He chose the one on the left, which led him outside, where he found the storefront of Côte D'Azur Immobilier.

"I've rented an apartment from your client, Mr. Rolf Swenson, and I'm supposed to get my keys here," Alan declared to the man inside, who himself must have just arrived, since he appeared a bit disorganized and had yet to turn on the lights.

The man, whom Alan assumed was a French real estate agent, unlocked a filing cabinet and retrieved some manila folders, where-upon he scoured various lists of apartments and sheets of names. After a few minutes he scratched his head and tossed the records onto his desk in resignation. "I unable to accommodate you—no paperwork," he said.

"You have nothing about my rental?"

The agent muttered defensively in French and replied, "Pardon, monsieur, I do not understand your word 'rental.'"

Alan consulted the translation app on his iPhone. "*La location* is the term, I believe."

"Ohhh," the agent exclaimed. "*Mais non, monsieur, elle n'existe pas.*"

Alan felt jet lag ganging up on him. "*Regardez*," he snapped. "This is an email from Rolf Swenson that documents our under-standing." He slapped a copy of the communication on the desk and tapped his finger on the part that supported his position.

The agent slowly read the email and lowered his unibrow-shaded eyes sheepishly. "I sorry, sir, but I have no paperwork and without paperwork you are, how you say in English, shit out of luck."

"But I paid 6,000 euros for this place!"

"There are other immobilers in Villefranche," the agent quickly reassured. "Perhaps there is some mistake, and one of them has your '*location.*'"

"No, Rolf said Côte d'Azur Immobilier—you're Côte d'Azur Immobilier, *n'est-ce pas?*"

"You say, *'n'est-ce pas.'* You want English or French now?"

The comeback did not impress. "What I want is satisfaction," Alan hollered, slamming his fist on the desk. "I've been on a plane seven and a half hours and a train five and a half." He paused and took a breath. He knew he was behaving like the classic ugly American; so he reined in his rage. He should relish the challenge of the unexpected as part of his new persona instead of further making a fool of himself.

"This man *Norvégien,* oui?"

Sighing, Alan conceded the fact.

"I know him—I tell you where he live—you fix this *merde* with him."

"How do I get there?"

"His apartment near church. Street, hmm, rue d'Église, *je crois.*"

The agent gave him the directions, telling him to watch for a large yellow bell tower, having a clock. "You find Rolf there, okay?"

"Oh, I will," Alan emphasized. "This is a matter of 6,000 euros, and I'm going to get to the bottom of this one way or another."

"Bottom of this? What you mean?"

"You know, get this worked out, hell or high water."

"Hell or high water?"

"Let's just say that he'll be made accountable."

"Ah, *vengeance,*" the agent cried out.

"Something like that," Alan responded. He strode from the office, determined not to worry, for worry in his new world was not supposed to be part of the equation.

* * *

On the way to the Norwegian's home, Alan descended a dark, narrow walkway, shadowed from the late day sun by a seamless array of old buildings and restaurant terraces. The path appeared to end at a massive stone wall, but at the last second snaked to the right. The wall constituted one side of an old church and was speckled by small holes that had been cut out by friars in the Middle Ages for nesting seagulls. In modern times, according to his exhaustive research of the area, the holes were covered by wire mesh to prevent entry of the birds and unpleasant streaks of excrement that such creatures would inevitably produce.

As he rounded the corner, the mottled stonework blended into yellow-painted plaster that rose to the top of a square bell tower. Each face of the tower had a large clock whose five- to six-foot hands jumped minute by minute toward four o'clock. At the final jerk of the big hand, the first of four resonating metallic clangs of the bell sent a chill down his spine, for their clarion call seemed to be omniscient and a witness to all that had transpired before that point.

Past the church Alan found a courtyard that cloistered a two-story apartment structure. Oddly enough the small quadrangle was cordoned off by crime-scene tape marked, *"Ligne de la Police—Ne Traversez Pas."* Numerous French police criminalists dressed in white booties, hair nets, and latex gloves carefully stepped about the ground and inspected its grey-slate tiles for clues. Amidst a group of red triangular-shaped evidence markers near the doorstep of the building, a motionless lumpy mass lay covered by a piece of black plastic. Outside the yellow tape, several onlookers gaped at the grim spectacle.

One of them, a hunchbacked old lady, stooped her small, feeble frame forward onto a dark-colored cane that she grasped for support. She looked as if she were dressed for mass, wearing a formal midnight-blue suit and a matching pillbox hat. When he got closer, he noticed her eyes, recessed and almost entirely white. She

was in fact blind, though there was something about her in a figura-
tive sense that suggested she could see very well. Since she may
have learned the particulars, Alan decided to query her. "*Qu'est-ce
qui s'est passé?*" he asked.

"*Il y a eu un meurtre,*" she responded ruefully. She held up her
thumb and forefinger in the universal sign for a gun.

A murder? The town seemed too small, too innocent, and too
beautiful for such a thing, he thought. Yet the tarp-covered body
confirmed the woman's words.

Alan asked his third French question of the day: "*Qui était-ce?*"

"*Rolf Swenson—le Norvégien,*" the blind lady answered. She
spoke of the man as though he were a unique figure in the town,
with whom everyone was familiar.

Recognizing the name, Alan blurted, "He's the one who ripped
me off for 6,000 euros!" So loud and forceful was his reaction, the
onlookers snapped their heads around and looked at him aghast, he
having disrupted their mournful gaze.

Within seconds, someone gripped his shoulder and asked in a
heavy French accent, "Did you know Rolf well?"

"Apparently, not well enough," Alan replied as he spun around.
Before him stood a man in his fifties, who sported a closely-
trimmed mustache, a dark fedora, and a grey blazer, worn from
years of use and wrinkled from neglect. He produced a card that
said, "Lieutenant Gustave Esnault, Gendarmerie Nationale."

"Ez-nalt, is it?"

"The correct pronunciation is, 'Ay-no,' monsieur."

"So you're a cop?"

Esnault smiled tight-lipped and replied: "In a manner of speaking."

"Look, I just arrived by train and have nothing to do with this—"

"Did Rolf owe you money?"

His lips quivering, Alan replied, "I rented an apartment from the man, paid the money, but got nothing in return."

"How unkind," the lieutenant said, his voice oozing with sarcasm.

"Are you making fun of me?"

"No no, quite the contrary," Esnault insisted. "I'm concerned about your plight. Please, tell me more. I imagine this development has placed you in a position quite untoward."

"What are you implying?"

"Simply that you have lost a great deal of money—"

"And what? That this would give me a motive for murder?"

"Your words, not mine, monsieur."

"So what do you want from me?"

As though the lieutenant were chiding an errant child, he said, "For one thing: the truth. For another: you must accompany me to an adjunct office of *la gendarmerie* along the Basse Corniche for a few more questions."

They made their way to a white Citroën having blue striping and the typical squad-car light package atop its roof. The lieutenant permitted him to sit in the front seat, not handcuffed or restrained in any way. He claimed he had extended this favor, because he didn't think Alan would be violent or a risk to flee. They drove to a brown-brick structure along the main vehicular drag of Ville-franche. The building had three flags draped over its entrance, one of which was the familiar tricolor of the Republic of France.

"Your card says you work for Gendarmerie Nationale. Is that like the FBI or something?" Alan asked.

"We are a branch of the French military that conducts police investigations of serious offenses committed in the countryside or in small villages. Our activities sometimes involve interrogation."

"Interrogation?" The word frightened Alan and put him even more on the defensive. "You have arrested me without any basis and now you want to interrogate me?"

"Technically it is an identity check," the lieutenant said. "Our law permits the detention of foreigners for up to four hours to determine who they are and the propriety of their presence in our country. Normally this occurs at transportation centers, but in some cases elsewhere. You mentioned you had come here by train and obviously, eh-hem, are not French."

"So now you plan to take advantage of this housekeeping procedure and question me."

"Quite naturally."

The lieutenant led Alan into a small office, where he hung his fedora and blazer on a rack in the corner. After he readied himself for the encounter by rolling up his sleeves and stretching out his arms, he took a place behind a desk cluttered with paperwork and pointed to a single chair in front of it. "Please, have a seat."

Alan complied and posed a simple question: "Do I need a lawyer?"

Esnault ignored him. Instead he fingered out some tobacco from a pouch that he had retrieved from his blazer and meticulously organized it into a neat pile on the desk. "Smoke?" he asked.

Alan declined and repeated his question.

As the detective calmly rolled a cigarette, he finally answered in a noticeably blasé voice: "You are entitled to inform a family member of your situation or anyone else of your choosing."

"Would such a person include a lawyer?"

"Why yes, though the term 'person' might be a bit generous. By the way do you have an avocat?"

"Not in France."

"As I thought," Esnault said. "Of course, you wouldn't need one for walking around here, unless you had something else in mind." He lit his cigarette and blew a smoke ring that rose upward like a halo in search of a saint. "Are you sure you don't want one of these?"

Alan shook his head and asked for the name of a local attorney with whom he could consult. But the French cop shifted back from his desk as though something vile had crawled across it and provided a sanctimonious reply: "That, sir, would be improper."

"Fine, I will call my American lawyer instead."

"An expert on French criminal justice, I trust?"

Conceding the lieutenant's point, Alan sighed and got out his iPhone and began scouring the local listings for an attorney. This constituted a laborious and frustrating process, for he did not understand the phone system and struggled with the correct terminology.

For a while Esnault seemed amused by such efforts, but as time went on, he decided to expedite things and offer some friendly advice: "Obtaining an avocat could take several hours, and in order to get you on your way as soon as possible, it might be more efficient to answer a few innocuous questions and forego such formality."

"All right, you win. Let's get this cleared up."

The lieutenant smiled approval. "Your passport, may I see it?"

Alan handed it to the cop, and he paged to his photograph, which had been taken long before his personality reversal and didn't reflect his many changes in appearance.

"You look much younger in person," Esnault complimented.

"How I look has nothing to do with this."

"You seem to have some animosity toward me, but I can assure you that I'm on your side as much as that of the République."

"I'm not convinced of that."

"I can tell."

"All I know is I'm not free to leave, which means I'm in custody," Alan said. "By this point in America the police would have read me my rights."

Esnault laughed, openly mocking the sophomoric irrelevancy. "As you no doubt have already observed, monsieur, your rights in France are very different."

The remark plainly summarized Alan's dilemma. Nothing he had learned about the law in his own country would assist him. "What if I refuse to answer questions?" he asked.

"I will report your lack of cooperation to the *procureur,* and he might view your unexplained recalcitrance as evidence you are hiding something," Esnault responded. He began pacing the floor with his hands clasped behind his back in a manner reminiscent of Sherlock Holmes. "Now, tell me why you were you at the murder scene again?"

"To find Rolf Swenson and get my money back."

The lieutenant pursed his lips and nodded slowly as he absorbed the response. Before he could comment further the phone rang, and he picked up the receiver. "*Oui.*" A pause ensued, then "*Oui*" again, followed by another pause and another "*Oui.*" Esnault hung up and resumed his pacing. "It seems you had a conversation with a real estate agent at a business called Côte d'Azur Immobilier. Can you tell me about that conversation?"

"The man there was supposed to have the key to the apartment, but he had no documents reflecting my agreement with Rolf."

"And what was your reaction upon being so informed?"

Alan hesitated, for Esnault seemed to know the answer before it came out of his mouth. "I was angry. Wouldn't you be?"

"He claims that you threatened revenge against the victim over the rent money."

"I never said anything about revenge," Alan replied, half laughing.

Esnault's face went stone cold and expressionless. "You said you wanted to get to the bottom of the matter—hell or high water."

"Those are English clichés that he didn't understand."

"He suggests otherwise."

"Well, he's wrong."

Esnault canted a disbelieving eye, at which point Alan began chattering in an attempt to justify himself like a teenager who had come home late with the family car. Plainly he had forgotten the most elementary advice any neophyte lawyer in the U.S. would have given him: shut the hell up when dealing with the cops. Esnault, on the other hand, said little, often maintaining uncomfortable dead air at every moment his willing subject paused for breath.

"I left the real estate office a few minutes before I got to the scene at 4 p.m., and the police were already there," Alan said. "The murder had to have happened some time before I spoke with the agent. However he has spun my words, they could not have been the motive for a crime that had already occurred before my arrival at his office. This is just a big misunderstanding!"

"Uh-huh."

The "uh-huh" offered little reassurance, so Alan continued his nervous babble. "Before I went to the real estate office, I had been on a train from Nice to Villefranche, and before that another train from Paris to Nice, and it arrived just before 3 p.m. When the murder occurred, I was still—"

"You seem very familiar with the time of the victim's death," the lieutenant interrupted. "How, pray tell, do you know when Rolf was killed? It could have been early in the afternoon or even this morning."

"I just assumed it was an hour or so before I got there."

Esnault responded with yet another "uh-huh."

"Before I was in Paris, I was on an overseas flight from the United States. Before that I lived a normal existence there." This statement was a bit of a stretch, but Alan went with it, figuring the cop would never learn about his troubles back home. "Even if Rolf were shot weeks ago, I couldn't have done it," he said.

"Shot?"

Alan straightened in his chair. "A-an onlooker told me that."

"Indeed, monsieur. Indeed."

"You're wasting your time."

"We can only hope."

"Why don't you let me go?"

"It has never been my intention to keep you."

"But I thought I was under arrest."

"As I explained, monsieur, this is only an identity check."

"Yeah, up to four hours to check my identity, right?"

"It's the law."

"And I suppose that makes it all good."

"Yes, as a matter of fact, it does. May I ask your profession by the way?"

"I-I'm a lawyer."

The lieutenant laughed again, this time more derisively. "Pardon monsieur, but I find the irony most entertaining."

All Alan could do was grunt.

"Before you leave, I do have one request," the cop continued.

"What's that?"

"Would you mind giving me that jacket?"

The wording of the question seemed deliberately designed to conceal the fact Alan would be giving formal legal permission to take his personal property. Figuring he had no choice, however, he removed the jacket and handed it to the lieutenant, who in turn gave it to another cop having a spastic facial tic involving his left eye.

"Why do you need it anyway?"

Esnault smiled coyly. "I have the right to remain silent."

"Very funny. Is there anything else, or can I go on my unmerry way?"

"Yes. Have you washed your hands lately?"

"Actually I did at a fountain in town."

"About what time?"

"Maybe a half hour ago. Why do you ask?"

"Again, I have my rights."

Esnault returned Alan's passport. He suggested that he sign in daily at the police station to show his good faith and avoid more severe terms of release that a magistrate might impose. The lieutenant then got permission to search his luggage and rummaged through his roller bag and backpack, but found no gun or weapon. "All right, we are finished for now," he said. "In the meantime, where will you be staying?"

"I have no idea. My apartment fell through."

"May I suggest an accommodation?"

"So long as it isn't a French jail."

"There's a hotel down the street on the left that you will find very much to your liking."

"What's it called?"

"Chez Betty."

2

Alan slowly made his way down the Basse Corniche, wondering why he had ever come to France. The doubting inner voice that had discouraged his departure re-emerged in the wake of the identity check and Esnault's interrogation. He bartered with the voice, telling it that he would gladly return to his former life, get rid of his new hairstyle, pawn his earring, and knuckle under to his wife's wishes, if the stress he now endured would go away. Simply put, he had taken a wrong turn in his voyage of self-discovery.

It was early evening, and a heavy onslaught of cars, buses, bikes, and scooters crammed the thoroughfare. As he trundled along, his suitcase in tow, he felt the whoosh of two motorcycles passing a bus in the oncoming lane at what must have been sixty or seventy miles per hour. "Aren't there any rules here?" he asked aloud. No one was listening.

He found other things odd in the town besides the traffic pattern, and their subtle variation irritated his lingering preference for the predictable. Inside a pharmacy distinctively marked by a neon sign in the shape of a green cross, employees dressed in white smocks gave the place the feel of a doctor's office, unlike a Walgreen's in America that peddled groceries, cosmetics, and the latest "As Seen on TV" products. Two men greeted each other still farther down the street by kissing each other on the cheek, back and forth multiple times as though they were long lost friends. Each kiss looked more like a momentary puff of air than lip-to-face contact.

Various businesses spilled their wares onto the sidewalk, including a barbershop whose waiting area blocked his path. And then there were the dogs—poodles, King Charles spaniels, Pomeranians, dachshunds, and terriers. So prevalent was their doo-doo that the local authorities had adorned the walkway with an official-looking dog-waste-bag dispenser. At least they're trying, he thought.

Two blocks from Esnault's adjunct office, he found a bar-hotel with terrace seating shaded by a large red awning. He crossed the street to get a more complete view, and from there beheld a four-story, nearly square building of 1930s vintage. To the right of a large second-floor window having dark shutters, a sign written in blood-red cursive left no doubt as to the place's identity: Chez Betty. For the moment, he believed he had arrived at the Bates Motel instead.

The patrons outside sipped coffee, beer, and wine, and eyed him suspiciously. They seemed to know he was not one of them before he ever opened his mouth. Of course his roller bag, backpack, rustic grayish-green shirt, and multi-pocketed cargo pants would have been their first clue.

Inside the business, he took in an ambience with which he was not wholly unfamiliar, for on this night Chez Betty had the racket of an American sports bar. But the sport was not baseball, basketball, or football, at least as he knew it. Indeed, what the crowd was watching on a large-screen TV constituted not a sport at all, but rather an obsession, one that the French pridefully called *Le Foot.*

White and sky-blue banners festooned the ceiling and rafters, and similarly colored baseball caps and team jerseys dressed nearly every part of the tavern. Trophies lined various shelves, evidence of the bar's participation in local tournaments. A deflated soccer ball, striped in light blue and autographed by player-heroes, rested atop a cooler. Every so often patrons of the establishment erupted in cheers as the TV announcer babbled excitedly at auctioneer pace, calling out the names of competitors who skillfully passed the ball about the field. The fact the score was 0-0 with five minutes left in the first of two halves did not seem to bore the onlookers. Significantly no one spoke about Rolf's murder, for *le foot* superseded this intriguing gossip opportunity.

At the bar, Alan approached the hotel manager about a room, but he was preoccupied with the game like everyone else. *"Attendez jusqu'à mi-temps*—Wait until halftime," he answered anxiously. Then without warning the crowd erupted into pandemonium and chanted, "*Allez, LO-M! Allez, LO-M!*"Its team had scored a goal.

With the mood more jubilant, Alan recommenced the conversation with the bar manager in simple English sentences and learned that the man's name was Thierry.

"Who's playing?" Alan asked.

"Marseille et PSG (Pay-Ess-Jay)."

"Who's Pay-Ess-Jay?"

"Paris-St. Germain."

"What's LO-M?"

Thierry appeared confused, if not offended. "Olympique-Marseille."

"And what does the L stand for?"

"Le."

"L apostrophe, right? Le precedes a vowel, so it should be L apostrophe."

"You geek?"

"So some have said."

Shaking his head, Thierry told him that a room would be eighty-five euros a night. "You pay cash."

Alan handed him the money.

"How long you stay?"

"One night, maybe two." Alan felt confident he would resolve his apartment problem quickly, and that Esnault would go fishing somewhere else. For now he would relax, refocus his energy in a positive direction and enjoy an intercultural experience with the locals.

The opportunity for the latter didn't take long, for a mass of spectators got up from their seats and approached the bar to purchase more beer and wine. *Mi-temps* had arrived.

One of them, a man who wore a backwards beret, a brown-leather jacket, and a light-blue LO-M scarf, made an attempt at conversation. "Ludovic," he said, while extending his hand. "*Et vous?*"

"Alan, Alan Newberg. Tell me something: How come you guys like soccer so much?"

Ludovic frowned. *"You mean le foot?"*

"Oui."

"J'sais pas. C'est comme l'amour pour une femme, je crois."

Ludovic's alcohol-induced slurred speech and poor diction blended his words into mush, so Alan asked him to write them down on a bar napkin. When he read them, he knew their meaning: *le foot* was like the love for a woman.

Ludovic laughed at Alan's sudden comprehension and slapped him on the back. "*C'est vrai, non?*"

Alan returned a lukewarm smile.

His new friend appeared to be in his mid-fifties, given his salt-and-pepper locks, well-trimmed grey beard, and bedraggled face. Despite his flamboyant dress and occasional drunken displays of emotion, he otherwise acted melancholic as though he bore a tremendous burden inside. While curious about the source of this pain, Alan did not inquire about it, since he didn't know the guy that well and had his own demons with which to deal.

In response to Ludovic's beckoning gesture for a drink, a tall woman in her seventies came over. Her long yellow-blonde hair and sweater, embroidered "Beauty," drew Alan's attention. "Is Beauty a way of saying Betty?" he asked her.

The woman produced a toothy smile, outlined by red lipstick, and corrected his pronunciation. *"C'est Bet-tee, monsieur."*

"C'est votre bar?"

"Tout à fait."

A sign indicated a small glass of wine would cost a couple of euros and a large one three. Feeling the need to wind down from the stressful encounter with Esnault, Alan ordered the latter in the form of rosé. "Want anything?" he asked Ludovic.

"Un whiskey."

Betty poured the drinks and deposited them on the bar, whereupon Alan slapped down ten euros.

"You nice guy for *Américain*," Ludovic said grinning. "Not cheap."

Alan nodded toward the big screen TV. "Tell me more about the game. Why is it such a big deal?"

"Not game. Match."

"Okay, match then."

"PSG won *Ligue Un* last year, but Marseille better this year," Ludovic emphasized, chopping the air beside him with his hand. "Tonight we get..."

"Payback?"

Ludovic's eyes lit up. *"Vous comprennez bien le sport."*

The second half started, and they swiveled their barstools around to watch. With a 1-0 lead, Marseille went into a defensive mode, not venturing as often into PSG's zone. A worried look invaded Ludovic's face, for he seemed to know that the strategy was ill-advised. Next to him another man began pleading with his hands at the TV in florid frustration, *"Allez! Allez!"* But the protective posture continued, angering him and the rest of the patrons. Playing not to lose got the team nowhere, Alan thought, though he himself had done this most of his life.

The inevitable came: a frenzied confusion of bodies caused the ball to roll randomly over the edge of the Marseille goal line. Now the score was 1-1. Ludovic waved his hands down in disgust toward the TV, as did everyone else in the bar.

At the end of ninety minutes of regulation plus some stoppage time, the score was still tied, so Alan asked his soccer pal another question: "What now?"

"La prolongation."

Anticipating overtime, they each had another drink, this time Ludovic buying. The match resumed, and the bar team finally caught a break. A PSG player tripped a Marseille one as he rushed all alone toward the PSG goal. The ref raised his hand in the air, and the crowd went nuts in triumph. A penalty kick had been awarded.

"We still gotta make it," Alan cautioned. "We" sat well with the bar's patrons as evidenced by their approving smiles in response. He now felt like one of the boys.

Ludovic and the others began celebrating before Marseille even attempted the kick, for they seem to know the odds. The ref precisely placed the ball on the ground twelve yards in front of the goal, and a Marseille striker stepped forward, faked his head slightly to the left, then launched the ball past the outstretched hands of the PSG goalie and into the right side of the net.

After overtime ended and amidst chants of "Allez, LO-M," Alan finished his wine and made his way to his hotel room. He had learned something new that night that had everything to do with his spiritual makeover; it was called passion. If he ever expected to succeed in finding himself in France, he could not ignore its direction, and if he played not to lose, victory would most assuredly elude his grasp.

* * *

Alan awakened the next day from a *Papillon*-like nightmare of solitary confinement in a rat-infested cell in French Guyana to the sound of someone knocking on his hotel room door. He got up and squinted through the peephole, half expecting to find Esnault, who had played the role of prison commandant in the dream. Instead it was the maid.

"*Femme de ménage,*" she trilled.

"Give me a few minutes, okay?"

Still nerved up from the nightmare, he looked out the window to assure himself he was in Villefranche and not prison. He noticed a sign across the street that said Boulangerie/Pâtisserie, and the thought of a French pastry delighted him. After dressing quickly, he made his way down the three flights of stairs that he had lugged his roller bag up the night before.

Inside the bakery, baguettes, stacked high on shelves and in baskets behind the counter, offered an enticing fresh-baked aroma. Customers pushed their way to the front of the establishment as though they were floor traders at a stock market and purchased and/or reserved loaves for evening pick up. The absence of a line bothered him, but his irritation subsided once he made it to the display case, where he eyed pastries, brioche, *pain au chocolat*, and quiches—Lorraine (ham), *épinard* (spinach), and *courgette* (zucchini)—and a tapestry of pies decorated by multi-colored fruits.

He chose the Quiche Lorraine and asked the woman behind the counter to heat it. As she did so, he fished his pocket for some euros to pay for the food, but realized he had none. While he went around the corner to an ATM machine to get some money, the woman graciously agreed to hold his purchases. After putting in his card and submitting his security code as demanded, much to his chagrin the screen read, *"Carte invalide."*

"Invalid?" He rushed to another ATM on the Basse Corniche, but the result was the same, and his mind began to race. He decided to check other establishments to see if they would take his credit card. The first was called Hotel de Méditerranée, a quaint place similar to Chez Betty down the street from the bakery. There the clerk politely ran his chipped card several times and offered nothing but a *"désolé."*

Alan desperately went to other hotels, even the most international ones closest to the water, but got the same response. If he did not have access to cash, he would not be able to pay for his room, and even if he conservatively used his emergency traveler's checks, he would only last a few weeks. Further, he couldn't go back to the States, since he had to sign in every day at the police station. "I'm a dead man," he told himself.

Back at the hotel, Alexis, the bartender, who identified himself as the grandson of Betty, offered him a free cup of coffee to assuage his troubles. *"Café Américain?"*

"Straight black, *s'il vous plait.*"

"Un double (du-bluh)?"

"Oui."

While Alexis prepared the coffee using the bar espresso machine, Alan quietly took in the ambiance that he had missed the previous night. Currency from nearly every country in the world was submerged beneath the bar's glass top. A giant framed photograph of the establishment in a different era prominently occupied a wall. Patrons ordered wine and tap beer, while others drank freshly squeezed orange juice and high-octane French coffee.

Alexis set a saucer containing a tiny teaspoon, a tube of sugar, and a wafer on the bar. A demitasse completed the arrangement, which appeared too refined and more appropriate for an old lady's bridge-club party. Toward the end of his coffee, Alan struck up a conversation with the young bartender. "*Ma carte ne marche pas*," he sadly said, waving his credit card. "Does this work here?"

Alexis took the card to Thierry for his examination, who sat at the end of the bar, doing some bookwork. After some words with him, Alexis returned and delivered more bad news: another *désolé*.

Alan asked for the passcode to the hotel's wireless so he could Skype his credit union up in his room. Given that it was noon in France and seven hours ahead of Chicago, the business was not yet open. Knowing Barry Simon, his divorce lawyer, got up at 5 a.m. and would now be awake, he called him instead. The phone rang repeatedly, but finally someone answered.

"Hello, Barry?"

A long pause ensued while the person at other end got his bearings. After a few minutes of hacking up phlegm and clearing his throat, he posed a logical question to Alan: "Who the hell's calling me at five a.m.?"

"Barry, please don't hang up. It's Alan Newberg." He could hear his attorney mutter to his wife, "Just another crank call, honey. Go back to sleep."

"Alan who?"

"Newberg."

"Ohhh, I remember you now," Barry Simon said. "You're the nut -bag who went off the deep end and split to France out of the blue."

"Actually I'm in Villefranche-Sur-Mer," Alan responded, showing off his best French accent.

"Yeah, yeah. Stop with the French crap and tell me what's up."

"My plastic won't work suddenly. Is there something wrong?"

"Uh, you took off in the middle of your divorce without telling me, and your wife got your accounts frozen," Barry answered. "She claimed you were making off with marital funds. Must be the judge's order just took effect."

Alan went from nonplused to angry, unable to utter a response.

"Just a moment. I got the decree in my briefcase," the divorce lawyer said. A few minutes ticked away, whereupon he returned to the decidedly depressing conversation. "It says, uh, 'Now therefore, to prevent further profligate spending and/or hiding of marital assets by Respondent'—that's you, Alan—'it is hereby ordered and adjudged that Respondent be enjoined from withdrawing funds or receiving credit from all accounts in his name or that of Petitioner, and that all financial institutions in possession of such accounts halt, stop, obstruct, thwart, and otherwise prevent any withdrawals or credit by or on behalf of said Respondent.'"

"What judge signed that?"

"Let's see. The Honorable M. Lewis O'Donald," Barry Simon said. "I kinda like the way he used 'profligate,' myself. My son's studying for his SAT, and I'm always looking for new words to challenge him."

"I'm four thousand miles away from home with no money! I have no time for fun and games."

"What was I supposed to do? Plead temporary insanity? You just left."

"All right. All right. How long will it take to get this undone?"

"Six weeks for another court date," Barry estimated. "But you need to get back here right away."

"I can't. I'm a suspect in a murder case."

"Say what?"

"The dead guy dirt-balled me on an apartment, so the detective thinks I got a motive. He wants me to sign in every day at the police station until I'm cleared."

"I don't do criminal work, but—"

"Would it do any good if I got you something from him saying this?"

"Might help," Barry replied. "But I'll also need an affidavit from you giving a legitimate reason for taking off in the first place."

"Is finding myself legitimate?"

"No!"

Alan sighed. "So what should I do about this murder investigation?"

"Don't tell the cops a thing."

"Uh, I had to say something—"

"What's the matter with you?"

"Truthfully, I don't know."

"Well, you need to get your act together, because right now you're in a world of shit."

"Tell me about it."

"Where are you staying in case the judge wants to know?"

"The hotel is Chez Betty."

"Spell that, will ya?"

Alan complied.

"And don't forget to send the documentation," Barry advised. "Maybe the judge will feel sorry for you and unfreeze a little money so you don't starve."

* * *

After the intense phone conversation with Barry Simon, Alan went to the bank, cashed one of his emergency traveler's checks, and paid for another night at Chez Betty. Thereafter, he returned to the bakery and squared up with the woman for the quiche. She hadn't thrown it out yet and warmed it up for him in the microwave.

While waiting for his food, something in the display case garnered his attention—meringue, and it covered more than pies. The sight of the ingredient atop cupcakes and other pastries sparked a thought; the French had dared to venture outside a conceptual box and invented something new. *So what prevents me from making such leaps?* Alan asked himself. *Fear of the unknown? Yeah, meringue.*

Emboldened by the metaphor, he exited the bakery with his breakfast-now-lunch and crossed the street to a large park, which seemed to offer the best opportunity to enjoy his repast and forget about his ever-growing predicament. In the background he heard an accordion playing traditional French music near the harbor that provided an ambience he had hoped to find in coming to the country.

The first attraction that caught his attention was the community soccer field. Along one of its sides, four rows of stone steps provided seating for local matches and offered an excellent place to munch down his quiche. A carpet of astro-turf covered the "terrain," an amusing military allusion the French used to describe a playing surface.

Beyond the "terrain," he marveled at the sea. The horizon stretched out far enough to see the earth's curvature, and he wondered what it would be like to travel beyond it. His eyes returned to the field, where he saw on the opposite fence a dark-blue sign that had a single word in white-capital letters: RESPECT. He pondered if he would ever have that for himself.

After he finished his quiche he continued his park tour. Amazingly he discovered a basketball court. The local government must have wanted to encourage a sport besides *le foot*, he thought. As he approached, he noticed some teenagers on lunch break from school, who had turned the court into a mini-soccer field, where they practiced their close-quarter kicking and passing skills. The rims and net were not worn in the slightest. It appeared that the powers-that-be had given up on the new sport idea, as the asphalt surface had been covered with a plastic grass carpet, useless for bouncing a basketball.

Despite their obsession for soccer, the French did like a few other sports. One was *la pétanque,* something Alan learned about at his next stop in the park. Several men in a dirt enclosure tossed croquet-sized metal balls at a smaller red one. He did not understand the game completely, but the gist of it was not unlike curling or horseshoes, in which players attempt to get as close as possible to a target, knock an opponent's mark out of the way, and protect their best shots with guards.

After each round of play, the men used magnets tethered to strings to pick up the balls without bending over. Then they recorded the result of the round on a small scoreboard. The players even had personal carrying cases for their equipment. Adjacent to the court, their jackets hung on hooks hammered into trees. The men acted the same as Americans at a bowling alley, laughing, bantering, and cajoling each other to victory.

In the main part of the park, he next took in what he thought to be a farmer's market, but a closer look revealed this was not the case. Instead men and women sold antique furniture, silver-service sets, picture frames, and household knick-knacks, while customers examined the various items and bargained vigorously. A food stand offered olives of every kind: green, black, some seasoned with basil and others mixed with peppers and pimentos. He purchased a bag, and it provided a salty supplement to his quiche.

Behind the market, French schoolchildren climbed on a series of brightly colored pieces of playground equipment, frolicking in a cacophony of tiny laughs, screams, and shouts. The fenced-in rectangular playground led to a school designated L'École Maternelle.

Alan scanned the area, left to right, suddenly stopping at a figure standing alone at the fence. It was a woman—thin, younger than he, with dark brown hair—the same one he had seen the day before on the train to Villefranche. His mood changed for the better.

He drew closer and noted she wore a lavender trench coat with large black decorative buttons, well-fitted slacks, and dark low-heeled pumps. The cuffs of her cream-colored blouse peeked through the end of the coat's three-quarter sleeves. Various matching accessories—a purse, a watch, and a silky black scarf—gave her a more sophisticated look than when he had seen her last. Though she could have leaned over the fence, she chose instead to stand tall and watch the schoolyard through designer sunglasses.

On the other side of the fence, several young girls, who appeared to be about five, engaged in a game in which each child took turns playing doctor, nurse, and patient. Periodically they switched roles, thereby learning something about empathy. When they tired of one profession, they went to another, becoming instead dancers, waitresses, chefs, bakers, teachers, and yes, mothers. The woman herself participated in these imaginary worlds as best she could from her position outside the playground. She had in her approach the creativity he lacked, and he found the quality mesmerizing.

He recognized the woman's daughter among the children, and she wore the same outfit as on the train. More precocious than the rest, she dominated the game, often assigning the other girls to professions or changing the context. It was clear she was in charge.

Approaching a barely familiar person of the opposite sex in public was not Alan's forté, to say the least. He hadn't dated since the demise of his marriage, and before that he had lived in a world where the mysterious notion of chemistry had always eluded him, causing him to be "just friends" with way too many women. As a result, he lacked the courage to expose himself to rejection, and while he had taken many risks lately, he was ill-prepared to leave his comfort zone. Or was he? Wasn't that why he'd come to France, to leave that zone? The thought of meringue returned.

He casually aligned himself along the fence, a safe but conversational distance from the woman. He summoned the courage to say something, albeit awkwardly: *"Est-ce que vous venez ici souvent*—Do you come here often?" Despite the pitiful cliché, his formal, schoolboy use of the language came across as sincere.

The woman scoffed a *"non."* Then, perhaps feeling sorry for him, she responded guardedly in heavily-accented English: "You're the man from the train."

Starting to relax, Alan said, "And you're the damsel in distress with the heavy bag." He should have chosen his words more carefully.

"Damsel in distress?"

"You know. Somebody who wants to be rescued by a man."

"I am not such a person," the woman said sharply and moved farther down the fence.

"No, wait. I didn't mean it that way."

Discontinuing her escape, the woman came back. She was kind at least.

"Sorry. I shouldn't have assumed that about you," he told her.

"That's quite all right, but please don't suggest something about me unless you know it to be true."

Alan nodded agreement and quickly changed the subject. "Your daughter is such a bright little girl. What's her name?"

The woman folded her arms. "And why should I tell you? For all I know you're a—"

"Child molester?"

"Yes, that's the English phrase, I believe."

Feeling miffed, Alan considered walking away, but the little girl strategically interrupted his offense. "*Maman, Maman, regarde-moi,*" she said, whereupon she managed three cartwheels in front of the jungle gym.

"*Trés bien, Chloé!*"

"Chloé, huh?"

The woman displayed an icy stare, so Alan gave up. "Nice to meet you," he grumbled sarcastically, even though they had never really introduced themselves. *She's like all the rest*, he thought. *My situation is no different now than it was twenty years ago, and the same here as in America. Always on the outside looking in.*

When he got a few steps away, the woman asked him to return, and he quickly did so and anxiously stated, "I'm Alan Newberg. I didn't mean to scare you, and I'm not a child molester—"

She put her forefinger over his lips to stop his neurotic prattle. "*Je m'appelle Jeannette Brouillet,*" she said calmly.

Something about her saying the name in French made the introduction special, and his heart warmed. "*Enchantez,*" he replied in a soft, sincere voice, having regained his composure. The word seemed perfect, for truly he was enchanted.

"Where are you from in the U.S?" Jeannette asked.

"Near Chicago."

"I want to go to New York, Washington, and Miami someday—maybe Vegas too."

"What about Yellowstone, the Grand Canyon, and the national parks?"

Jeannette's face dissolved into an empty look. She seemed to know little about America, save from what she had seen on Canal Plus and other French television stations. "Why did you come here?" she asked. "Are you a tourist?"

Alan shrugged.

"No seriously, why?"

"Not sure."

"A man who has no goal or purpose makes me nervous."

"I came here—to escape purpose." The words he had spoken surprised him, but they were the right ones, for he had piqued the woman's interest. "I was wondering," he slowly began to ask, "if you would like to get together sometime."

"You Americans move quickly, don't you?"

"Yes, but not for just anyone."

Jeannette smiled.

"In my prior life, it would have taken me months. So give me some credit."

"And now?" she asked, suppressing a flirtatious giggle.

"I—"

"Go for it?"

"Yeah, I guess."

"I like a man who acts without thought or consequence. Tell me something: Is there a damsel in distress in your life these days?"

Alan did not answer, staring instead at the ground.

"Surely you are married."

"Almost divorced," he finally responded.

She looked at him dubiously. "Almost?"

"Scout's honor," he pledged, holding up three fingers.

"What's that?"

"I swear it's the truth," he said, explaining the slang and the gesture.

Chloé interrupted again. *"Maman, il est treize heures moins cinq."*

Five minutes to one, Alan thought.

"Since I bought her that watch, she keeps reminding me of the time," Jeannette explained with resignation. "She thinks she's helping me."

"Is she?"

"In a way, yes."

"Why's that?"

"I don't want to get into it right now, but I'm not a person who worries about time."

Alan was the opposite, of course. He longed to change this, though he knew he would never give up wearing a watch.

"Anyway," Jeannette continued. "Chloé must return to school in a few minutes, so I must go."

"Darn."

"No really, scout's honor," she replied, smiling again.

"How do I get ahold of you?" he asked.

"I work at the flower shop next to La Presse across the street."

At this, Jeannette moved farther along the fence, passed through an opening, and took Chloé by the hand. They disappeared inside the school, out of sight but not out of mind.

3

An idyllic sun-splashed vista soothed Alan's spirit on his way to Nice. As Bus 100 of Lignes D'Azur travelled along the hillside far above the Mediterranean Sea, his "fancy lightly turned to thoughts of love," in the words of Tennyson. Despite not having had a date with Jeannette, he adored her, unrestrained by caution or thought of failure. This was the new Alan after all, spontaneously driven by heart and uninhibited by mind. If it did not work out, so what—he'd find another woman, and still another if need be. If only he had that same attitude with respect to his upcoming meeting with Esnault.

About a half kilometer before the city, the bus came to a sudden and unscheduled halt. Instead of the PA system's computerized voice routinely announcing the next stop, the driver himself came on and barked, "*Descendez á cause de la manifestation.*" Without complaint the passengers exited, as though they had experienced this inconvenience before. Alan asked one of them what the street demonstration was all about, and she told him that a small tax had been imposed on cellular phone use, and that bus drivers, as union members, typically honored such protests, however petty. The manifestation together with his gross miscalculation of the walking distance to Esnault's office delayed him forty-five minutes and put him even more on edge.

The Nice *gendarmerie* didn't look like any cop shop Alan had seen in America. Instead it had the appearance of a military installation, with a gated check point, a series of barracks, and a fenced perimeter. After he explained at the guard house that he had an appointment with Esnault, an officer in combat fatigues marched him up several flights of stairs in the main building to a hallway, where he waited outside a door. After several minutes a voice gave him a start.

"You're late."

Alan turned and saw the lieutenant. He was leaning against a wall with his arms smugly folded across his chest.

"A manifestation delayed me."

"I would expect a man whose life is so organized to have left early in anticipation of such diversions," Esnault observed. "Why the change in approach?"

"Have you been talking to my wife?"

"A background check was necessary under the circumstances," the lieutenant said. "I must admit her hyphenated name suggests she has had only one foot in your marriage. I imagine this has bothered you to some degree?"

"Whatever. Can we get on with this?"

Esnault politely gestured to his office, and Alan followed him inside, where he observed a government-issue desk and a large bookcase loaded with French code manuals. The meeting provided yet another opportunity for interrogation, so the lieutenant jumped right in. "How long have you been married?" he asked.

"Twenty years," Alan replied, thinking the cop already knew the details.

"And your wife is a professional as well?"

"Yes, an accountant."

"How nice. I assume as a result of your hard work you have accumulated a moderate amount of wealth."

"We've done okay."

"*Financially*, that is."

Alan drew out a long exasperated "yeah" in response. The French detective was like a horsefly, doggedly buzzing a hiker on a hot summer day. Whenever Alan would take a swat at the insect, it would elude him and attack from another direction. It didn't help that he was already in a sweat from his hasty walk.

"*Emotionally*, however, I suspect there were problems," Esnault continued.

"And that is your business why?"

The lieutenant quickly circled the desk and angled his head close enough for Alan to smell his breath. "Is my desire to understand you upsetting?"

"Yes, as a matter of fact, it is."

Esnault retreated to his chair and opened up a manila-file folder, the contents of which were unknown to Alan. "You mentioned you wanted to see me, but you never got into the specifics."

"I need something in writing stating that I have to stay in France during your investigation."

Esnault stared contemplatively out the window, tilting his head upward and striking an erudite pose. "And what is the purpose of such documentation?"

"So my divorce judge will know I can't return to the States right now."

"Is there some hurry?"

"He froze my accounts. If he understands that I'm stuck here, he might unfreeze them, so I have access to money while I'm here."

"And why did he do this in the first place?" Esnault asked, still gazing out at the clouds.

"Because my wife's lawyer told him I might be hiding marital assets."

The response caused the lieutenant to change his mood. He pressed his palms on the desk, leaned over it and sharply asked, "Was Rolf Swenson helping you squirrel away such funds?"

"No!"

"A business arrangement, perhaps, that would launder the money so you could live happily ever after in the Riviera?"

"No!"

"Did Rolf threaten to expose this scurrilous artifice to Sara Elliot-Newberg?" By now the lieutenant's voice had risen to a mild yell.

Again Alan denied the accusation.

Esnault dropped down into his chair and clasped his hands on his desk, returning to his previous even demeanor. "Why stay in Villefranche so long?" he asked. "Most stay a few weeks."

"I came here," Alan replied, "to refocus."

"Ah, a cathartic resolution of internal pain and conflict. Very chic."

"Look, I'm not here for a therapy session—just type me up something that says I have to sign in at the police station, okay?"

Esnault looked puzzled. "And this favor should be extended to you out of my detached, disinterested largesse?"

"Oh, I see. You want a bribe."

"No, but something else would suffice."

"What's that?"

"Documentation of your alibi."

"Would my train ticket to Nice help?"

"Perhaps."

"Why only perhaps?"

"Even with the ticket, I have nothing to prove you were on that train," Esnault said. "You could have manufactured the conductor's punch hole and simply not boarded."

"So what are you suggesting? That I bought a ticket, but did not use it in order to fabricate an alibi, arriving here earlier by some other means of transportation?"

"It's been done," the lieutenant noted with quiet confidence.

"If you're really concerned about this, you should get the video footage from the surveillance cameras at Nice-Ville—there all over the place there."

"Yes, I have already thought of this. Unfortunately one camera was broken that day, and the others did not get a view of your face."

"And what about my flight from Chicago to Paris?

"Again your boarding pass might help, but we will need the airline manifest to prove you were actually on that flight." Esnault began to tap something on his computer. "That is if we can still get it." He printed the document he had typed and requested that Alan follow him down the hall.

"Where are we going?"

"Don't you want something official?"

At another office, a woman notarized Esnault's signature on the statement. A second one notarized the first's signature. Alan wondered if there would be a third. Finally, the lieutenant handed him the double-notarized paperwork and said, "I look forward to the pleasure of your company in the near future."

"The near future?"

"For the boarding pass and train ticket, of course."

"I thought you said they wouldn't do any good."

"They are not absolute proof, but with them I might be able to help you."

"Help me?"

"Why, yes. Don't you trust me?"

* * *

After his appointment with Esnault, Alan wandered about Nice, trying to find the right bus back to Villefranche. He was not familiar with the streets that wound their way around without the pretense of a grid. Stores and businesses ending in "erie" repeated in a never-ending cycle, and *épiceries, boulangeries, crèperies, confisseries,* and *charcuteries* all looked alike after a while. He might as well have been lost in a rain forest.

He asked for directions from someone selling gyros, frites, and pizza at a small stand on a corner, but the fellow couldn't speak French, and English didn't work, either. A businessman rushing into an office building offered a better alternative. To avoid an undecipherable onslaught of verbiage, Alan asked the man closed-ended questions. This worked well, as it forced him to answer with *oui* or *non.*

A full hour passed before Alan finally found what he thought to be the right bus stop, about the time his feet had started to blister. He noted a schedule for Bus 100 on one of the stop's walls, so he believed he was in the right place. He patiently sat on the bench, and in time spotted down the street a bus with the correct number displayed on a sign above its windshield. By now he knew the drill: enter, put a euro and a half in the tray by the driver, take a ticket, and validate it in a composting machine near the door. He performed the procedure without a hitch, feeling ever-so-proud of his mastery of the local transportation system.

And so his trek back began. At first he relaxed and enjoyed the sights, but after a few minutes, he noticed the sea was not on his right, as it should have been if he were returning to Chez Betty. He asked in his best French a professionally dressed older woman with beady eyes and pouty lips if the bus went that way, but she gave him a haughty sniff.

"My English is perfect and exact," she said. "There is no need for you to resort to your elementary Americanized version of our language."

Alan recoiled, understandably irritated by the putdown.

"You, sir, are on the right bus going the wrong way," the woman noted, seemingly amused by his confusion.

Her voice grated on his already frayed nerves. As a result, his filter didn't work well. "Whatever shall I do?" he asked in a saucy tone.

"You must descend posthaste and catch the right bus going the right way, of course."

"No kidding, really?"

The woman closed her eyes and raised her brows.

"And how might I signal the driver that I wish to exit the bus?" Alan asked, mocking the lady's snotty syntax.

"You must press the red button on the metal pole, and when you embark upon the correct bus, pay the driver again," she said, eyeing his ticket. "You can only use that to transfer to a bus going in the same direction."

"Well, thank you very much for that information," Alan replied, pressing the button. He waited in silence, doing his best to ignore the woman.

But Miss Perfect wouldn't let it go. "I have been to your country many times, and when I visit, I familiarize myself with your laws and customs," she said. "I'm quite surprised you have not done so here."

"Must be because I'm not as sophisticated as you, what with your perfect French and English."

"Yes, in fact I speak many languages well, something of which you Americans are so incapable."

The snooty bitch, he thought. *She knows nothing about me or my country.* With the exception of Spanish, English prevailed for thousands of miles in the U.S., unlike in Europe where in the same distance five languages might be spoken. It was absurd to suggest that Americans were ignorant simply because they didn't know as many languages. "You should feel lucky," he retorted.

"In what respect might I inquire?"

"If it weren't for us, you'd be speaking German."

Several onlookers, who understood English, gasped at the dig.

"Touché," the woman responded roundly. "But since I also speak perfect German, I would have no problem." She turned her head away and glared out the window, palpably offended.

* * *

Alan finally got off the right bus going the wrong way. When he attempted to verify with the new driver that he was going to Villefranche, the man pointed to a sign that said, *"Défense de parler avec le conducteur."*

A video screen confirmed things instead, providing Alan with some much needed relief. As he looked down from the screen, he heard another woman's voice, one considerably less annoying than Miss Perfect's. *"Je me souviens de vous. Vous étiez sur le scène du meurtre*—I remember you. You were at the murder scene," she said.

It was the blind lady to whom Alan had spoken before Esnault's identity check and initial interrogation. She wore the same pillbox hat and dark suit. He asked her how she recognized him.

"By your voice. I listen well, as I'm blind."

Alan appreciated the switch to English. He sat next to her, hoping to learn more about what her keen ears had heard. Perhaps she was lonely and would oblige him by openly chatting about Rolf Swenson. Their conversation flowed easily despite periodic interruptions of the monotonous bus PA system that foretold upcoming stops.

"How long did you know Rolf?"

"He was my neighbor for two years."

"I only knew him through renting an apartment," Alan said. "What did people think of him around Villefranche?"

"Most didn't like him. He owed them money, you see."

"For what?"

The woman rapidly blinked so as to emphasize her response. "He gambled at Monte Carlo too much."

Alan looked out the window as the bus made its way around the mountainside and down a hill toward Villefranche. During this time, the blind lady, who obviously was missing the glorious view, darted her head about, reacting to the slightest sound like a nervous sparrow.

"So what did he do to cover his losses?"

"Several business ventures—taxis, rentals, maid services."

"And did he make enough money to pay off his debts?"

"Sometimes."

"He must have had a lot of enemies."

The woman smiled and nodded.

"Prochain arrêt, L'Octroi," the PA system called out. This was the stop for Villefranche. Alan got off and helped the woman descend from the bus. She then tapped her way down the sidewalk with her cane in the general direction of the bell-towered church.

While Alan strolled along the Basse Corniche from the stop, he reflected on what the blind lady had told him. Rolf had many irons in the fire, any one of which might have bitten him in the butt on the day in question. No doubt the man had ripped off other tourists in order to pay his markers, his life being one of robbing Peter to pay Paul. Esnault should have known this from a tertiary investigation of the facts.

Across the street from the Octroi bus stop, Alan noticed Jeannette in front of her flower shop, so he changed his channel from Esnault to the blissful mood that had started his day. His flame fussed over arrangements displayed on large stands, adding or adjusting a flower here and there, seemingly on a whim. Sans her lavender coat, she wore the same outfit she had on when he saw her last. The arrangements over which she fretted had a spring theme: red and yellow roses, lilies, carnations, daisies, and tulips.

After jaywalking at a slow trot across the street, he greeted her in English, since his brain was too fried to speak in her native tongue. "Hey, remember me?" he asked, tactlessly.

Jeannette ignored him and continued working.

He tried again, thinking she was playing hard to get. "Did Chloé make it back to school okay the other day?"

"Bien sûr, monsieur," Jeannette replied as if he were a customer.

Maybe that was how she wanted to keep him—at a distance. He decided to switch to French, hoping to bring her out. *"Depuis combien de temps est-ce que vous travaillez ici?"* Asking her how long she had worked at the flower shop was a question more appropriate for a job interview, but it was the best he could do.

"I've been here three years, and you can speak English."

"For a minute there, I thought you were blowing me off."

Her face contorted, so Alan restated himself. "I thought maybe you were ignoring me and possibly didn't like me."

Jeannette responded with a quick "hmm" and started taking down her flower arrangements.

"Closing up shop early?"

"I have to pick Chloé up after school."

"I thought you weren't a clock watcher."

"She called me on her cell phone to remind me."

"A cell phone? She's what, five?"

"Five going on fifteen, I guess."

Alan laughed and shifted closer to Jeannette. "Need some help taking down those flowers?"

"Only if you're very careful."

Together they loaded a small cart and took them inside. Alan's OCD brain winced at the jungle of paperwork behind the counter. "Given how much trouble you have keeping track of time, how do you manage your books?" he asked.

"Everything seems to work out," Jeannette said.

Alan wasn't so sure about that. For him things never just happened, and anything good was the result of diligent pursuit. "Maybe I can help you with that sometime," he offered politely.

"And what experience do you have with such things?"

"I used to own a title company."

"A title company?"

Alan searched for the equivalent in French. "I was," he said, snapping his fingers, "a *notaire.*"

"And how does that qualify you to balance my books?"

This was cause for him to babble on and on about the various debits and credits of a closing sheet. Finally he shut up, once he realized his lecture didn't impress. He needed to learn to state his thoughts in sentences and not paragraphs, but often found it difficult to do so.

Inside the store, Jeannette took off her sunglasses and set them on the counter. Beneath one of her brown eyes he noticed a small bruise. "Hard day at work?" he asked, nodding toward the contusion.

"I tripped and fell. I must have hit my face on a flower stand," Jeannette replied.

Alan doubted the story, but said nothing further about it, as he had a different mission. He plucked a red rose from a cooler in the back and put it on the counter by the cash register, a bold departure from his previous playbook and an abrupt change of pace in their conversation. "How much do I owe you for this?" he asked with as much confidence as he could muster.

"*Ça fait deux euros,*" Jeannette said, returning to her all-business tone.

Alan handed her the money together with the flower. "*C'est pour vous,*" he announced with a smile.

Jeannette silently moved to the other side of the store. "*C'est pour toi,*" she corrected.

Smitten by the fact she had given him permission to *tutoyer*, something the French reserved for people close to them, he repeated: "*C'est pour toi.*"

Jeannette thanked him and performed a slight curtsy.

"So what about that date you promised me?"

"Promised?"

"You said I could contact you here about it."

"What do you have in mind?"

Alan didn't have a ready answer. He didn't think Jeannette would agree to do anything in the first place. "Uh, I thought maybe we could go for a hike. *Randonnée* is the word for it, right?"

"Where would you like to go?"

Since Alan didn't know the area well, he said, "You tell me. Maybe something with Chloé."

"How about Mont Boron? It has a park and a trail leading up to an interesting old fort."

"That's between Nice and Villefranche, right?"

"Yes. On Sunday my shop will be closed, so that works best for me."

"Sunday it is then. How about eight sharp at Chez Betty?"

"*Tu plaisantes*—You've got to be kidding."

Alan recovered and suggested a range of time instead. "Is between nine and ten okay?"

"*C'est beaucoup mieux.*"

Much better indeed.

* * *

It could have been a lot of things. It could have been he'd left his airline boarding pass in the seat pocket of the plane between the vomit bag and the safety instructions, and forgotten about it in all the excitement of touching down at Paris-Charles De Gaulle. Or perhaps in a moment of nonchalance, he had decided that he didn't need the document and discarded it in the international terminal concourse or left it somewhere while wandering about trying to find ground transportation. He could have done the same while in one of several train stations in Paris, or even at Nice-Ville.

The ticket from Paris to Nice was also missing. Maybe the *femme de ménage* had thrown it out as well as the boarding pass when she cleaned his room. Perhaps the documents had fallen off the nightstand and onto the floor, and she swept them up with the dirt. Or worse yet, she worked for Esnault or some other mysterious force that had conspired to create his current devastating coalescence of circumstances. Maybe Sara Elliot-Newberg had something to do with it.

Alan checked everywhere: his clothing, the numerous folds and pockets of his backpack, his roller bag, the desk, the nightstand, the dresser, the covers, the floor beneath his bed, the bathroom, even his shaving kit. But he had no luck.

Regardless of the reason for the missing paperwork, without it, he was genuinely screwed. The airline boarding pass would have accounted for his whereabouts up to his arrival in Paris, and the train ticket to Nice through 3 p.m. He saw the police at the murder scene at four, and they had to have been there some time before that. With these documents he could have eliminated himself for all but a small window of time. Yet he did not have them.

"Why?" he yelled, pounding his fist against the wall. In his prior life, he had been the clearinghouse for all records associated with a real estate closing, and at home he had retained every receipt, warranty agreement, utility bill, and oil-change invoice. Nothing slipped his mind. But now, when it really mattered, he had become scatterbrained. The price of change was steep.

He went down to the bar, where he found Betty immersed in an afternoon French soap opera. He grabbed a stool in front of her and tried to explain his situation. During his recitation of events, she motherly corrected his errors in pronunciation, grammar, and diction.

"*Vous avez besoin d' un verre, monsieur*—You need a drink, sir," she said, while pouring him a *grand ballon* of white wine.

Alan got out his wallet to pay, but she waved him off. She then told him that an American regularly came in the bar at one o'clock and might be able to help him with his economic woes.

As he began to sip the wine, he contemplated what this man might have in store for him. Instead Ludovic arrived and sauntered over. He bragged that he had won fifty euros on the lottery at La Presse, but when he noticed Alan's morose mood, he asked, "You not look so lucky. What wrong?"

"Long story."

"Hey, maybe I cheer you up."

"Yeah, sure."

"You like Marseille?"

"You mean for Le Foot?"

Ludovic raised his eyebrows as if to say "what else."

"I guess. But why do you ask?"

"You want go match?"

"You have some tickets?"

Ludovic fanned his face with the fifty euros he had won and said, "I got two for Nice-Marseille. Match two weeks from today. Nice Stade."

"Me and you?"

Ludovic nodded. "Meet here. *Dix-huit heures.*"

"Six o'clock, right?"

"Oui."

"You're on," Alan said, now more upbeat. His friends at home would never believe this. It was one thing to see a museum or a tourist attraction in France, but quite another to experience a League One soccer match.

Ludovic chugged down a whiskey and left without another word. As he did, Alan yelled to him, "Hey man, thanks." His soccer-devoted friend tipped his backwards beret as he walked out onto the sidewalk.

Alan looked at his watch. It was 1p.m. Not a minute later, the front door swung open, and a six-foot-four-inch man, wearing a ten-gallon cowboy hat, a tan leather duster, and snakeskin boots, swaggered in. He paused dramatically, surveying the customers as if he owned them. They in turn gawked at him in silence.

"*Ça c'est l'Américain. Son père est un homme d'affaires au Texas, dans le pétrole, je crois*—That's the American. His father is a Texas businessman, oil, I think," Betty whispered.

Alan asked her why the guy wore a cowboy hat.

"*Il pense qu'il se moque de nous*—He thinks he's making fun of us."

The Texan strode over and ordered some bourbon, tossed it down his throat and banged his shot glass hard on the bar.

"I thought this was Chez Betty, not the Long Branch," Alan joked.

"I wish it were the Long Branch," the man drawled, loud enough to fill the whole bar, despite the competition from the television. He appeared brash, purposely graceless, and unrefined, everything the French hated about Americans. "What part of the good ol' U.S. of A are you from anyway?" he asked.

"A suburb of Chicago."

"Chi-town, huh? Gotta a sistur livin' thar." The man turned to Betty and ordered another shot, racing in French with her about something. His perfect accent contrasted his own in English and seemed to mollify any objection she had to his rough manner.

"Where are you from?" Alan asked.

"Houston via Pa-ree."

"How come you speak the language so well?"

"My ma is French and daddy American. I'm what you call a half-breed."

Alan smiled at the man's self-deprecating frankness. Though he was politically incorrect, he had a certain refreshing charm.

"Buck Treadway," the Texan suddenly announced, offering a massive hand.

"Alan Newberg."

"You know what? You oughta change your name to Al."

"I thought the same thing, but my wife wouldn't let me."

"What?"

"I didn't want a name to get between us."

"Appeasement never works, my friend."

Alan looked down, feeling ashamed. "Yeah, I know. We're getting a divorce."

"Well, from now on you're Al to me," Buck said. He poked the bar with his finger so as to emphasize his point. "Tell me somethin', Al, what in the hell are you doin' all the way across the pond?"

Buck waved his hands wildly as he spoke. Alan learned quickly it was best to step back a little when conversing with the man, for fear an errant gesture might whack him in the face. He explained his financial situation in an effort to seek his help.

"You gotta a mega, mega problem, pardner."

"And it keeps getting worse."

"You ever thought about workin' in France?"

Confused, Alan asked, "How can I do that? Don't I need a work permit or something?"

Buck provided a long explanation about the French economy. While many people worked for regular employers, the government required companies to pay a great deal of money for fringe benefits. Consequently they preferred to hire workers under the table for less money as black-market labor. "You could work here without anyone knowin' on account of the fact everyone else does the same damn thing," he said.

"But what could I do?"

"Work for me. Yourself, I mean."

"I don't understand. Doing what?"

"Drivin' people around."

"You mean as a cab driver?"

"Hell, no!"

Buck explained that he had set up an Uber-like company in which independent drivers took customers around the area. The customers used an easily downloadable app to connect with his service. The drivers weren't cabbies and most certainly not employees, since they used their own vehicles. All he did was bring people together.

"How many drivers do you have working for you?"

Buck cleared his throat and lowered his voice. "You'll be the first."

"But I don't have a vehicle."

"I'll lease you one of mine."

Alan worried about getting on the wrong side of the law even further. But he had no choice, for soon his money would run out. "All right, I'll do it," he blurted, surprising even himself.

"Thatta boy, Al—take the damn bull by the horns," Buck said, with a throaty voice. He threw down another shot.

Alan stuck out his chest, though cautiously. "I may need some help with the streets," he said.

"Most jobs are airport runs, and that's nothing but drivin' up and down the Promenade des Anglais," the Texan replied.

"How much do I get per run?"

"We charge fifty euros a pop. You take half. The other half is for the lease and my cut."

"How many customers will I get?"

"Maybe thirty a week."

Still not having lost his penchant for numbers, Alan quickly calculated his share to be 750 euros, enough for hotel and food, at least until he got his accounts unfrozen. "All right, when do I start?"

"Monday morning."

"Here?"

Buck slapped him on the back. "Where else, Al?"

4

Alan's first date with Jeannette took forever to arrive. Since his last conversation with her at the flower shop, he had been looking forward to their *randonnée*. But looking forward was one thing, and obsessing was another. Habits from his past still controlled him in times of stress, causing him to plan, forge goals, and visualize or even fantasize outcomes that never occurred. Such an approach suited him well at work, but did nothing for him socially.

In the case of Jeannette, he pondered many possibilities, all way ahead of the game: whether they'd fall in love, whether her child would accept him, what his role would be, where they'd live, how he'd support them in America or France, who the girl's father might be, what interference he would run, and of course, what type of lover this woman would end up being.

He perseverated in this manner, despite the fact he knew little about Jeannette. She could be a drug addict, an alcoholic, or a psycho with a borderline-personality disorder for all he knew, and Chloé, a defiant devil-child from hell. Simply put, he needed to live in the moment, but hadn't found the wherewithal to do it.

As a result of this inherently anxiety-producing mentality, he commenced a clock-watch vigil at Chez Betty at 8:45 a.m., a full fifteen minutes prior to the one-hour range of time he and Jeannette had agreed upon. At exactly 9:00 a.m., he ordered his usual "*double café*" from Alexis and some *pain au chocolat*. He ate and drank quickly, finishing by 9:15. From 9:15 to 9:30, he talked soccer with the young bartender, who worried about the possible demise of Marseille due to injuries and its players' prima-donna arrogance.

From 9:30 to 10:00, he observed bar characters: a portly old man wearing a sport jacket who ordered a breakfast of two grand ballons of red wine; the grocery store owner who stopped by for coffee before his morning bike ride; and a mentally ill guy, who every day without fail, according to Alexis, bought two panini ham and cheese sandwiches and three Oranginas.

By 10:00, Jeannette had not yet arrived. Maybe she had forgotten. Maybe something had happened to Chloé. Maybe she was blowing him off. Maybe she was messing with his head. Maybe she thought he was a loser. All manner of speculation flooded Alan's brain, and by 10:30 he had worked himself into a lather.

The bar phone rang, and Alexis answered. "Oui, oui," he said. He hung up and announced that Jeannette's alarm clock didn't work that morning, and she'd be a little late.

"My ass," Alan said loudly, now sounding more like Buck Treadway. He labeled his new crush passive-aggressive, irresponsible, and undisciplined. Of course his premature thoughts about a life with her before ever having gone on a single date evinced his own psychological issues. Self-help books he had read suggested a long list of "rule out" diagnoses: obsessive-compulsive disorder, generalized anxiety, dysthymia, and intermittent-explosive anger syndrome.

Finally, Jeannette and Chloé made it, and Alan noted the exact time of their arrival on his multi-function watch: 11:15 a.m. Yet he did not deliver a critical word, for his desire for the woman glossed over his anger and repressed his many hang ups. Besides, it would have been bad form to complain about tardiness in front of her daughter, especially on their first date.

Jeannette offered no apology and did not appear to be in any hurry. She had dressed down for the excursion, in a pair of khaki pants, a grey t-shirt, and hiking boots. Chloé had donned blue jeans and tennis shoes. Alan wore nothing different, since his clothing already conveyed an L.L. Bean look.

After they had some orange juice and chatted about one of Chloé's École-Maternelle activities, the hikers set off. Their route took them a kilometer or two down the Basse Corniche to St. Estève Escalier, an intimidating tower of zig-zagging stairways that disappeared high above them into a mountainous forest.

"Do all the stairs in Villefranche have a name?" Alan asked.

"Most," Jeannette replied. "They're like streets to us."

Alan looked upward, wondering if his heart would make it. "We may have to stop once in a while—to take in the view, of course."

Chloé, being a little explorer at the tender age of five, led the way, and Alan took up the rear, tightly grasping the wooden railings in order to pacify his fear of heights. Their arduous climb left little room for conversation.

Eight flights later, Alan stopped, his respiration having become labored and his shirt dampened with sweat. After catching his breath, he encouraged Chloé to ride him piggyback in order to demonstrate his worthiness as hiker and potential father figure. Needless to say his effort in this regard didn't last long. In general he was hardly a match for his companions, who had climbed the hilly terrain all their lives.

The stairs gave way to trails that wound their way up. "Soon there will be exercise stations," Jeannette announced with the vigor of a gym teacher. "We must try them." After one switchback, they saw a balance-beam, after another monkey bars, and following a third, hurdles—yes, hurdles! Chloé and her mother availed themselves of each apparatus, while Alan waited in the wings. Eventually the child raced to an area having stationary bikes and elliptical machines, and Jeannette joined him on a nearby park bench so they could talk.

"So who's her father?" Alan asked.

"*Capitaine de bateau,*" Jeannette answered quickly. In her next breath, she asked, "Isn't it wonderful they have this equipment? They've planned two more stations."

Alan ignored the not-so-subtle hint to change the subject, for missing social cues was another one of his deficits. "Given he is a boat captain, I don't imagine he spends much time with her. Does this clown even pay child support?" Class was also not one of his strong points.

Jeannette called out to Chloé, telling her in French it was time to get going. She grabbed the girl by the arm and stormed ahead—a bit over-dramatic but justified nevertheless.

"Wait, I'm sorry. I didn't mean to upset you," Alan yelled, chasing after them. After a few minutes he caught up. As he tried to explain himself further, Jeannette suddenly deviated from the marked path and into more difficult ground, thereby stimulating his fear of heights. "W-where are you going?" he asked, as he brushed aside tree branches and thorny bushes that scratched his hands and arms. At one point he even slid down a steep embankment on his butt rather than risk losing his balance while on his feet.

"I want to show you something," Jeannette finally replied. "Come, it's this way."

Alan didn't understand his date's mercurial attitude. First she acted calm, then she got pissed, and now she wanted him to accompany her on an off-trail expedition to parts unknown. "It's a long ways down, and we could get lost, or seriously injured," he protested.

"The sea is on the right and the mountaintop left, and Ville-franche is down there— just do what I do, and you'll be okay," Jeannette reassured.

After a few more minutes of braving the slippery hillside, they stopped at a boulder, carved with weathered initials of lovers past. Way down below, Alan could barely make out the church bell tower, though he did recognize the soccer field immediately, as it took up so much space. In the distance he savored a breathtaking expanse encompassing several nearby towns, the cape, and Villefranche Harbor. A feeling of peace replaced his vertigo.

"This is my secret place," Jeannette said quietly. "My mother took me here when I was Chloé's age."

"And now you do the same for her?"

"*Ça c'est oui.*"

While grasping the boulder, Alan thought of his own safe havens growing up: a favorite tree, a closet at his grandmother's house, and a small waterfall deep in the woods near his childhood home. "I'm glad we came here," he said. He turned to Chloé and tried to give her a geography lesson. "*Corsica est au-delà du cap,*" he said, pointing to the south.

"*La Corse,*" the little girl corrected.

After acknowledging his mistake, he continued, speaking of Tunisia, Morocco, Algeria and other African countries that existed far beyond the reaches of the French-island territory to which he had referred.

"*Et par là?*" the young girl asked, gesturing toward the west.

"*L'Amérique.*"

"*Est-ce que tu m'y emmèneras*—Will you take me there?"

Feeling the need to comfort the child, he managed two words. In English, they were someday and maybe.

"*Tais-toi, Chloé,*" her mother interrupted.

"Why are you telling her to be quiet?"

"Because it's not good to fill her heart with hopes and dreams that will never come true."

"Hopes and dreams are sometimes all we have."

"But when it comes to her, I need more than that."

Jeannette's response made Alan nervous. He wondered if she meant financial support, something he could not offer at the moment, but again he had gotten way ahead of himself.

Next they took a shortcut, with Chloé marching in front yet again, and came to an embankment that rose up to a stone fence that bordered a narrow road that led to a large edifice farther up the mountain. He gently lifted the child over the barrier, whereupon he and Jeannette climbed atop it and jumped down.

"*C'est Fort Alban,*" Chloé declared, dancing as they approached the building. Obviously she had been there before.

The greyish-brown medieval castle, forty feet high and a hundred square, was no work of art, but rather an intimidating display of military prowess. Crenellated walls, where soldiers must have hidden and shot arrows, were punctuated by square-corner towers having strategically placed murder holes from which boiling oil and water was likely poured upon attackers. Alan had a tough time imagining how they could possibly have scaled the rocky cliffs without falling, let alone dodged an onslaught of arrows while doing so.

He and Jeannette ascended a set of stone steps that led to an eight-foot-high wooden door, the only entrance to the building. Unfortunately the caretakers had padlocked it, making it impossible to explore inside. Instead they sat together on the stoop, while Chloé played in the courtyard below.

"I'm sorry for prying earlier," Alan told Jeannette. "But it seems like Chloé's father left you high and dry."

"It's for the best," she replied, her eyes morosely fixed on her child. "I don't want him around her anyway."

"What about a different kind of guy?"

"You mean, you?"

"Yeah, me. What's wrong with me?" It was a question he often asked himself.

"Well, for one thing you need to slow down. This is our first date, and we may not have anything in common."

"Uh-huh."

"So what do you like to do for fun?"

Alan struggled for an answer. His activities in his prior life were downright boring, and if he mentioned them, she'd likely have nothing to do with him. So he replied in a very non-committal way about his preferences going forward: "Seeing the sights around here would be cool, I guess." It was not much of an answer, but at least he had one.

"The bigger problem is we come from different worlds," Jeannette continued.

"How so?"

"Your life is in America, and mine is here. It's as simple as that."

Alan had reached a profound fork in the road. In the past he would not have decided which direction to take without considerable research and investigation, but now things were different, and he would allow himself risk if for no other reason than to prove he could tolerate it. "What if I stay?" he asked.

Jeannette gasped, obviously annoyed by his inability to listen.

"What's wrong?"

"You don't get it, do you?"

"Get what?"

"I barely know you, and you're already talking about moving to another country."

"Don't you like men who act without consequence?"

"In some ways, yes. But others, not so much."

It appeared Jeannette was becoming the person Alan knew well. He, in turn, seemed to be behaving more like her. If the relationship lasted, perhaps they could learn from each other and both become better people. The key was "if."

"I don't know. You're just such a geek," Jeannette said.

"Not anymore," Alan answered, plucking his cool-guy-messy hair. Despite his social incompetence, he did have a sense of humor, something that served him well at moments like this.

"Well, at least Chloé likes you." Alan put his arm around Jeannette, and she leaned into him and said, "Just don't hurt her, okay?"

"*C'est promis, ma chérie.*" French had finally found a way to roll off his lips. If only the rest were that easy. While relishing the view and romantic interlude, he took out his iPhone and snapped several pictures of the sea and coastline. He posted them on Facebook with the caption, "Pure Heaven." For the moment it was.

Just as he put the phone away, their attention was drawn to Chloé, who had been performing a balancing act on a four-foot-high wall in the courtyard. "*Fais attention!*" Jeannette yelled, but her daughter had already jumped off the wall and in the process sprained her ankle. As the girl wailed in pain, Jeannette examined the injury. Though she didn't notice much swelling, she suggested they go back to her apartment just in case.

The child's tears stopped as soon as Alan lifted her upon his shoulders and began carrying her down an asphalt path on the opposite side of the mountain. This time he wasn't trying to impress as he had done earlier while climbing the *escalier*. Instead he picked her up because he genuinely liked her and wished her no harm, something which Jeannette clearly noticed. "You're not such a geek after all," she whispered to him as they walked.

The three slowly made it to the Col de Villefranche, a business district at the peak of the village. Thereafter, they trudged down stairway after stairway to Jeannette's apartment near the bell-towered church. After Alan had lain little Chloé on the living room couch, he asked if they should take her to the doctor.

Jeannette pinched the child's ankle. Drawing no tears, she shook her head.

"Are you sure?" Alan asked.

"Yes, of course. But why are you so concerned?"

"I just don't want anything to happen to my damsel in distress."

"Wait a minute. I thought that phrase was reserved for me."

"I guess it could apply to any of us."

"Us?"

Jeannette paused to reflect, then slowly nodded approval. So too did Chloé.

Finally something had gone right.

* * *

Alan's mind churned all night after his first date with Jeannette, alternating between giddiness and anxiety over whether the new relationship would work out. She was correct, of course: they were from different worlds, making the prospect of success in such an endeavor minimal at best. Even so, it was worth pursuing.

After taking a shower and getting dressed, he made his usual pilgrimage to the corner bakery for a slice of quiche and returned to Chez Betty to wash it down with some espresso. Before he could practice his French with Alexis, Buck Treadway dropped his cowboy hat down next to him at the bar and ordered a *petit café*.

Due to his obsession over Jeannette, Alan had nearly forgotten about his first day of work for the man.

"Sleep well, Al?"

"Not really."

"Something botherin' ya?"

"I don't know if 'bother' is the right word."

"All right, what kept you up? A pack of yowlin' cats outside yur winder?"

"Not quite."

"Happens 'round here, ya know."

"What's that?"

"Yowlin'cats." Buck laughed his way into a coughing fit, grabbed his napkin, spit into it, and examined the phlegm. "Goddamn French cigarettes."

"Maybe try vaping instead."

"Or get some real honest-to-god smokes."

"Like what, Marlboros?"

"Yep. The ones in a box." Buck resumed his hacking until his eyes watered. Finally when he composed himself, he said, "They used to call me the Marlboro man."

"If the shoe fits, I guess."

Buck stirred some sugar into a demitasse of coffee with a dainty spoon given to him by Alexis, providing an interesting contrast to his Wild West look. After taking a sip, he asked, "So what is it, a lady friend?"

"Huh?"

"That's causing you to fret."

Alan gave a bashful smile. "How'd you know?"

"Saw you helpin' Jeannette Brouillet with some flowers the other day at that shop of hers," Buck replied. He looked around to see if anyone was listening and lowered his voice, something which he strained to do. "I'd be real careful if I were you, pardner."

"Why's that?"

"Put it to you this way: she's got some tough hombres in her life."

"Like who?"

"Rather not say—just keep it in mind before you go deep."

"Now you got me going."

"If and when it becomes an issue, I'll let you know," Buck said. "But right now we need to talk business."

"The cab business, right?"

The Texan backed away from his coffee. "First thing you gotta learn is it's not a cab business."

"But I thought you said I'd be driving people around town."

"In your own vee-hee-cul," Buck stressed.

"Yeah, the one you're leasing me."

"Pure business, my man. Pure business."

"How so?"

"Taxi licenses cost 250,000 euros."

"But you aren't a taxi business."

"Exactly. It's called redefining the problem. Trouble is the cab drivers don't cotton to it very much."

"What do you mean?"

"Par-ree, they went on a *grève* and blocked traffic clear up and down the Champs-Élysées all on account of Uber."

"Yeah, I heard about that."

"The gumint wouldn't outlaw it, and it pissed 'em off. And that's when I decided to get in on the action, bein' the risin' entrepreneur that I am."

Alan nodded slowly.

"Anyway, numero uno, we're not a cab company," the Texan emphasized. "We don't get in a rank or let anyone hail us. Just meet the customers where I tell ya."

"Where's my cab, or uh leased vehicle rather?"

"Follow me."

They left Chez Betty and went around the corner to a red 2014 extended-cab Chevrolet Silverado. It had no taxi-light on its roof, of course.

"How does a customer know who to look for?" Alan asked.

"Come this way."

They went to the front of the truck, where Buck smiled like a proud father at a pair of longhorns that garnished its hood.

"Did you get 'em in Texas?"

"Hell yeah, I did," Buck replied. "You shoulda seen them Frenchie customs agents at the airport. Must have thought I'd come back from a safari."

"I can just imagine."

"The customers are told to look for them, and case they don't understand what a longhorn is, put this on the dash when you pull up," Buck instructed. He handed him a sign that read *"Véhicule Privé de Transport."*

"And how do I know where to go?"

"I'll call you with this." Buck stuck a company phone in Alan's shirt pocket.

"And how do people pay?"

"Cash or credit. If it's credit, use this here app," Buck said. "We settle up at the end of each week at Chez Betty. Understood?"

"I guess."

"Got any other questions?"

"Yeah. Don't I need a chauffeur permit?"

Buck slapped a fifty-euro bill in Alan's hand.

"What's that?"

"Your permit."

* * *

Alan's first five days of work went down without a hitch, and he quickly became accustomed to the highways and byways of the area: the Moyenne Corniche, or the upper main drag that complemented the lower Basse Corniche; convoluted streets that curled around to the hotels by the water; and the route to the Nice airport. He learned to negotiate the hilly parts of town as well, which sometimes had only one lane for two-way traffic and plenty of hairpin curves. In between runs, he listened to French tapes and memorized vocabulary while sitting in the pickup, though he would have been better off conversing with Betty or Alexis at the hotel bar.

Most of his customers that week were students from the local French immersion school who wanted to go to the airport in order to return home. They included a hot Russian model and her mother, a singer from Canada, a chef from England, a Red Cross worker from Ethiopia, and an American diplomat from D.C, all interesting people. The diplomat reminded him of himself before he went off the deep end and came to France.

After the student runs on Friday, Buck gave Alan one more customer: an unusually short Norwegian woman who had flown in from Oslo. She provided only her first name—Eva. At her direction, he drove her from the airport to a swank apartment atop Ville-franche. As he was dropping her off, he asked what had brought her to town.

"My husband died, and I'm returning his body to Norway," she said.

Norway? Must be Rolf Swenson. I mean, how many dead Norwegians are there around here? Alan thought. He confirmed the fact with Eva, but did not bring up the sordid details of the man's death. Nor did he tell her he was a suspect in his murder. Instead he offered her a free fare to assuage her loss. She declined, and he drove back down the hill to Chez Betty for his accounting with Buck.

As he did so, he noticed in his rearview mirror two taxis tightly trailing him. Every time he accelerated out of a hairpin, they quickly caught up and closed within inches of his rear bumper. The chase escalated when one of the cabs dangerously swerved around him and blocked his progress, whereupon the other rammed the rear of the pickup, nearly pushing him off the road. He would be pinned between the two taxis if he didn't take evasive action.

So he veered to the left and attempted to pass, but was quickly cut off by the forward cab. He did not have enough time to avoid this vehicle and collided right smack dab in the middle of its front quarter panel. Somehow he managed to slip by the French taxi, but not before one of the cabbies flipped him the bird and screamed: *"Putain triche!"*

When Alan finally made it to the bar, he anxiously greeted Buck, who was already waiting. Wiping off the sweat streaming down his face from the intimidating encounter, Alan told him what had happened and asked what the phrase meant that the cabbies had used.

"Fucking cheat," Buck replied bluntly. "It's a reference to us getting around the rules. The bottom line is they don't like the competition."

Alan suggested they check the pickup for damage. They went to the truck's rear first.

"Looks good," the Texan said. "Bumper must've done its job."

"Better check the front. I rammed one of them with it while getting away."

When they circled the vehicle, to Alan's astonishment, Buck began to bawl like a baby. One of the longhorns had been broken off during the collision. "Mercy, Jesus," he shrieked. "Look at what them Frenchies done now."

Alan attempted to console his new boss. "Maybe we can find the horn and glue it back on," he suggested.

"Glue it?"

"You know, Superglue."

Buck shook his head in disgust. "Ain't no Superglue in these parts."

"I'll get you another longhorn, okay. Just stop crying."

Buck wiped his tears away with the top of his wrist and slung his arm around Alan. "That's okay, pardner—price of doing business, I guess."

"Especially when the business involves driving a cab without a taxi license."

Buck growled. "Private vee-hee-cul for hire."

"Whatever."

"Next time one of them Frenchies bothers you, park the truck and take this to 'em," Buck said angrily. He reached under the driver's seat and pulled out a tire iron.

Alan backed away in alarm. "Aren't you worried someone will get hurt?"

"Nah. They'll run like the devil, just like they did in dub-ya dub-ya two."

"But this isn't war, Buck—"

"It is now!"

* * *

In anticipation of going to the soccer match with Ludovic, Alan had purchased some Marseille gear: a sky-blue baseball cap and matching jersey, each embroidered with the team badge and motto, *Droit Au But* (right in the goal). It cost him about seventy euros, but he felt flush due to that week's earnings being more than expected. He thought that wearing the clothing would demonstrate his loyalty to the team and endear him to the regulars at Chez Betty.

Ludovic arrived pretty much on time, dressed in his standard uniform of a reverse beret and leather jacket. But he had skipped his light-blue scarf. As a matter of fact, his entire ensemble included not a single color or emblem of Marseille. He approached the bar with a look of great concern.

"Something wrong?" Alan wondered if there was a problem with the tickets.

"If you go match, must change clothes," Ludovic said, pointing to the brand-new Marseille jersey and hat. He shook his finger back and forth in front of Alan's face as though he were scolding a child. "*Ligue Un* not NFL."

"In America we show support by wearing team colors, even at away games."

"Seats in Nice section. That not safe."

"Anything else I need to know?"

"Oui. When Nice mark, clap—but not for Marseille." Ludovic put his hands together as though he were a priest praying at an altar and tapped his fingers together softly, his way of demonstrating how to feign support for the opposition all the while saving face.

After Alan ditched his outfit in his room, he met his soccer match companion outside Chez Betty, where the latter had parked his dark-purple Renault. "How much do I owe you for the ticket," he asked.

"Thirty euros."

Alan handed him the money, got in the right front passenger seat, and off they went. Ludovic took the back way to Nice, which consisted of a perilous ride through a series of narrow streets and alleyways. He explained that this was how'd they get to the Voie Rapide, Nice's only expressway. On the way, he nearly hit two parked cars, ran six stop signs, and caused a pedestrian in a crosswalk to dive into a ditch.

"You sure drive fast."

"Drove cab. Quit," Ludovic answered.

Rather than discuss his own questionable participation in the business, Alan asked, "So where do you work now?"

"Sweep *escaliers* and overlooks for Villefranche."

"Do you make good money?"

"Not like taxi."

After going through a long tunnel and around several mountains, they came to a semi-rural area, where a brightly lit stadium known as Allianz-Riviera emerged from a murky mist. Its undulating top gave it the appearance of a giant space ship that had landed from a faraway planet. At any moment Alan expected alien creatures to exit its many portals and invade the Cote D'Azur.

Ludovic left the car in a dirt lot a quarter mile away after paying an exorbitant parking fee and they walked to the stadium. Unlike in the States, nobody tailgated, and the smell of brats, hamburgers and hotdogs that pervaded the air at games back home was missing. Hundreds of Nice fans made their way to the entrances, wearing red and white scarves and jerseys imprinted OGC-Nice. Sky blue could not be seen.

"Where are the Marseille fans?" Alan asked. Ludovic told him they were given their own parking area and a separate entrance on the other side of the stadium for safety reasons.

As they got closer to their destination, they saw several gangs of red-and-white-clad men crowded around small arrangements of green beer bottles on the ground. The men eyed them carefully for their allegiance. Perhaps they should have worn Nice colors to camouflage their loyalty to Marseille, but likely Ludovic wouldn't have gone that far. Near the entrance they climbed a long ramp that led up to an outdoor concourse. Farther down the walkway some cops patted them down, but did so very superficially.

Inside, the stadium had a state-of-the-art feel: wide concession concourses on multiple levels, broad stairways and escalators, comfortable auditorium seating, and a soccer field with the latest in turf technology. They easily found their seats in the highest level on what would have been the ten-yard line at an American football game.

As they sat down, Alan asked his companion if either team had a name besides the city they represented. He footnoted his question with the fact that U.S. sports teams had designations like Bears, Packers, Colts, and Broncos.

Ludovic shook his head.

"What about a mascot?"

The response was the same. Le Foot did not mess around with triviality apparently.

Alan scanned the seating on the other side of the venue and noted that one part looked different, since it offered a splash of light blue amongst a blanket of red and white. *Marseille fans*, he thought. The triangular-shaped section contained perhaps fifty rows that stretched from field level to the top of the facility. Two twenty-foot-high Plexiglass partitions flanked the section and protected the people inside from angry Niceans. Additionally, a buffer zone, perhaps twenty to thirty seats wide, ran along the barriers that numerous burly security cops kept empty.

Suddenly, a loud chorus of whistles erupted and jolted Alan back in his seat. The goalie for Marseille had taken the field to warm up. He ran back and forth and jumped up and down while stretching his white-gloved hands skyward, taunting the crowd into an angry frenzy. Ludovic smiled proudly, then turned to Alan and circumspectly said, *"Notre gardien de but est bon*—Our goalie is good." Fortunately his words could not be heard by those who surrounded them due to the steady barrage of taunts and sneers that were being lodged against the player.

The goalie for Nice ran out next. In contrast the crowd greeted him with thunderous acclamation. A few minutes later the rest of the players from both teams slowly dribbled out onto the field and went through a series of drills with their feet, passing and kicking soccer balls around in magician-like fashion.

As the stadium filled, a mob of several thousand Nice fans behind the goal on Alan's right began rhythmically chanting, "Nee-sa, Nee-sa." Some of the fans waved giant red and white flags while others hacked the air violently with their hands, impatient for the blood-bath to begin.

The announcer drew people's attention to the center of the closest sideline. Players from both teams faced the crowd in a queue and rested their hands on the shoulders of young girls and boys in front of them, who were dressed in soccer clothes. It was supposed to show mentorship and support for youth sports, but the display ended shortly when a cherry bomb exploded.

Alan snapped his head in the direction of the Nice goal, where more firecrackers went off and the crowd flag-waved, whistled, and vibrated like a hive of angry bees. He noticed the orange glow of fire in various spots and red and white pieces of cloth cascading down the crowd onto the "terrain." Worried that the series of conflagrations would engender a mass stampede, he started to get up. But Ludovic calmly remained seated, so Alan dropped back down. As the fires subsided, smoke still obscured the field, but lifted, thereby revealing the methodical grind of professional French soccer.

"Wow, that was something," Alan exclaimed. "But I thought the police searched everyone."

"Flares and fireworks *interdit* but flics don't care," Ludovic replied. "They hate Marseille too."

By *mi-temps* neither team had managed a goal. The only noteworthy event in the back-and- forth defensive battle was when the ref gave a Nice player a yellow card for an aggressive tackle. This caused the crowd to whistle the rest of the match even on the most obvious calls. Alan's ears soon hurt, and his head pounded at the continuous shrill.

During the break he went down to the concession stand and bought some popcorn, the only game food he recognized. On the way back he climbed a flight of stairs leading to his section. Between the stairwells, he saw far below a contingent of about fifty cops, who had donned full riot gear in preparation for the decisive second half and a possible donnybrook after the game. The gear included helmets, face masks, shields, tear-gas canisters, and billy clubs. While this may have been overkill, Alan knew the police wouldn't have done this unless prior experience had dictated it. So far his own experience dictated it.

Fortunately, the Nice fans adopted a better mood toward the end of the game, when the ball somehow wandered into the Marseille goal. From that point forward, they faithfully sang a song over and over, with each stanza being accented by three hard unintelligible chants. Valiantly Marseille tried to get back into the game, but their efforts went for naught. Both Alan and Ludovic politely clapped at a Nice insurance goal in the non-committal manner that they had agreed.

After stoppage time had expired and the head ref raised his arm, signaling the end of play, they left the stadium and tried to make their way back to the car. They never got there. A rowdy gang of hooligans charged after them with obvious acrimonious intent.

Alan didn't know what motivated the attack. Maybe someone had recognized Ludovic as a Marseille fan, or worse they had become caught in the cross-fire of a larger fight. Perhaps Buck's rivals were engaged in yet another round of intimidation. Whatever the reason, they had to get out of there quickly, as their very lives depended on it.

At first, the pursuit went across the stadium grounds, where Alan and Ludovic easily made themselves scarce among thousands of departing fans and cars. But after they got to the other side of the Voie-Rapide in an area of hotels, strip malls and farmland, no longer was there security in numbers. Ludovic spotted one of the attackers and yelled to Alan, "*Vas-y par là!*"

In response Alan sprinted in the direction instructed in paranoid frenzy, while Ludovic split off, thereby drawing the posse his way. After several hours of searching for him, Alan gave up and rode a shuttle bus safely back to Villefranche and Chez Betty. He worried all night long about his friend and the reason for the attack. There was more to this than Le Foot, he thought, though he wasn't sure he wanted to find out what that might be.

5

The nurse at the reception desk at Hôpital L'Archet refused to give directions to Ludovic's room or acknowledge his status as a patient. Alan knew otherwise, of course, for Betty had told him the poor guy had been severely beaten and taken by ambulance to a medical facility close to the stadium. A quick Internet search revealed this had to be the place.

Undaunted by the nurse's response, Alan cruised several hallways and found the right room. The patient was alive and awake though obviously not well. His left arm was in a cast, and his ribs were wrapped in beige medical bandages. Stitches above his eyebrows highlighted a swollen and bruised face, and a wired-shut jaw disrupted communication with him more than usual.

Alan's reaction to the pathetic scene was mixed. On the one hand, he felt lucky to have escaped the marauding gang. On the other hand, he wanted to exact some measure of revenge, perhaps with the assistance of Buck. But after fuming beside the bed for several minutes, he came to his senses. "Who did this to you?" he whispered to his soccer friend.

Ludovic moaned something unintelligible through his teeth and swollen lips.

Alan searched the room and retrieved a crumpled-up piece of paper from the waste basket. He gave it to him together with a pen. *"Écris le nom ici,"* he instructed. Ludovic started to scrawl something, then suddenly relaxed his hand and dropped the pen to his bedside.

"I see you and your friend have become reconnected," a French-accented male voice said quietly. "I didn't want to interrupt your heart-to-heart talk, but I found I could no longer resist."

Alan saw Esnault at the door. "What are you doing here?"

"Funny, I was about to ask you that same question," the lieutenant replied while snatching up Ludovic's note. "Who won the match, by the way?"

"Nice. Two nil."

"What a pity. I too am a Marseille fan, you see."

Esnault circled Ludovic's bed, inspecting his many injuries. He shifted his eyes back to Alan. "Did you recognize the men who chased you after the match?"

"No, but how'd you know we were chased? For that matter how'd you know we were even at the match?"

The cop turned to Ludovic's bed without acknowledging Alan's questions. Perhaps he believed the patient's weakened condition would loosen his lips despite the wired merger of his teeth. "I don't suppose *he* recognized anyone either."

Ludovic garbled what seemed like a response, but his words could easily have been the result of a hallucination induced by a heavy dose of French Oxycodone.

"*C'est un oui ou non?*"

Not liking the belligerent tone of Esnault's voice or knowing what he would do next, Alan attempted to divert his attention by asking him if he had any other leads.

The lieutenant nudged Ludovic's casted arm enough to draw a wince and coldly said, "Further investigation shouldn't be necessary, provided our witness is willing to cooperate."

"Look, if he doesn't want to say anything, he probably has his reasons."

Esnault stuck his face within inches of Alan's and presented a disquieting smile. "He has his options, and I have mine."

Ludovic grimaced, though it was difficult to tell if it was born out of pain or fear.

"One other thing," the lieutenant said before heading out the door. "Have you found your boarding pass or train ticket?"

"No, I must have thrown them out."

Esnault raised his thick eyebrows. "As I might have guessed. As to your newly acquired penchant for Le Foot, you may wish to confine your observation of such competition to the large screen television at Chez Betty."

* * *

Buck Treadway was happy as happy could be. In front of him on the bar lay a brand-new set of longhorns a friend had Fed-Exed him from Texas. He caressed the adornment as if it were a long-lost love. "Al, you got to promise to be more careful next time."

"Yeah, I know. Just confront the bastards with the tire iron and no power moves with the pickup."

"And stand your ground," Buck added.

The two went outside Chez Betty where the Texan screwed the horns on the truck's hood.

While Buck worked, Alan gave his rendition of the soccer-match mélée. "Do you know who might have roughed up Ludovic?"

"Not sure—probably has to do with a feller named Christophe." Buck put his screwdriver back in his toolbox, wiped his hand off with a rag, and stood back. "There, much better."

"I haven't met Christophe yet. Who's he?"

An angry, determined look invaded Buck's face. "Ludovic's former employer and our chief competitor."

"In the cab business, right?"

Buck sighed impatiently. "Al, you need to stop talking like that."

Inside the bar, the Texan ordered a whiskey, and Alan bought a Perrier from the vending machine. But the topic of the soccer match would not go away.

"Did Christophe have Ludovic beaten up?"

"No doubt."

"But why?"

"That would involve a long discussion that my time does not permit."

"Okay, I get it, but just answer me this: Was Christophe behind the cab-ramming incident a few weeks back?"

"Most likely."

"Why did Ludovic quit working for him in the first place? Sweeping overlooks and escaliers isn't exactly a lateral move."

"He didn't like Christophe's methods, or maybe Christophe didn't like his."

"I guess those methods include violence."

"Apparently so," Buck replied, nodding toward the front door.

Ludovic limped to the bar, his backwards beret, leather jacket and L'OM scarf on full defiant display. His arm was still in a cast, but the swelling had gone down on his face.

"I see you've made it out of the hospital," Alan noted pleasantly. But the mood was hardly festive.

Ludovic couldn't speak, since his jaw was still wired shut. He did, however, communicate better than at the hospital, though said communication came in the form of grunts, growls, and snarls.

"Get 'em a whiskey," Buck said. "He needs one."

Thierry, the bar manager, rushed over and poured a shot, and Ludovic withdrew a straw from his leather jacket with his one good hand and stuck it in the glass.

"You're looking better than a few days ago," Alan noted, again with upbeat inflection.

Grunt.

"Feel like going to another match soon?"

Snarl.

"You'll be back to work in no time; don't you worry about a damn thing," Buck said.

Ludovic tried to smile, but for obvious reasons his attempt fell short.

"So did the people who beat you up at the match think you were a Marseille fan?" Alan asked.

Ludovic shrugged.

"Well, if it wasn't that, what was it?"

There was no response.

"Was it Christophe?"

Despite his pain meds, Ludovic moaned.

"Better get him another," Buck told Thierry, who quickly replenished the shot glass.

Alan persisted. "Did you do something your former boss didn't like?"

This time Ludovic growled.

"Maybe we should let it drop, least 'til he gets stronger," Buck said. He threw some euros on the bar and got up to leave.

After Buck departed, Alan turned to Ludovic and described how he had been a victim of a different act of violence several weeks back, when he was chased by the cabbies. Since his friend was not much of a talker that evening, Alan performed a monologue of speculation about the events that had transpired and Ludovic's former boss's involvement. Eventually he popped a question without considering its consequences very carefully. "Tell me something, my friend: Is there a way to get a gun around here for self-defense?"

Ludovic spit out his whiskey on the bar.

* * *

Alan went up to his room after his encounter with Ludovic. While propped up on his bed, he scoured the Internet on the topic of guns in France, his mind having now spiraled completely out of control. The beating at the match, the game of bumper cabs, what Buck had told him about Christophe, and Rolf's murder had put his brain on overdrive, something that happened very easily anyway.

He discovered France regulated four categories of guns: A) fully automatic weapons that were generally illegal for civilians to possess without special authorization; B) handguns and semi-automatic weapons; C) hunting rifles and semi-automatics with non-detachable magazines; and D) everything else. To legally possess a firearm, it was necessary to obtain a sport-shooting permit, meaning he would have to be an active member of a gun club, get a doctor to attest to his physical and mental capacity, and pass a police background check to make sure he wasn't a criminal or some other nefarious person.

With respect to the last requirement, he thought of Esnault and quickly discarded the notion of lawful gun ownership. He closed his laptop, determined to move on to something else, but the obsession returned. So he opened his computer back up and began researching the elements of self-defense in France, or *la légitime défense*.

First, the danger had to be imminent, that is immediate. Second, a gun could not be used to stop a fleeing aggressor. Third, the threat had to be an illegal one. In other words one couldn't use force against police officers who were acting with lawful authority. Fourth, self-defense could not be employed aggressively or in revenge for an initial interference with one's person. Fifth, it had to be necessary. Finally, it needed to be proportionate to the threat—with the aggressor exerting a similar level of force upon the defender. While the burden of proof was normally on the person claiming the defense, he or she was not required to sustain this burden with respect to preventing entry into or evicting an intruder from his or her home.

Alan doubted he would be able to think through all these permutations in the heat of battle. So he reviewed the law's application regarding the use of a gun in the scenarios he had experienced thus far: being run off the road—maybe, depending on whether he could escape; receiving a beating at a soccer match or somewhere else on the street—probably not, unless the thugs used a deadly weapon to exact it. But if someone was in the middle of breaking into his hotel room while he was present, deadly force might be justified.

A Skype message from Barry Simon diverted Alan's attention from these sinister musings. It was still afternoon in America, so he called him back.

When the phone picked up, Barry said, "I'm afraid I have some bad news."

"What now?"

"I got your paperwork from France, the statement from the cop, and your affidavit explaining your presence there."

"Uh-huh."

"I filed a motion to dissolve the judge's injunction freezing your accounts."

"And?"

Kenneth Farmer

"The judge denied the motion without a hearing."

Alan flopped backwards on the bed with one hand on his brow and the other on his iPhone. "What?"

"Your wife's lawyer gave a response," Barry said flatly. "He argued that since you had fled to France, you could no longer avail yourself of the laws of the U.S."

"I didn't *flee* a damn thing."

"His citation to the Fugitive Disentitlement Doctrine was brilliant."

"*Fugitive!*"

"I know, I know. It's a bit strong," Barry said. "That's for wanted criminals who sue the cops."

"I am *not* a criminal!" Alan hollered. Of course he had moved closer to that label by becoming a suspect in a murder case, contemplating the illegal purchase of a handgun for protection, and associating with the less-than-above-board vehicle-for-hire operation of Buck Treadway.

"It gets worse," Barry continued.

Alan wondered how that could possibly be.

"Your wife's attorney filed a motion for default judgment, since you've not been present in court."

"But I gave you an appearance authorization."

"Yeah, I know. But given your rather precipitous departure, the judge doesn't care."

Alan grabbed a pillow and screamed into it, using every profanity in the book. Then he pummeled the bed with his fists.

"You still there? Alan...Alan?"

Regaining his composure temporarily, he grabbed his iPhone and asked Barry Simon what would happen next.

"Well, the judge took the default motion under advisement."

"And if he signs it, she gets everything?"

"Not everything. Just most of it."

"Do me a favor Barry, will ya?"

"Depends on the favor."

"Kill me! Get a gun or a knife or whatever, and kill me!"

"Can't do that, Alan."

"Why not?"

"You're four thousand miles away."

* * *

Despite his problems with his wife and his crumbling world in France, Alan's relationship with Jeannette continued to flower. Lately they had agreed to spend the day in a little town called Èze, some twenty minutes away from Villefranche by bus. One of the main attractions in the village was the Fragonard perfume factory.

The date started off much better than the hike up Mont Boron. Jeannette arrived at Chez Betty within the broad time frame they had agreed upon, and Alan traded in clock-watching for reading the paper while he waited. She had purchased him a card, a minor expression of affection. He hadn't gotten her anything yet, but figured there would be plenty of opportunity in Èze.

The long climb to the Col de Villefranche, where they would catch the bus, provided yet another opportunity for rigorous exercise, something that by now Alan had grown accustomed. After departing Chez Betty, they rounded the corner of the hotel and walked through an alley to a set of stairs. This led to another, and a third that went straight up as far as he could see. In all, Alan counted 277 steps. Yes, he counted every one. At the top of the last stairway, he turned to Jeannette and smiled victoriously, where-upon she smiled back and told him they were only half way up.

A series of steep and winding streets followed the stairs. Due to the bedrock next to the road that could not be easily chopped back, there wasn't enough room to build a normal-size sidewalk, much less a terrace between it and the street. Where a narrow walkway did exist, it flanked only one side of the road. Sometimes it went to the other side, requiring them to cross the street. At a few points it didn't exist at all, and they had to duck between parked cars and hug rocky cliffs whenever they heard the drone of a vehicle or moto approaching. "Heard" was the operative word, since the sight of a vehicle did not occur until it was too late because of hairpin turns and curves.

At the front desk of the Fragonard perfume factory, a receptionist told them a tour would be free and assigned a guide who was somewhat fluent in English. The guide, a thick-waisted middle-aged blonde, escorted the couple down some stairs and into the production area. There she demonstrated with a large chart the eight flowers grown near Grasse from which the main scents of perfume were obtained. They included roses, orange blossoms, mimosa, jasmine, lavender, violets, genet, and tuberose. The flowers were distilled into fragrance on location, where their power was the greatest. Thereafter the resulting essence was transported to factories and made into perfume or added to soaps and various cosmetics. In addition, other scents and spices from all over the world were used.

"Perfume has the highest amount of floral extraction, followed by ésprit de perfume, eau de perfume, eau de toilette, eau de cologne, perfume mist, and splash," the guide rattled off. "The concentrations are determined by the amount of water and alcohol employed, and they are carefully regulated by industry standards."

The highlight of the tour was a glass-enclosed room containing a multi-level console that looked like a church organ. The console held several hundred small vials of scent. The organist, of course, was the *Né* or Nose.

"The Né creates the perfume," the guide said. "Nés go to specialized schools in France, and only when they are able to distinguish over three-thousand fragrances, do they receive their certification."

"How long does the schooling take?" Alan asked.

"Ten years total, seven to learn the scents and three to become educated in perfume chemistry."

"Wow. They must have a helluva of memory."

"That is very true, sir. But their most cherished asset is their creativity."

"They're so artistic," Jeannette chimed in, clasping her hands together blissfully.

"As well as structured and organized," Alan countered.

The guide smiled, obviously amused by their divergent perspectives. "A combination of such attributes is the most important thing," she emphasized cheerfully. "A balance for which we should all strive."

They finished their tour of the factory at a gift shop, where they found an expansive perfume inventory and sampled selections to the point where they could not well separate them. Jeannette fixated on some *eau de toilette* having a heavy-evening accent, so Alan purchased it for her. It was a good choice, for she smiled and immediately dabbed some behind her ears.

After Fragonard, they ascended a steep cobbled walkway through town and up to Nid d'Aigle, or Eagle's Nest, a 1,400-foot-high overlook that sat atop Èze. Its features included a botanical garden of cacti among ancient castle ruins and a limitless panoramic view, accented by a brilliant sun-induced column of light that stretched out to sea for miles. They stood hand in hand in silence, mesmerized by the awesome display of nature's beauty and power, and spent well over an hour at the nest. This set a romantic tone for the rest of the day.

Following a late lunch at a local café, Jeannette brought Alan to a walking trail that started not far from the entrance to Nid d'Aigle. It traversed back and forth all the way down to the sea. "It's called Nietzsche Path," she said. "He climbed it every day in the summer."

"I remember learning about him in college," Alan replied. "The heat gave him hallucinations and inspired him to write."

"Or perhaps the drugs he took."

At Jeannette's insistence, they descended the rocky trail that often narrowed to a few feet. As usual Alan's fear of heights slowed him down. He crept along, being careful not to trip on rocks that sharply protruded. If he fell, the least that would happen would be embarrassment, and the worst, a trip back on a stretcher in a French med-flight helicopter. Jeannette, by contrast, forged ahead fearlessly, tiptoeing up, down and around all obstructions with the precision of a ballet dancer. Since the distance to the bottom was five kilometers and would take at least an hour, Alan warned that darkness would make their route back dangerous. Jeannette responded, almost parenthetically, that they could always catch the bus to Villefranche on the highway far below.

Toward the end of the trail near the sea, the sunny day turned to an auburn dusk. At this point a safer stone path with walls on either side emerged, and Alan felt relief. This didn't last long, since Jeannette ran ahead and disappeared. He kept walking, figuring she would come back soon enough and end her game of cat and mouse, but she did not. Had she fallen and hurt herself? Had one of his cab-company enemies taken her? Had she ditched him, having experienced second thoughts about their relationship? Finally, without warning, she grabbed him from behind, startling him. He pulled her around and into his arms, and his feeling of paranoia transformed into delight.

"*C'est bon, non?*"

Overtaken by Jeannette's accent, Alan pondered what it would be like to have sex with a French woman, naïvely believing that somehow it would be different. At first he resisted the enticing fantasy, then gave in as he smelled the fragrance he had bought her. His lips met hers, but as quickly as the passionate tryst had begun, she put her hands on his chest and pushed him away. "I must know you better first," she said.

With the exception of his title company job, he had told her little. So he went into his failed marriage and changed outlook in more detail, albeit cautiously. He mentioned that his wife had frozen his bank accounts, forcing him to work for Buck, and that the police wanted him to stay in France due to "a legal problem." Before he could get into the specifics, she interrupted him and asked if he would be returning to the States given his money issues. "Maybe to settle my divorce," he replied.

Jeannette turned away from him and walked farther down the hillside, but he caught up with her, put his hands on her shoulders and said, "I wouldn't leave you, really I wouldn't."

She kissed him in return, but this time less passionately. "Come, we must go."

"But it's too dark," he protested, ominously looking at the mountainside that now towered above in a shadowy mist. Eventually he gave in, however, and they made their way back up. Luckily Jeannette stayed close by. Whether this was due to the growing darkness or the marginal intimacy that they had achieved, Alan could not determine. As they reached the top, he finally relaxed and asked, "What was the name of the work that Nietzsche wrote here?"

"*Thus Spoke Zarathustra.*"

Alan perched himself atop a large rock along the trail and pulled out his iPhone. He looked up the title and found a quote from the philosophical masterpiece that seemed to epitomize his journey of self-discovery while in France. It said: "I am a forest, and a night of dark trees: but he, who is not afraid of my darkness, will find banks full of roses under my cypresses."

The words seemed to justify his pain, not to mention his newfound relationship. He vowed never to live by fear again and instead to be guided by the still, quiet muses that emanated from deep inside him. By that process, he believed, he would once and for all find the bank of roses he so desperately sought. Now it was time to wander deeper in the dark forest.

6

The Quai des États-Unis, a mile-long boardwalk that divided Old Nice from the Mediterranean beachfront and ran parallel to the Promenade des Anglais, offered an interesting history. Originally, it had been a stone rampart that protected the city from naval attack. After World War I and various redevelopments of the surface over the years, the French dedicated it to the United States in recognition of its defense of their country against the Triple Alliance of Germany, Austria-Hungary, and Italy. In modern times the quai had become a haven for joggers, walkers, cyclists, and artists.

Alan went there alone with Chloé. Jeannette had called without notice and asked him to babysit, because she needed to take her mother to the podiatrist. The elderly woman lived a considerable distance down the coast in Saint Paul, and from time to time would request her assistance.

Alan's reaction to the proposal was one of reticence and apprehension. Being isolated with a five-year-old girl presented the potential for all manner of accusation, something particularly concerning since accusation had become so much a part of his life. Further, he had had little experience with children, as his marriage to Sara had produced none. Finally, while Jeannette and he had gone on various day trips with Chloé, the prospect of an extended one-on-one conversation with the child struck him as daunting.

When he had raised these issues with Jeannette, she said she understood his reservation, but claimed she had no reasonable alternative; her mother's ailing foot required immediate medical attention, and Jeannette was her only means of transportation. Taking Chloé along was not an option, as she would likely be a constant source of distraction while Jeannette tended her mother's needs. Enter Alan, who, despite his lack of confidence in this realm and general ineptness, needed to buck up. To make things easier, Jeannette suggested he take her daughter to Nice and the Quai des États-Unis, where there would be much diversion.

"Puis-je t'appeler, Alan?" Chloé asked as they stood next to a small ebony replica of the Statue of Liberty along the boardwalk. Her precocious politeness in asking what to call him entertained him. Nevertheless it put to the forefront a significant point: What was he to this child? A father figure? A mentor? A friend? And just as important, what was she to him? He told her to refer to him as Alan, his name when he wasn't around Buck Treadway.

Chloé pointed to the statue. *"Alan, c'est quoi?"*

He gave the little girl a long lecture about France's gift of friendship to America and how the real Statue of Liberty constituted a universal symbol of freedom and democracy. He described its dimensions and went on at length about how people could climb up inside it and look out the crown. Even though he spoke in French, the child stared blankly, as his words had fallen into the category of too much information.

As he tried to recover, Chloé asked him where the statue was located, and he told her. She then wanted to know if he lived in New York, and he explained that he resided in a town near Chicago. She seemed satisfied with this response, which was fine with him, as he didn't particularly want to get into the rest of the story.

They returned to their walk along the quay, where they took in the beach that by this time of year was full of sun bathers, some of whom were topless. He felt embarrassed and wondered if he should shield the child from the spectacle. But Chloé was oblivious, no doubt because she hadn't reached an age in which breasts had any sexual significance, and she lived in a culture where no one really cared.

"*Est-ce que t'as une famille à Chicago?*" she asked next, bringing up the subject that Alan had avoided: his family back home or lack thereof. Her persistence disarmed him, and in an odd sort of way, she came across like a junior Esnault. He told her curtly he was married and going through a divorce. He hoped she would drop the subject. She did not.

"*C'est quoi—le divorce?*"

After groping for the correct words, he explained as best he could what it meant for a legally married couple to break up. Apparently Chloé's mother and father had not been married, or if they had, failed to pursue a French divorce. Thus, he got another blank look.

"*Pourquoi est-ce que t'as voulu divorcer?*"

Telling a child so young why he and his wife wanted a divorce, when he himself did not fully understand it, made him uncomfortable to say the least. Instead he said that they didn't love each other anymore, which was probably a worse answer than another lecture.

Chloé frowned in a way only a child could—pouty lips and doughy eyes. After a long pause, she asked, "*As-tu des enfants?*"

With this question, Alan felt enormously empty, if not guilty. Heretofore he had repressed such a shortcoming, if it were one at all. Now in the presence of this little girl, he had become exposed and felt as though he were confessing a sin to God. He considered telling her the truth: his childlessness was the result of an evolution of circumstances most of which were beyond his control. But instead of overthinking the problem and going into something she would not understand, he simply said he had no children and left it at that.

Yet the interrogation didn't stop. Chloé asked him why he had come to France. He knew that kids her age could not think in the abstract. Accordingly, he struggled to explain his desire to change himself. He indicated he was looking for something, but didn't know what it was.

"Est-ce que t'as perdu un truc ici?"

He hadn't lost anything, of course. He decided it best to use an analogy to offer the child some measure of understanding and maybe fend off her probing questions once and for all. So he asked if she had ever wanted a toy or piece of clothing, but didn't know the exact kind.

Momentarily confused by the metaphor, at first Chloé did not respond. After a few seconds, she nodded and told Alan that some time ago she had wanted a watch, but was unsure of the brand. Her mother had taken her shopping at Nice-Étoile, the local mall, and on that day she had seen for the first time the watch she pre-ferred—the pink-banded Mickey Mouse one currently on her wrist. He explained that in coming to France he had hoped to find what he was looking for too—his own Mickey Mouse watch. Finally the questions stopped.

They decided to sit on a metal bench facing the sea. He pointed to various objects around them: the water, its waves, different boats, seashells, sand, and rocks. She provided the word in French, and he translated it in English. After they exhausted all possibilities around them, they resumed walking, until they came to a group of in-line skaters, who demonstrated their skills along the boardwalk with great precision.

The skaters had cordoned off an area and placed on the ground a line of twenty orange pylons, each three feet apart. They took turns charging rapidly at the pylons and dancing back and forth between them. Occasionally they missed one, but seldom did they fall. For ten minutes, Alan and Chloé watched, mesmerized by the amazing demonstration. It would be impossible, he thought, to learn such a skill, much less master it. He might hurt himself and spoil his trip to France, but he felt the tug of the little girl on his arm. *Oh no, please no,* he told himself.

"*Trouvons des patins à roulettes et faissons du roller*—Let's find some roller skates and go skating," Chloé said. Her eyes sparkled, and she began jumping up and down in an effort to get her way. "*S'il te plaît, Alan. S'il te plaît!*"

He hesitated initially, but gave in. The child from within himself had been brought out by another child. He asked her if she knew how to skate, and she told him that she had done so since she was three. He scanned the boardwalk, and a short distance away a man stood by a stand that rented sporting equipment. The man must have overheard their conversation, as he smiled and waved them over.

"*Est-ce que vous louez patins*—Do you rent skates?" Alan asked.

"*Des patins,*" Chloé whispered from behind his leg.

Alan quickly corrected himself. In English it would have been okay to omit an article before a plural noun, but not in French. Here the article should have been "des" or some.

The man examined their feet to determine the appropriate size and gave them each a pair of skates. Alan searched his brain for the words for helmet, elbow and knee pad, and wrist guard, for he knew such equipment would be of great value, given his lack of experience in the sport. Before he could find the words on his iPhone translation app, Chloé took over: *"Aussi, nous voudrions des casques, des cordiéres, des genouiliéres, et des protégé-poignets."*

Alan shrugged, and the man shrugged back.

After they put everything on, the French lesson quickly evolved into a skating one. Alan grabbed onto a metal rail for balance. The first thing he had to learn, Chloé explained, was how to stand without holding on. She demonstrated this by putting one foot at an angle behind the other. *"Alors, à ton tour,"* she said.

Alan did as instructed, but wavered about as he tried to maintain his balance.

*"Fléchis les genoux comme ça—*bend your knees like this."

He did his best. For several minutes they stood together until he gained confidence by maintaining a more athletic position.

Next she taught him to walk forward and backward. He asked her why he had to learn to do this when he was supposed to be skating. She said that in order to skate, he first had to be able to walk. So he did so, looking like a duck waddling on a shoreline and causing the child to giggle.

"Es-tu prêt à patiner?"

He was ready to skate all right, and also ready to fall down and bust his ass.

Chloé showed him how to stop, push off with his feet to gain momentum, and roll along. Endeavoring to persevere, he started to move forward ever-so slowly, periodically using the metal rail for assistance. As time went on, he needed it less and less, and started to become more proficient. While he got the hang of things, Chloé skated circles around him and back and forth along the quay.

*"Essayes de patiner en arrière—*try skating backwards," she suggested, showing him how to do it. Instead of pointing his toes outward and pushing off to go forward, he had to angle them inward. He followed the child's lead.

"C'est bien, Alan, c'est bien—"

Splat! He had fallen on the hard asphalt, and boy did it hurt. He looked up pathetically at Chloé, who stood over him, but she offered no sympathy. *"Vas-y, relèves-toi*—Come on, get up," she insisted.

He rolled onto his knees and hoisted himself up using the railing. By then a small group of onlookers had surrounded them, and when he made it to his feet and started skating again, they clapped for him. "*Bravo! Bravo!"* they cheered.

Bravo, indeed, Alan told himself. He had learned to skate, and more importantly, achieved the adoration and acceptance of this wonderful child. The latter gave him meaning and purpose and a respect for himself that heretofore had been absent in his life.

* * *

Over the next five weeks, Alan continued to see Jeannette as well as Chloé. Since he had proven himself worthy as a caregiver, Jeannette permitted him more time with the child. Their play dates included the movies, hikes around Cap Ferrat across the bay, and even ice skating at an indoor rink in Nice.

He and Jeannette had plenty of opportunities to be alone and familiarize themselves with each other as well. They went to a competition in Villefranche Harbor in which carnations and mimosas were used to decorate boats, travelled to Cannes, the site of the famous film festival, toured another perfume factory in Grasse, and had many private dinners together. He helped her with the bookkeeping as promised.

During the course of their time together, Jeannette told him more about her background. She was born in Nice thirty-two years before and grew up in Villefranche. Everyone knew her in the small town, and despite her best efforts to maintain a low profile, the people there were well aware of her comings and goings and especially her relationship with Alan.

Her mother owned the flower shop and once worked there herself. Jeannette's dad had been a garbage man, who died in a bizarre work-related accident. He had become caught in his truck's compacting mechanism when he tried to fix it, and ended up compacted himself. After his rather unseemly death, her mom moved in with her older sister in Saint Paul down the coast, since she could no longer stand living in Villefranche, where the accident had occurred. This led to Jeannette taking over the shop. Unfortunately her mother's plans in staying with her sister didn't work out, as the sister contracted Alzheimer's and died from a myriad of complications associated with the disease.

Jeannette had one brother, but he lived in Paris and rarely came to Villefranche. As a result, he hardly knew Chloé. But he did send his sister money to tide her over in the low season, when business slowed down. He could afford to do so, as he went to college and got his degree in finance. This enabled him to get a real job at a bank, investing its assets at La Bourse (the Parisian stock exchange).

While Jeannette received her Bac (the French equivalent of a high school diploma), she did not go to college like her brother. She chose instead to become a townie. Besides working and caring for Chloé, she spent her free time on artistic hobbies: painting, crafting, and doing pottery. She sometimes made flower pots for her more expensive arrangements. Not being a driven person, none of her moves in life were calculated. Planning, staying organized, and managing her finances were not her forté. Thus, she and Alan constituted a good match.

Despite their time together, the couple never had sex. Oh sure, foreplay and many episodes like the one at Èze occurred, but never the ultimate act. They hadn't gotten to know each other well enough yet, she claimed, and "yet" seemed to be taking a long time. This was especially so, since Jeannette had a peculiar knack for coming onto him and later retracting her affections.

No doubt her reticence in this department had a lot to do with Alan's camping-out status in France. He lived in a hotel, for Chrissakes, and worked at an under-the-table job for a guy who wore a cowboy hat. Jeannette must have thought that any moment he would leave, or worse something would happen to him. Despite his best efforts to convince her otherwise and get her to surrender unto him, she refused. So he waited her out, earnestly believing that she was worth waiting for.

At times he wondered if she truly cared about him or simply wanted a father figure for her daughter. In other words independent of Chloé, did Jeannette really give a damn? When he looked at the relationship objectively, however, his doubts and fears evaporated. She actively communicated with him, expressed interest in his daily activities and experiences and shared her deepest thoughts. She often initiated conversation via phone and email and didn't wait for him to do this.

Though his involvement in her family was limited to Chloé, at least she trusted him with her. Most importantly, Jeannette seemed happy when around Alan, often maintaining eye contact, responding with displays of physical affection, and being attentive to his welfare and personal growth, even to the point of motherly concern.

As far as the rest of Alan's life, he kept his job with Buck, and the war with the rival cabbies fortunately achieved a state of temporary détente. While he still had to sign in with the cops every day, Esnault pretty much left him alone. As to the divorce proceedings, a settlement had not yet been obtained, but fruitful discussions had been taking place among the attorneys, and the judge hadn't ruled on Sara's default judgment motion, forcing such talks to continue. Overall, life was good, at least until the 30th of June.

That evening Alan went down to Chez Betty for his usual *grand ballon* of white wine after a hard day at the office, a.k.a. Buck's pickup truck. "*Votre francais est meillur depuis quelques temps*—Your French is better these days," Betty complimented after pouring him his glass.

"*Merci bien, madame.*"

The bar owner wiped down some tables with a wet towel and collected several empty glasses left by some tourists, who had been drinking there for hours. Her yellow apron, accented by fancy red embroidery, protected her navy sweater and matching silk scarf from bar grime. A makeup-caked face, rouged cheeks, and red lipstick, combined with her broad smile, gave her a friendly look. Her incessant correction of his grammar and gracious attitude reminded him of his own mother.

When he was about to head upstairs to his room, Betty's jovial face switched to a frown. For reasons unknown, a burly, bearded man stood squarely at the door, blocking any opportunity for exit. His companion, another creature of large dimension, approached the bar and sat down next to Alan. He was one of the thugs who had chased him and Ludovic at the match.

Before the man did anything to Alan, Betty whispered, "*Poussez la vitrine là-bas. C'est une porte cachée*—Push the window over there. It's a hidden door."

Alan eyed the floor-to-ceiling glass pane, the farthest to the right on the front of the establishment. But when he tried to get up to leave, he felt a massive hand grip the flesh between his neck and shoulder and mash him back down on his stool.

Betty headed to the phone, apparently to call the police. She quickly returned and transferred some dirty plates and silverware to the bar. They were easily within Alan's reach.

The thug at the bar had underestimated the old woman's guile and didn't seem to notice the potential weaponry. *"Est-ce que vous comprenez le mot triche*—Do you understand the word cheat?" he asked Alan. He had no neck and tiny black eyes that receded beneath a square forehead. His dim look suggested he was in fact very dim.

"Me no speak French," Alan replied, doing his best to look confused despite the fact Buck had long ago familiarized him with the word "triche."

Betty dropped a dish on the floor. Its loud crash gave Alan the opportunity to lunge for a fork in the pile of dishes she had set down. He jammed the utensil into one of the smallish eyes of the man next to him, dashed for the hidden exit, pushed it outward and eased out onto the sidewalk.

He considered running across the street toward the park, but this was too obvious and would keep him in view of his pursuers for some distance. Instead he circled the corner to his right and up a narrow street jammed with parked cars. The street had many nooks and crannies and might provide refuge until the hoods passed. But as he searched for a place to hide, he spotted the thug he had forked at Chez Betty, coming at him from the opposite direction. When Alan turned around to go back the other way, he saw the other thug rushing toward him like a linebacker about to execute a tackle at a football game. An image of Ludovic at Hôpital L'Archet came to mind.

Before he met the same fate as his soccer friend, he heard the roar of a car engine. The cavalry had arrived in the nick of time; Buck Treadway raced up in a red, white and blue Camaro and swung its right front passenger door open. "Looks like you found some Frenchies with some balls," he yelled.

Alan hopped in, and they sped up the hill. "The truce is over," he told Buck, while trying to catch his breath.

"You can say that again, Al."

The large men did not give up easily, however, and pursued them in their own car, whose headlights blinded its make. The vehicle converged on Buck's rear bumper as he headed into the first of many hairpin turns, but his acceleration after each curve put distance between his car and theirs.

As they wove their way along the Moyenne Corniche, Alan asked Buck how long he thought the chase would go on. Buck glanced in his rearview mirror and replied, "about another minute." He floored the Camaro, whose powerful engine had obviously been souped up with several after-market adjustments. Seemingly to toy with the pursuers, he thereafter slowed down just enough to entice them closer.

"What are you doing?" Alan asked desperately. He didn't know if he was better off with Buck or the thugs who gave chase.

"Just having a little fun is all," the Texan answered.

"What are you, nuts?"

A sharp curve approached a short distance ahead, and Buck began to accelerate to encourage the car behind them to go a wee bit faster. He seemed to know the exact speed required for his upcoming entertainment. Once he made it to the curve, without warning he jammed on the brakes, causing his Camaro to spin 180 degrees. The abrupt move forced the thug car to screech out of control in order to avoid a head-on collision and careen down a short hill. Luckily for its occupants the drop-off didn't go down far, and a brick wall stopped their descent into an even deeper abyss.

The brawny men stumbled out and screamed profanities at each other in French, while gesturing at a plume of steam escaping their radiator. Buck yelled at them as well, using a few choice obscenities of his own. Naturally he offered them in perfectly accented *Français.*

"You could have gotten us killed," Alan yelled.

"Maybe. Maybe not," Buck replied. "Either way it would have been fun."

"What?"

"I told you, Al: appeasement never works."

Alan felt like walking back. Instead he remained in the car, not knowing what further menace awaited him. "Where are we going now?" he asked Buck, as they started back down the road.

"My place. We need to talk."

Three kilometers later, a driveway guarded by an iron gate appeared. Buck buzzed the entrance open and drove up a long curvy road that led to his less-than-humble abode. The outside of the villa appeared the same as the others in Villefranche—heavy on pastel walls, lime-green shutters, and arched verandas.

The inside, by contrast, had the feel of the Ponderosa on the TV series *Bonanza.* At any moment Alan fully expected Hoss or Little Joe to pop out. Above the stone fireplace, a five-foot-diameter wagon wheel, garnished by tumbleweeds and sage brush, rested on the mantel, and animal-head hunting trophies, lassos, riding chaps, paintings of horses, and of course, a Texas lone star, overwhelmed the rest of the living room.

Buck motioned Alan to one of two brown-leather easy chairs that flanked the hearth, while teasing coals and ashes in the fireplace with an iron poker. He dumped a couple of dry logs on, which immediately went ablaze, noting that even in summer he could burn wood due to the breezes that came off the sea. While grabbing a metal cup, he asked, "Coffee?"

"Sure, why not."

Buck poured them some from a blue and white speckled pot that dangled above the burning embers. "It's decaf so it shouldn't keep you up."

After they watched the fire crackle for a while, Buck said, "Them two losers that rousted you at Chez Betty were Christophe's boys, you know."

"I figured as much. One of them asked me if I knew what a *triche* was."

"*Triche*? Hell, they're the cheats."

"Anyway," Alan continued diplomatically, "if it weren't for Betty and later you, I would have ended up like Ludovic."

Buck leaned forward, set his coffee cup on the hearth in front of him, and said, "I'd ride with that old hag any day."

Alan smiled weakly at the imagery. "How'd you know I was having a problem with Christophe's thugs?" he asked.

"Betty called, and I was nearby."

"Why not the cops?"

"She knows better."

Alan began to sweat from the fire, so he took out his handkerchief and wiped his brow. "So you think the cops are in league with Christophe?"

"Yep."

"Are there any who aren't?"

"Maybe Gustave Esnault, but I wouldn't bet the ranch on it."

"He's the one who wants my ass for Rolf's murder." Alan detailed why he was a suspect, his alibi problems, and the detective's annoying interrogations, while Buck tended the fire.

"Esnault's in over his head," the Texan said.

"Why do you say that?"

"Talks smart, but frankly he's incompetent."

"So Christophe runs circles around him?"

"Darn tootin'."

"Tell me more about this man. You only gave me half the story at Chez Betty after Ludovic got out of the hospital."

"Christophe imports hash from Morocco and heroin from Turkey." Buck went on to explain that while the drug lord's money came mostly from this source, he also owned legitimate-appearing businesses in order to diversify his risk and maintain an air of public respectability. One of them was his cab company.

"Was Ludovic privy to this?" Alan asked.

"Yep. That's why he got beat up after the match."

"What do you mean?"

"Christophe don't want him shootin' his mouth off about his operations—his way of granting a severance package."

"Sounds like he's a pretty dangerous guy."

"He's in with some people who enforce their will in Marseille with drive-by shootings and message killings such as 'barbecues.'"

"Barbecues? Didn't they originate in Texas?"

"Actually in France," Buck said. He pinched the stubble on his chin and patted his butt. "The French word for beard is *barbe*, and the one for tail is *cue*. But with Christophe it ain't no picnic, if you know what I mean."

"So he and his men barbecue people like pigs?"

"After shooting them in the head," Buck said. "Usually they leave the charred remains on a rival's doorstep."

Alan gulped. "Aren't you afraid of this guy?"

"Nah."

"Why not?"

The Texan laughed into a smoker's hack as he banged the bottom of a box of Marlboro reds on his knee. While dangling a cigarette in his mouth, he got up and retrieved a 30-30 rifle from a gun rack on a wall near the fireplace, opened its breach and carefully examined the inside of the barrel. "Cuz he don't know what I'd do," he said, gritting his teeth.

Alan wondered if he needed to be a little more unpredictable himself to avoid being skewered and turned over a fire pit. "So tell me more about Rolf Swenson," he said, changing the subject.

"What do you want to know?"

"Did Christophe have something to do with his murder?"

"Rolf ran a vee-hee-cul-for-hire company, just like me. Plus he owed Christophe money."

"That's what the blind lady said. She mentioned Rolf had a lot of gambling debts."

"Helène Picard's her name. Lives by the old church."

Alan paused, not sure if he wanted to pose his next very sensitive question.

"Something else botherin' ya, Al?"

"Yeah, how does Jeannette fit in? You told me to be careful about her some time back."

"Now I ain't gettin' involved with that," Buck replied. "But I can guarantee you one thing. She does fit in."

They went outside for some fresh air, since the cigarette smoke had begun to bother Alan. "How come you stereotype the French so much?" he asked Buck, as they seated themselves on the villa's veranda. "I mean, your mother was born here."

"She was a wonderful woman—for a while," the Texan said, his eyes starting to glisten.

"Was?"

"Was," Buck underscored.

"Why do you say that?"

"When I was five, she took off with a French guy, and I never saw her again."

Alan noted Buck would have been Chloé's age. "Sorry, I didn't mean to salt old wounds."

Buck's eyes welled up even more. "That's all right, pardner."

"So your dad raised you in Texas after she left?"

"Yep."

"Why'd you come back here?"

"Couldn't stay away from paradise, I guess."

"Paradise? Barbecues and people like Christophe don't exist in paradise, Buck."

"A few bad apples don't spoil the bunch, and even the bad apples have good parts."

"That's pretty insightful coming from—"

"—a redneck from Texas?"

Alan smiled. "You got me there. Guess I'm guilty of some stereotyping myself."

Alan now knew Buck better. Really the Texan didn't dislike the French. He was just pissed off about his mother's abandonment and needed a way to express it. Macho, brusque, and willful, he fancied himself as the ultimate hard guy, who took no prisoners. This amounted to compensation for the ugliness he had endured. Alan had to be careful not to absorb all of such characteristics. On the other hand, a few would do, for he had in his own life ugliness that needed compensation.

They spent the rest of the night exchanging stories. At dawn they could see the fog rise above the harbor as the sun peeked out from the eastern horizon. A U.S. destroyer had settled in there overnight.

"They come here for R and R," Buck said.

Without warning, the ship began blasting *The Star-Spangled Banner* from its speakers, a form of reveille for its sailors that had the same effect for the denizens of Villefranche. Buck snapped to attention and put his hand on his heart, for even though he was half French and half Texan, he was all American. Even more importantly, he was all heart.

* * *

Ludovic's last name was Renard, the French term for fox. While he had not been very cunning in avoiding the wrath of Christophe's men after the Nice-Marseille match, he had survived at least. Others had not been so lucky. For this reason Alan believed he had much to learn from the wily soccer nut and trusted his advice and possible assistance. In this spirit he agreed to have lunch with him at the "terrain."

Alan arrived at the community soccer field with the bakery *dejeuner* formula in hand: a ham and cheese croissant, a piece of apple pie, and a soda. Ludovic brought a small baguette, a chunk of brie, and a deerskin of white wine. After they watched the local team practice while sitting on the concrete steps that edged the field and ate their food, the conversation became serious.

"So you worked for Christophe, but quit?"

"Took different job."

"Sweeping the stairwells and overlooks, right?"

"Fringe benefits better," Ludovic said, not very convincingly. He nervously glanced about to make sure no one was around and changed the subject abruptly. "You ask about gun. Still want gun?"

"As I said, for self-defense."

Ludovic snickered and took a hit of wine from his flask. He didn't appear to be impressed by the justification. After they listened to the soccer coach yell out instructions to his team for a while, the Frenchman poked him in the chest and said, "I get gun for you."

Alan wondered about the urgent tone, but was very much interested in the proposal nevertheless. "After you got out of the hospital, you didn't seem to think this was such a good idea. Why the change of heart?" he asked.

"No heart change. You want gun, I help." Ludovic threw the rest of his baguette on the ground for the seagulls to fight over and got up to leave.

Thus far, Alan had been all talk and personal research about obtaining a firearm. He hesitated to take the next step, since this would represent a considerable departure from his law-abiding character. On the other hand, he had to do something to stay safe. As Ludovic walked away, Alan quickly caught up with him and asked, "What are we talking about in terms of money?"

"*Deux cent*—two hundred."

"And the bullets?"

Ludovic waved a hand in annoyance. "Yes, yes, bullets too."

"I guess we have a deal then."

"Man home. We go now."

They walked to Ludovic's Renault and drove to Nice.

"Where does he live?" Alan asked, as they sped along the Promenade des Anglais.

"*Les Moulins.*"

Alan knew *moulin* meant windmill. "Are there *moulins* in Nice?"

"*Non, ce sont des logements sociaux*—No, they're public housing projects."

By now Alan's job with Buck had taken him to many parts of the city of 400,000—the airport, hotels, and train stations. But housing projects hadn't graced his list. He had naïvely assumed that they didn't exist in France. "Where are the Moulins? "he asked.

"Saint Augustin, *une banlieue*."

This seemed bizarre. Low-income apartments in the States were in the city, not the suburbs.

As they stopped for a traffic light, Ludovic said coldly, "Need money first."

Credit didn't seem to be an option, so Alan paid him the euros.

They continued along the main road to the airport, then to the perimeter of the Moulins, where a series of high-rises housed 12,000 poor people in 3,000 densely packed apartments. A sign proclaimed the project to be part of the ZRU *(Zone de Redynamisation Urbaine),* and large demolition machines leveled the land to make room for more buildings. The machines droned in the background so loudly, it was hard to think.

Ludovic parked his car. "Stay here," he instructed. "Lock doors."

"Why? What kind of people live here?" Alan asked.

His friend leaned in the car window and said: "*Les Maghrébins.*"

Alan recalled an article he had read in the *Nice-Matin* about France's immigrants. Thirty percent of them came from Algeria, Morocco, and Tunisia. Known as *Les Maghrébins,* they were the largest ethnic group in the country and constituted the vast majority of the prison population.

While France had a wonderful system of social benefits, they were predicated on a person having had a job in the first place, something North African youth couldn't get due to rampant employment discrimination, and at times, their own unwillingness to assimilate. Consequently forty percent of this youth group spent their lives hustling, dealing drugs, working under the table, and otherwise existing on the edge in gangs. Most were Islamic, and

Chez Betty

places like the Moulins, sometimes amounted to breeding grounds for radicalization.

"Why can't I come with you?" Alan asked Ludovic. "It's pretty scary out here."

"Man not know you," he replied. "No sell to strangers."

Alan surveyed the area near their car while he waited for Ludovic. Above him, several twenty-story dismal-looking buildings presented a complicated jigsaw puzzle of apartment homes, some empty, some with small children on the balconies, and most displaying that day's wash.

On the streets below, various Arab-looking persons milled about. A few conversed with each other, but most sat idly on curbsides, park benches, and stoops, surrounded by litter blowing in a lonely wind. He felt as though he were in the now-torn-down Cabrini Green, a former housing project in Chicago where not even the police wanted to go. He dared not interact with anyone, for fear he would reveal his accent and ethnic status as an American.

After twenty minutes, Ludovic returned and gave him the handgun. On its black plastic grips, Alan noticed the letters RF with a circle around them. "Republic of France," he said, pointing to the mark. On the right side of the gun's frame, he saw a crescent shape over a vertical line; the image looked like a palm tree. "What's this?" he asked.

"Moroccan police," Ludovic replied.

"So it's stolen?"

"Want gun, no?"

"Okay, okay. What kind is it anyway?"

"Semi-auto, 7.65 millimeter," Ludovic said, using his best English yet. He grabbed the weapon back and removed its clip, loaded it with nine rounds of ammunition, and handed it to Alan. "Now you defend."

After Ludovic dropped him off, Alan went back to Buck's pickup, which he had left in front of Chez Betty. He ensconced himself behind the steering wheel while traffic passed, holding the gun and marveling at the new purchase. A bus stopped for a light next to the truck, whereupon he looked upward at its many windows and people inside. He recognized a familiar face, Miss Perfect, the woman who had advised him on the right bus going the wrong way. Her eyes fixed intently upon the gun. Alan hastily hid it under his seat, but it was too late. As the bus slowly drove off, Miss Perfect smiled with satisfaction, as if to say to him "your comeuppance is nigh."

7

Alan blew off the fact that Miss Perfect had seen him with the gun. While at first he considered getting rid of it, he eventually convinced himself he was overreacting. The woman didn't even know his name in order to report him to the authorities. Plus, she likely couldn't describe the weapon in sufficient detail so that the police could conclude it was in fact a gun. Finally, he had better things to do than worry. One of them was a trip to Old Nice with Jeannette and Chloé.

Initially the excursion went well. After getting off the bus they visited a fancy candy store that specialized in crystallized fruit of every conceivable variety—oranges, lemons, limes, kiwi, and apples, to name a few. The *confiserie* even sold sugar-coated rose and violet petals, packaged in plastic funnels that gave the appearance of bouquets. Only in France, Alan thought. He purchased one of them for Chloé, which was a nice touch.

In Old Nice, a maze of narrow passages, darkened by four-story yellow-stucco buildings, sent them to medieval France. The massive number of tourist shops, however, returned them to the present. After Jeannette bought veggies, pasta, cheese, and shrimp for dinner, they came to a square near a small fountain, and Alan's ability to divert his attention from his legal troubles became overwhelmed.

Before him stood the regional courthouse for the Département des Alpes-Maritimes, or more simply, Le Palais de Justice. He gave

Jeannette some euros and asked her if it would be okay for him to take a look inside while she and Chloé got some gelato. The young girl's ears perked upon hearing of the treat, weakening her mother's power to resist. They agreed to meet back at the fountain in thirty minutes.

As he ascended the courthouse steps, Alan stopped for a moment to take in its classic exterior. Three archways separated an equal number of doors and above them appeared the words *liberté, égalité,* and *fraternité,* a battle cry of the French revolution. Over the archways, thirty-foot-high columns went to the top of the building. He noted an interesting juxtaposition of two abstract concepts carved in stone inside the outer columns: *Droit* and *Loi.* The purpose of French justice, he thought, was to achieve a balance between rights and law, the former inhering in the individual and the latter in government. He wondered how this dichotomy would apply to him.

Marble floors and walls greeted him inside, but he couldn't experience their beauty until he passed security. In that regard the courthouse was no different than in the States, with plastic trays for valuables and a doorway having metal sensors. He set off no alarms, and nothing in his appearance caused the guards concern, at least until he asked them if he could take pictures. Then they looked at him like a terrorist who was there to case the place and told him this would be *interdit.* Fortunately, he had left the gun at Chez Betty.

After security, he glanced up at an open expanse that towered high above the middle of a large concourse. On the floor, men and women, dressed in black robes and frilly white neck-scarves, chatted in groups and scurried about doing business. He assumed they were lawyers or avocats. Unlike English barristers, they did not wear wigs.

"Excuse me," he opened with one of them. "I'm an attorney in the United States and want to ask you some questions about your system."

The avocat cautiously nodded agreement and spoke in educated English, while Alan used informal American vernacular. "Do you guys wear those robes all the time while working?"

"Only in the Palais de Justice," the avocat replied. Underneath his own outfit, he wore blue jeans and carried two items in his hands: a briefcase and a motorcycle helmet. "When we leave, we take them off."

"What are they called?"

"*Les robes d'avocat.*"

This seemed odd to Alan, since only judges wore robes back home. He pointed to a black sash with white fur on the end that draped over the man's left shoulder. "What's that?"

"*Une épitoge,*" he said.

"And the scarf around your neck?"

"*Un rabat.*" The avocat smiled and quipped, "We used to wear hats or *toques*, but no one wears them today except three people."

Alan knew several lawyers like that in the States, so he laughed. "Where are the courtrooms?" he asked next, thinking there had to be many in a city the size of Nice.

The French lawyer pointed to only two. "That one is called *La Chambre de Correctionnelle*, and the other is *Le Cour d'Assises*," he said.

"Why so few courtrooms?"

"Le Tribunal de Police deals with traffic matters and minor offenses in another building, and the volume of cases in France is lower than in your country."

Still, Alan thought.

"Would you like to see Le Cour d'Assises?" the avocat asked. "A trial will start soon, and the chief judge may otherwise veto your presence."

Naturally Alan agreed, and they passed into a large courtroom, two times as wide as it was deep. Stadium-like, it advanced down to a fifty-foot-wide counter. Nine high-back chairs appeared behind it, with the one in the middle being the largest. Facing the console was a lone chair.

"Who sits there?" Alan whispered so his voice would not echo off the marble walls and disrupt the courtroom's solemnity.

"Witnesses when they are interrogated," replied the French lawyer, also in a whisper.

"Pretty darn intimidating."

"It's meant to be."

"Who occupies the seats behind the counter?"

"The judges and jury. The prosecutor stands on the *parquet* in front."

"Why do they call it a parquet?"

"It refers to the wooden floor," the avocat said. "The point is to separate the prosecution from the triers of fact, who sit above the fray and consider the matters at hand objectively. Today parquet is a term broadened to include the entire prosecutor's office."

"Where do the judges go to school?"

"The same institution as the parquet—L'École de la Magistrature. All judges and prosecutors are considered magistrates, a life-long civil-service calling."

"Better than in the States," Alan said. "Most judges there are elected. What about defense attorneys?"

"They attend a different school."

"Does that make it so the judges feel more kinship with the prosecutors?"

"Officially they maintain their independence, but unofficially—"

"Maybe not, right?"

The French lawyer smiled, but expressed no commitment.

"Where does the defendant sit?" Alan asked.

"In the *box d'accusé.*" The avocat pointed to a glass-partitioned cage on the left side of the courtroom a good thirty feet from the counter and a similar distance from the witness chair. Its only exit was a rear door through which defendants were presumably brought from the jail. "It prevents any attempt to fly," he said.

"Sure doesn't facilitate communication between attorney and client."

"You don't understand; the defense lawyer stays in the box as well."

"Even when addressing the court or a witness?"

"Yes, of course."

Alan imagined the attorney straining to make a point over the cavernous distance, all the while cloistered from the rest of the courtroom players. He or she would be on Mars and the others on Earth.

"You seem troubled by this," said the French lawyer.

"Well, the segregation of the defendant and his avocat conveys the impression that they do not have equal footing with the prosecution."

"Yes. Yes. I've heard this argument."

"Plus it makes the accused look guilty."

"How he looks is not as important as what the evidence shows."

"Maybe, but when one looks the part, he becomes the part."

The French lawyer managed a polite chuckle. "You seem to take this very seriously, almost as though you yourself were the accused."

While this was true, Alan didn't want to explain the embarrassing details of his life to a veritable stranger, so he simply thanked the man and left the courtroom. When he passed back into the hallway, he saw a notice tacked on a bulletin board next to the Cour d'Assises. It announced a sentence for a man convicted of murder *"avec la circonstance aggravante de préméditation."* The sentence or *"condemnation"* was *"réclusion à la perpétuité,"* a deeply troubling notion for him, given his current situation. While France didn't have the death penalty, the idea of perpetual separation cut to his core.

"Something wrong?" Jeannette asked back at the fountain.

Alan stared off into space, then turned his eyes to Chloé, who had a ring of chocolate gelato around her mouth. He started to cry.

"Please, tell me what is wrong," Jeannette implored.

"I just can't right now," he said with his voice cracking. "Maybe later."

The three hiked back to the bus stop and got on the right bus going the right way. The wrong way appeared to be the direction of the Palais de Justice.

* * *

Alan hadn't been to Jeannette's apartment in a while, so he looked forward to going there for dinner the night of their visit to Nice. Before they went through the front door, his girlfriend greeted her second-floor neighbor, who was hanging out her wash on the balcony above. He recognized the neighbor as the blind lady from the murder scene, Madame Helène Picard. Given his experience at the courthouse, he felt the need to ask the woman some questions, and did so while Jeannette and Chloé proceeded inside.

"Where were you the day of Rolf's murder?" he asked the woman. Though the question bordered on accusatory, given his mood, he didn't feel like mincing words.

"*Ici*," the blind lady replied, pointing toward the floor of her balcony with a clothespin. She then meticulously felt her way to a laundry basket, retrieved a sheet and hung it on a line that extended to the building from the balcony.

"Why did you go to the murder scene?"

"I heard a single gunshot," she said. "It occurred at the moment the church bell chimed."

"What?"

"Yes, it was quite unmistakable."

"How many times did the bell chime?"

"Three."

"You're sure?"

"*Absolument.*"

Alan considered the implications. The murder occurred at precisely three o'clock, but he had been in Nice at that time. He could now speak with authority about the time of Rolf's death for the purpose of his alibi.

"Did you tell Lieutenant Esnault this?"

"Yes. I was the one who called the police."

Alan grew angry, thinking about his conversation with the cop at the identity check. *Son-of-a-bitch knew all along when Rolf was killed!* "What time did the police arrive?" he asked the woman next.

"*Quinze heures quinze, monsieur.*"

The perfect use of the liaison and accent reminded him of a small voice that had uttered the same phrase months before. He entered Jeannette's apartment and urgently posed a single question: "*Where's Chloé?*"

* * *

Alan was no idiot, despite his social deficits. He understood like everyone else that relationships depended upon open communication and an elusive notion called trust. Even so he had not done enough to foster this fundamental concept with Jeannette. Nor had she with him. Secrets remained.

For his part, he had neglected to tell her he was a prime suspect in Rolf Swenson's murder. While he had mentioned his job with Buck Treadway, he had not disclosed that this arrangement exposed him to violence at the hands of a gangster named Christophe and his cabbie goons. And then there was the gun and his trip to the Moulins with Ludovic.

So far Alan had rationalized these omissions and half-truths based on the time-honored principle of need-to-know. What difference did the perils he faced at work make or how he defended himself? The important thing was he earned money. As to the murder, he hadn't even been charged yet, and the case would likely go away on its own. If he told Jeannette, she would undoubtedly freak out, especially since she was already paranoid about him abandoning her. But now with the prospect of Chloé being an alibi witness, he could no longer avoid the subject. He would have to come clean.

"There's something I need to tell you," he opened.

His ominous tone caused Jeannette to drop the knife she had been using to chop vegetables, and she sank onto a chair at the kitchen table. "So is this where you dump me?"

"No, no. Nothing that dramatic," Alan replied, feeling surprised she even knew the slang. "I would never do that before dinner!" His feeble attempt to liven the mood before telling her the bad news fell flat.

"What is it?"

"I-I'm a suspect in the Rolf Swenson murder."

"*Quoi?*"

"No biggie. I just need to clear up a few things with the police."

"The police? Why didn't you say something earlier?"

"I didn't want to upset you."

At this point Alan did what any red-blooded American male would have done under the circumstances. He nuzzled his arms around Jeannette, thinking that physical affection might placate her and diffuse the awkward moment. Instead she wrested his hands away and jumped over to the stove, where a pot of boiling water awaited the pasta she had purchased in Nice.

"Uh, you're not thinking of pouring that over my head, are you?"

Jeannette did not respond, perhaps not wanting to reveal her plan of attack. Alan moved nervously to the other side of the table.

"Look, I tried to tell you about this on that path near Èze. Don't you remember? I said I had a legal problem, but before I could explain what it was, you changed the subject—"

"Did you kill Rolf Swenson?"

"No!"

"Then why are you a suspect?"

After taking a breath Alan recounted the misunderstanding that he had had with the real estate agent, his blundering outburst about Rolf taking him for the 6,000 euros, and Esnault's unwarranted persistence.

Jeannette groaned and started to walk into another room. "La Gendarmerie doesn't investigate innocent people."

Alan followed her, put his hands on her shoulders and turned her toward him, for he wanted to make his next point perfectly clear. "In my case they're wrong," he said sternly.

"And why should I believe you?" Jeannette asked, rushing away from him.

"Your neighbor heard a shot from Rolf's apartment when the church bell chimed for three o'clock. Then she found him dead and called the cops."

"So?"

"So I was in Nice at three that day and couldn't have done the murder."

Jeannette slowly nodded understanding.

"I was with you and your daughter on the train after that."

"We were coming back from my mother's in Saint Paul," Jeannette reflected, now becoming circumspect for reasons unknown. "W-we were late for a visit with Chloé's father."

"Her father! I thought you said he was as a yacht captain and long gone." Apparently Alan was not the only person in the room who had disclosure issues.

"All right, I lied," Jeannette confessed. "It was our first date."

"So lies on a first date are okay?"

"You're the one who failed to mention a murder charge!"

"Investigation," Alan corrected.

The conversation stopped, while both parties gathered themselves. The only sound in the room for several minutes came from the boiling water on the stove that fortunately had remained in that position during the entire argument.

"Please. Listen for a second," Alan started up again.

His pathetic tone caused Jeannette to relent. "So what do you want from me?"

"On the train ride from Nice to Villefranche the day of the murder, Chloé indicated the time," Alan explained. "I completely forgot about the conversation until your neighbor jogged my memory."

"So what's your point?"

"Chloé might remember the conversation and be able to say—

"You're not thinking of making her a witness."

"I have no choice!"

"She's five years old!"

"That doesn't mean she's a deaf-mute."

"Come on, Alan."

"All she has to do is tell the police the truth, and they'll exclude me. She won't even have to go to court."

"That would still be too traumatic for her."

"And if I'm charged with murder, what would that be? A walk in the park?"

The water continued to bubble. Finally Jeannette turned it off and yelled, "Chloé."

"No, wait. Don't ask her yet. We have to think this through."

Alan believed Esnault would accuse him of suggesting the time of the train encounter to the young girl. "If we casually bring up the subject and ask her open-ended questions, it will be better," he said.

"But the police will still say you manipulated her."

He showed Jeannette the voice-memo recorder of his iPhone and set the device on the table. After she finished making dinner, she called her daughter from her room, where she had been taking a nap. Chloé slowly obliged, rubbing sleep out of her eyes as she sat down.

The three ate the veggie-pasta-shrimp ensemble that Jeannette had prepared without broaching the subject of the train ride. When Chloé became focused on dessert, Alan activated the voice recorder, then raised the issue indirectly; he asked Jeannette how long they had known each other.

"*Quatre mois*—four months," she replied, following his lead in French, so her child would understand.

"*Souviens-toi la première fois que nous nous sommes rencontrés*—Do you remember the first time we met?" Alan asked.

"*Oui, au parc.*"

"*Mais non, Maman. Il était dans le train*—It was on the train," Chloé piped up. "*Nous étions en retard pour ma visite avec Papa*—We were late for my visit with Dad.*"

"*La visite à quelle heure?*"

"*Quinze heures, comme d'habitude*—Three o'clock, as usual," the girl said.

Alan asked her if she could recall the conversation she had had with him on the train.

With a giggle, she responded, "*Tu m'a demandé quelle heures est-il, et je t'ai dit quinze heures quinze*—You asked me the time, and I told you 3:15."

Alan nearly broke down in tears, since he now had his alibi locked down. But the next thing that the ingenuous child said sent his emotions farther over the edge.

"*Ça c'était la jour où Papa a frappé Maman, parce que nous étions en retard*—That was the day that Dad hit Mom, since we were late."

At the mention of this, Jeannette gasped and ran into the bedroom crying, leaving Alan alone with Chloé.

The precious child looked at her Mickey Mouse watch and sadly said, "*Ne t'inquiète pas. Ça n'arrivera plus jamais*—Don't worry about it. It'll never happen again."

* * *

For some dumb reason, Alan believed the French justice system would exonerate him once he mentioned his alibi to the police. He fostered the naïve conclusion that things were better in France than in America. At home he had sometimes associated with criminal lawyers, who told him stories about innocent people being convicted, the existence of racial disparities and other inequities in the system. The rate of violent crime in the States was astronomical, despite the fact that prisons burgeoned with inmates incarcerated under mandatory-minimum-sentencing schemes enacted in response to get-tough-on-crime lobbies.

Europe, on the other hand, with its excellent social service system and progressive attitude on various issues such as gun control, the death penalty, and decriminalization of certain offenses, was safer, fairer, and perhaps better. As a result, he thought that telling Esnault about Chloé would settle everything, enabling him to return to a life in paradise with his new-found family. The lieutenant agreed to a *rendezvous* and suggested that they hook up at Place de Masséna in Nice.

Alan took the train rather than Bus 100 for the meeting. After exiting at Nice-Ville, his rosy view of France took a hit. Outside the station, under a palm tree, he saw three homeless men sleeping together on a filthy mattress while other members of the SDF (*Sans Domicile Fixe)* wandered about begging for money. On the sidewalk in front, an Arab-looking woman lay asleep, but her two-year-old boy, grimy from not having had a bath, crawled about unattended. Alan put a couple of euros in a basket next to her that had a small card that read, *"Merci."* He could tell her desperation was no act.

Farther down the street, he encountered several Armenian prostitutes who propositioned him. The language barrier between him and the women did not hinder their overtures. After declining them, he went past some rowdy teenagers who bore a boom box that blared French rap music. Yes, there was such a thing, and it raged ugly about the police.

Alan reflected on this milieu and about what he had otherwise seen in the country. France had divorce, single parents, domestic abuse, racial discrimination, homelessness, housing projects, poverty, street violence, illegal guns, and a growing undocumented immigrant population the same as in America. Likewise, it had pop music, sports bars, favorite teams, electronics of every dimension, the Internet, Facebook, and reality TV. However much the two countries differed, they had far more in common, good and bad. The notion evoked a tentative feeling of kinship before his discussion with Esnault, and as well a portent of things to come.

At Place de Masséna, Alan waited near a pool, where a hundred-yard-long shallow veneer of water mirrored in perfect symmetry a lighted pavilion with three domed turrets. As he pulled out his phone to photograph the beautiful attraction, he noticed the lieu-tenant approaching from the pavilion's center in the watery reflec-tion.

"I see you've learned to be more prompt," Esnault said.

"A manifestation didn't delay me this time," Alan replied.

The lieutenant laughed, his mood more pleasant than when they had met last. He proposed a walk, and the two strolled about the square together, until they came to an amusement park. There Alan announced he had uncovered some information that exonerat-ed him.

Instead of responding, Esnault gazed upward at a Ferris wheel that had eighty spokes of brightly-lit LED lights that periodically changed color. "Do you want to give it a try?"

"I thought we were here to discuss my case, not go on rides."

"In due time," the cop said. "Come on, it will be fun." He gestured at the attraction's four-person carriages that slowly climbed to a peak of perhaps two hundred feet in the night sky.

Alan reluctantly agreed. When he reached into his pocket to get out the money for his ticket, Esnault stopped him. "No, my treat," he said chuckling. "You should accept my generosity. It may be the last I ever extend you."

A carnival worker locked them in the first-available carriage. In the background Alan could hear classical violin music that offered a majestic ambience. Despite the melody he felt uneasy, for now he had no avenue of escape. "I have found some people who can put me on the train from Nice to Villefranche at 3:15 p.m. the day you found Rolf's body," he told the cop as their carriage began to rise slowly. "You can now eliminate me as a suspect, and I can get my life back."

"Usually alibi witnesses are friends or family members of the accused and have little credibility," the lieutenant responded dismissively.

"But I have one who is beyond reproach."

"Oh, really. Who might that be?"

The Ferris wheel by now was halfway up. "The five-year-old daughter of my girlfriend, Jeannette," Alan replied, starting to shake.

"You seem nervous. Perhaps you lack confidence in this claim."

"No, that's not it. I just don't do well with heights," Alan said. "The girl is, in fact, very believable."

"You understand a child is not considered a valid witness in the French courts."

"Huh?"

"If you are ever charged, the judge will listen to her, but cannot rely on her statements to establish facts."

"But *you* can, right?"

Esnault sighed. "Very well, go ahead. What does she have to say?"

Alan recounted his conversation with Chloé at Jeannette's.

"Frankly I have difficulty with this. How can anyone, much less a child, possibly remember a conversation on a train that occurred months before?" Esnault asked. "Did you suggest this alibi to her?"

"I knew you'd say that. That's why I recorded our conversation when the subject came up." Alan retrieved his iPhone from his pants pocket and offered it to the cop, but he pushed his hand away.

"What did you tell her before you activated the recorder?"

"Nothing!"

Alan's emotions had gone from fear to anger. When the Ferris wheel carriage stopped at the ride's pinnacle and began swinging in the night wind, they returned to fear.

Esnault, by contrast, calmly took in the picturesque nighttime coastline. "When, might I ask, are you going to give up this fantasy of innocence and tell me the truth?" he asked.

"It is not a fantasy!"

The lieutenant moved to Alan's side of the carriage, causing it to become imbalanced. "They say fear is like a prison, and that if we conquer it, we become liberated," he said. "I have a different opinion. I believe truth sets us free, since the pangs of guilt are so enormously restrictive."

"Whose truth?"

Esnault moved still closer and said, "My truth, monsieur, for *it* is all that matters to you."

The ride finally started moving again, and the lieutenant returned to the other side of the carriage and proceeded to the less abstract aspects of the case. "Even assuming this child can recall the time and circumstances of the train ride, you cannot prove the exact moment Rolf Swenson was killed, unless, of course, you know that yourself."

Before the blind woman had told Alan when the shots were fired, he had researched the ability of a pathologist to determine time of death. Due to a myriad of factors, some controlled and others not, such an expert would never opine this with exact certitude, unlike on TV. "I understand it's hard to reconstruct when someone has died," he told the cop, having now regained his composure.

"Unless someone has seen the crime or was present at the moment of death," Esnault replied.

"Or *heard* it."

The remark caught the lieutenant off guard. He removed his fedora, which he had thus far held on his head during the ride. "You have an ear witness?"

"Quit playing dumb," Alan said. "All along you've known about her and that Rolf was shot at 3 p.m."

"You must be referring to Madame Picard."

"She heard the shot when the church bell tolled for three o'clock," Alan said firmly. "And more importantly she told you this." He couldn't resist the opportunity to turn the tables on the lieutenant and make accusations against him. "You, sir, have your own issues with the truth."

Esnault waved his hand. "She is nothing more than a lonely old lady in desperate need of attention."

"So she's lying?"

"Stretching things, more likely."

"For a full hour?"

The Ferris wheel ride finally ended. Had Esnault not left so soon, Alan might have had a legitimate charge for punching him in the nose. No matter what he told him, he wouldn't believe him, and this was frustrating. Even worse, his key witnesses had been divulged. Now his case, like the Ferris wheel carriage, fluttered helplessly in the wind.

* * *

After the train ride back to Villefranche, Alan arrived at Chez Betty for his weekly Friday-night accounting with Buck Treadway. The Texan was in a particularly good mood. "Business has been rolling," he said cheerily.

"Must be the high season," Alan replied.

They decided to celebrate their success, and Betty poured them each a glass of champagne.

"As the French say, *'santé,'* "Buck said, tapping Alan's glass.

While they savored their drinks, the Texan mentioned that he believed the key to their good fortune had been their willingness to stand up to Christophe, who had backed off after the last chase along the Moyenne Corniche. "We sure set him straight," Buck bragged.

"We?"

"You're the one who helped lure his loser friends into that trap; don't underestimate your contribution to the cause."

"The cause?"

"Hell yeah—the cause of showing Christophe who's boss."

Alan did not respond. Instead he fixed upon his champagne glass.

"What's the matter, Al?"

"Esnault."

"What about him?"

"Jeannette's daughter can give me an alibi on the Rolf Swenson case, so I told him about it, and he cut it to shreds."

"I wouldn't trust a French cop period," Buck emphasized.

"Yeah, you're right. No matter what I say, he's dead set against me."

"Probably hates Americans, too."

Alan finished his champagne and poured himself another glass.

"Not tellin' you how to handle your business, but I'd blow that French fucker off," Buck said, raising his already loud voice. "He ain't got dick on you."

"So you think he's playing me?"

"Does a steer have horns?"

Alan smiled for the first time in the conversation and returned to the topic of Christophe and his thugs. "I bought a gun, Buck."

"That tire iron not workin' for you, Al?"

"Not really."

"Where'd you get it?"

"Ludovic and I went to the Moulins."

"I'd be careful if I were you."

"Why's that?"

"Ludovic's got his feet in two different commodes, if you know what I mean."

"And what might those commodes be?"

"Well, one's Christophe."

"I thought Ludovic had nothing to do with him anymore."

"Friendship is one thing. Fear is another."

"So he still does Christophe's bidding?"

"Yep, especially after the beating at the match."

They finished their champagne, whereupon Buck suggested they get some real "I-talian" food. The two went out to the pickup. Buck wanted to admire his longhorns before they left to eat. But as they approached, they noticed an unwelcome sight; all four of the truck's tires had been slashed.

"Goddamn cowards!" Buck yelled.

"I guess they haven't learned," Alan said.

"Nope."

"So is there going to be some payback?"

The Texan said nothing.

They drove up the hill toward the Moyenne Corniche in Buck's Camaro ostensibly to get some "I-talian." "Where's the restaurant?" Alan asked.

"A little ways farther," Buck said as they exited a tunnel that went through a mountainside. "But first I gotta git gas." His voice was unusually pleasant.

They pulled into an all-night mini-mart, where Buck opened up the trunk for some reason. Alan paid him no mind, as he was checking his emails on his iPhone. After they got back on the road, he said, "I didn't know the Italian place was this far."

Without responding to the remark, Buck made a quick turn and parked his car next to the entrance to a villa. He claimed he was "takin' a piss."

Alan heard the trunk open again. He rolled down his window while he waited, since he needed a break from the stale odor of cigarette smoke inside the vehicle. Instead of getting a breath of fresh air, he got a whiff of something else—gasoline. He turned around for the first time and saw his boss stuffing a rag inside a wine bottle.

"Buck," he shouted, but the cowboy had already lit the wick with a flick of his lighter and tossed the resulting Molotov cocktail toward a dark-colored BMW inside the gate of the villa. If Alan were not mistaken, based on the car's front end damage, it was the same one that had chased them the night Christophe's thugs had confronted him at Chez Betty.

As the BMW exploded in flames, Buck got back in the driver's seat of his Camaro. "Pansy-ass motherfuckers," he said. "If they want a guerilla war, they picked the wrong monsieur."

* * *

Buck waited several days after the firebombing to buy four new tires for the pickup at a discount store in Nice. While Christophe likely knew who was responsible for the incendiary reprisal, Esnault did not become involved. According to Buck, reporting the matter to the authorities wasn't the mob lord's style.

At the end of the short work week caused by the repair job, Alan asked Jeannette if she wanted to go to Monte Carlo. He had several reasons for this, besides the fact it might be a good date. First, however much his travels constituted a spiritual journey, he still had a little tourist in him. Second, the blind lady mentioned Rolf had gambled there. Seeing the place first hand would add depth and color to a possible motive for the Norwegian's murder. Finally, Alan liked James Bond, and several scenes from the character's movies had taken place at the iconic gambling mecca.

Jeannette enthusiastically endorsed the idea. She told him she had been there many times and considered it a place of intrigue and mystery. She agreed to go, provided she was able to take Chloé to her mother's and that he could find a sport coat.

They met at the hotel. Alan had borrowed Buck's pickup so they wouldn't have to take the bus or walk from the train station in Monaco to the casino. He wore a dark evening jacket, a white shirt and a black bowtie that Thierry, the bar manager, had lent him. Jeannette dressed up in an elegant low-cut cream-colored gown, her one other formal outfit.

To get there, they drove along the Basse Corniche in the opposite direction of Nice, a scenic route that took them through Beaulieu-sur-Mer, Èze, and Cap-d'Ail. On the way they discussed Esnault's reluctance to believe Chloé and his insinuation that Alan had been manipulating the child into providing him a defense. It was hardly a romantic topic.

"After this horrible investigation ends and you are exonerated, are you going back to the States?" Jeannette asked. Once again she had brought the issue up.

Despite all the other distractions he had to deal with, Alan had looked into how he could legally remain in the country. His passport allowed him a total of three months, and he had already exceeded that. Absent crossing international borders periodically to extend this time, he would have to obtain a visa, a long and bureaucratic entanglement. For that he would have to be a student, be employed legitimately, or prove he had enough money to support himself and maintain health insurance so that he wouldn't be a drain on the French social-service system. The latter alternative was possible, assuming his divorce was finalized, and he ended up with enough assets.

After more discussion about his immigration issues, they arrived in Monaco. Its skyline of modern twenty to forty-story condos, bank buildings, and swank hotels contrasted greatly with the architecture of Old Nice and Villefranche. The three-quarter-mile-square city had about 36,000 citizens, according to Alan's travel books, making it the most densely populated town in the world. The country's principal industries were tourism, gambling, and banking, and the casino was, for some unscrupulous types, a convenient way to launder money. The latter topic made him jittery, for he feared his wife would somehow find out he'd been there and raise more suspicion in divorce court about his travels.

Alan got his first look at the casino when he drove past it on a circular drive. The famous attraction's Belle-Epoch-style architecture diverted his attention, nearly causing him to plow into a Ferrari, a Rolls-Royce, and a Bentley that waited for valets to whisk them away. He knew immediately that Buck's red pickup and longhorns didn't belong, so he drove to the bottom of a hill and parked in an underground garage.

Before entering the building, he and Jeannette had to present identification to prove they were not citizens of Monaco, for ironically such persons could not legally gamble in their own country. The purchase of two *Carte d'Entrées* for ten euros apiece admitted them into the main part of the casino, where they took in gilded rooms, Beaux-Arts nineteenth-century décor, ornate ceilings, large crystal chandeliers, and beautiful paintings and sculpture.

The couple decided to try their hand at roulette. The French version of the game had different terminology, of course. Instead of Even and Odd the table read Pair and Impair. For one to eighteen the designation was Manque, and for nineteen to thirty-six, Passe. The lower end of the board indicated P-12 (*première,* or first 12), M-12 (*moyenne,* or middle 12), and D-12 (*dernière,* or last 12).

The table also had Racetrack Betting, and it had nothing to do with horses. Here three bets existed: *Les Voisins* (the Neighbors) for a mix of sixteen numbers flanking the zero on the roulette wheel; *Les Tiers* (the Thirds) for twelve possibilities directly across from *Les Voisins;* and finally, *Les Orphelins* (the Orphans) for the eight remaining numbers.

Jeannette consistently bet on Les Orphelins, riskier but nevertheless closer to her affinity for the unfortunate. He, on the other hand, stayed with Les Voisins. She won twenty-five euros, and he lost thirty. Later he put ten euros on seventeen black and lost yet again. On that note, Jeannette led Alan to a high-roller room called

La Salle Médecin. She must have thought the high minimum tables would keep him from betting and losing more money.

A well-dressed man at the entrance stopped them initially, for the room was member only, but he recognized Jeannette for some reason and allowed them inside. Alan did not ask how she knew the casino worker, nor why she could enter so easily, for he was distracted by the room's magnificent décor. It included a half dozen orange-felted Black Jack tables, empire green and bronze walls, mahogany woodwork, and a carpet having a complex mix of purple, orange, and green. Though the stakes were high, no screams, threats of suicide caused by heavy losses, or other antics transpired. The place had too much class for that.

Then it happened. Jeannette clutched Alan's arm in a vice-grip that left bruises in the shape of her fingers. *"Allons-y,"* she urged, forgetting her English in a moment of stress. The phrase literally meant "let's go," but the context suggested something much stronger. "Let's get the hell out of here," would be a more apt translation. Though Alan got the drift, he froze, not knowing the origin of the threat.

Jeannette pulled his arm still harder. *"Tout de suite!"* she hissed, as her eyes swept across the room to a short, blond-haired man in his forties who was playing roulette at a fifty-euro table. He wore a purple-velvet smoking jacket with a large collar, and underneath it, a black silk scarf and a white dress shirt. One of the men beside him had a black patch over his eye.

As the couple rushed out of the casino and toward the parking ramp, Jeannette anxiously spouted out between breaths: "That was Christophe!" After she gathered herself further, she quickly explained she had dated him five years prior and somehow extricated herself from him and his physical abuse. "If he were to see us together, he'd be jealous," she said. "I don't know what he'd do."

"Christophe, huh? He wouldn't be the owner of a taxi cab company, would he?"

"Yes, as a matter of fact."

The revelation nearly dropped Alan in his tracks. He was in even deeper than he had thought. But instead of reacting with shock or alarm, he put on a gritty front. "What would the asshole have done if we'd stayed, sicked his dogs on me? He already tried that, and it didn't work. Didn't you see the guy with the patch over his eye? I was the one who gave him that."

"Oh, you're real tough, aren't you, Alan."

"I can hold my own," he replied, not very convincing even to himself.

When they got back to Villefranche, they decided to go to a local restaurant called La Grignotière and decompress. Alan assumed the eatery would be of moderate size, with four to five waitresses and thirty tables. But after opening the place's heavy wooden door that stuck on its frame, they were greeted by a single server. She was in her fifties, had short salt-and-pepper hair, and wore a white blouse and black sweater. "Oui, monsieur?" she asked.

"Une table, s'il vous plaît," Alan responded confidently. He wanted to demonstrate a take-charge attitude, since Jeannette hadn't exactly believed in him at Monte Carlo.

"Combien de personnes?"

He held up two fingers.

The waitress seated them in the back of the quaint restaurant that was the size of a living room in a ranch-style home. She scooted each person close to the table, being careful to attend first to Jeannette. After babbling in French several specials and passing them menus, she left for the kitchen, where a lone chef prepared a dish for the only other customer. Of significance to Alan was the absence of ice water.

The room had the feel of his grandmother's house. A beige antique chest of drawers holding knickknacks stood on one side, and a wine rack hung high above the other. The place's peach-colored plaster walls had sconce lighting and were adorned with framed pictures of Villefranche, including a large one of the harbor in the far back corner. Shaker-style chairs surrounded the restaurant's tables, which were covered with white linen, silverware, and wine glasses.

The waitress returned to the table with a dish of green and black olives as an appetizer and asked, *"Avez-vous choisi?"*

After carefully examining the menu of French, Italian and Mediterranean dishes, Jeannette selected *Le Loup Portion Frais Cuit à l'Huile d'Olive et Citron* (fresh sea bass cooked in olive oil and lemon), and Alan picked something closer to his American heart: *Le Filet de Boeuf Béarnaise.*

"Et pour le vin?"

They decided to share a bottle of the house red. While waiting for the wine, they talked more about Christophe, being careful to keep their voices low.

"So it's been five years since you dated him?" Alan asked.

"In a small town where it is hard to escape gossip, it seems like yesterday."

"I understand, but why have anything to do with him?"

Jeannette's eyes shifted downward and away from Alan's. "There's something else I haven't told you."

"What now?"

"It has to do with Chloé."

Alan began to connect the dots. "Christophe wouldn't be her—"

"Yes."

"No wonder she has lighter hair than you," he replied, displaying his knack for making inappropriate remarks at key points in a conversation.

Jeannette next detailed the rest of her ever-evolving story. The part about a yacht captain having been in her life was true. She did have a boyfriend having such an occupation. In fact, he had been her *lycée*-sweetheart, and they had lived together in her apartment in Villefranche, when he wasn't driving rich cats around the Med in a boat. It was also correct that said yacht captain had disappeared, but not for the reasons Alan had thought. The young man had lost a large shipment of Christophe's hash while being waylaid by some Tunisian sea pirates. After that, Jeannette never saw him again and started dating Christophe on the rebound.

During Jeannette's explanation of family history, she conceded she had once had a curious addiction to bad boys: men of violence, those who were on the wrong side of the law, and risk takers. Both the yacht captain and Christophe fit this persona well, but after having experienced enough excitement, she had changed her tastes. Something about physical abuse at the hands of the man had been influential in this regard. Then too, the mysterious disappearance of her previous boyfriend had been a factor. A guy like Alan met her requirements better, for fundamentally he was a good boy, albeit one in serious need of tweaking.

The waitress brought the bottle of wine, uncorked it and efficiently poured them each a glass. At this juncture Alan needed a drink, since the frank discussion together with the quick exit from the casino had caused him to become a bit unhinged. "Your daughter said that on the day of the murder she was supposed to have a visit with her father," he observed.

"That's right. He has visitation at three on Saturdays."

"You left the train station in Villefranche in the opposite direction of your apartment. Was that because you were going to Christophe's?"

"Yes."

"And when you got there, he hit you?"

"For being late."

"That explains the bruise you had at the flower shop, and as well Chloé's obsession about time."

Jeannette nodded sadly.

"Rolf Swenson owed Christophe money, so he must he a prime suspect in the murder," Alan said. "But if Christophe was waiting for a visit with your daughter at his house at three, he couldn't possibly have been at Rolf's in time to kill him."

"I guess Chloé is an alibi witness for him too," Jeannette said with a twisted smile.

"Maybe that was his intent all along," Alan responded, pouring himself another glass of wine. "That's why he got mad when you didn't show up on time, since your being late spoiled his little plan. Someone else must have done it for him. The question is who."

"In case you haven't noticed, he has plenty of options."

"No doubt. So, are you afraid Christophe could do something to you besides give you a black eye?"

"He would have killed me long ago if it weren't for my daughter."

"Now that part I don't get."

"Believe it or not, he wants a good mother for her," Jeannette said. "Still, I worry every day about what he might do. He's capable of most anything."

"You think he'd ever hurt her?"

"If it suited his purposes. So far it has not."

The server brought them their food and removed the dish of olives. Alan asked for some catsup for his fries, since no bottle of it was on the table. Jeannette shook her head in disgust at the request.

After they finished eating, the waitress cleared away their dishes and asked, *"Ça vous plait?"*

Jeannette told her that everything was fine, whereupon the server announced the desserts. While the *Crème Brulée* and *Tarte Tatin*, a pastry of apples caramelized in sugar and butter, seemed enticing, they both declined. *"Désirez-vous d'autre chose—un digestif peut-être?"*

Alan ordered some *café au lait*, and Jeannette kicked him under the table, this time not tolerating his boorishness. "We French hate it when you Americans order that as an after dinner drink. To us, it's like wearing black socks with shorts."

Eventually they left La Grignotière for a walk on the beach, but the subject of Christophe would not go away. As they went along together hand in hand, Jeannette said, "Your job with Buck is very risky."

"Uh, I got that point some time ago."

"Then why do you continue to work for him?"

"Money."

"I must insist you do something else," she stressed. "I can't have my child's new father exposed to the wrath of a crazy man."

"Maybe my divorce will settle, and I can quit."

"Please, Alan—I care about you—You must do so immediately."

"With no money I'll need a place to stay."

"You can live with me," she promised. "And maybe find another job."

They reached the shoreline, where an overcast sky gave them privacy. The serious conversation about Christophe having finished, Jeannette suddenly became more spontaneous, much to Alan's delight. She took off her shoes, left them by a large boulder, and said, "Come on, let's go for a swim."

"Swimming? *Au natural?*"

"*C'est ça oui.*"

Ça oui indeed.

Alan removed his shoes, bowtie, shirt, and sport jacket. Jeannette gathered up the bottom of her dress with her hand and ran with him toward the sea. There the couple enjoyed the surf until their remaining clothes became drenched. At the water's edge, they removed them, and began swimming. The salt stung his eyes, but not enough to blur his view of her naked body.

After returning and grabbing their clothes, they hid behind a boulder where they finished what they had started in their trek down the mountain near Èze. This time he initiated things, kissing Jeannette passionately. Instead of resisting as she had done before, she permitted his advances, and ultimately they had spirited sex to the cadence of the pounding surf. He had finally learned what it was like to make love to a French woman, and Jeannette most certainly did not disappoint.

8

At precisely 6 a.m. the day after his hot date with Jeannette, a sharp rap on Alan's hotel room door interrupted his deep and restful sleep. Still relishing the sex-on-the-beach tryst, he felt self-assured, not believing anything could possibly go wrong that day. He was in love after all, and love trumped everything, everything except the long arm of French law.

"Police! Ouvrez la porte!"

Alan jumped out of bed and slipped on his pants, which were still laced with sand from the events of the night before. The knock turned into a relentless hammer, so he reached for the door without bothering with his shirt. After cracking it open slightly, he peeked outside, where much to his disappointment he discovered a swat team of French cops poised to pounce. Their automatic weapons, bullet-proof vests, military-style fatigues, and camouflaged faces turned his blood to ice.

"May I help you?"

The intruders' response was not so polite. They stormed inside without hesitation, mashed his face down on the floor, and screamed commands in French in a manner that reminded him of the American TV show *Cops*. Amazingly, the tune *Bad Boys* played in his head, though the situation hardly evoked amusement.

The leader of the police brigade, Lieutenant Gustave Esnault, instructed his overwrought helpers to handcuff Alan to a chair in front of the desk. "My apologies for the forceful manner in which you have been treated," he said. "Unfortunately our protocol requires 'shock and awe' when it comes to searches for firearms. I'm sure you understand."

"I don't understand a damn thing," Alan snapped.

Esnault positioned an official-looking legal paper in front of him. "This is a *perquisition*, or a search warrant in your parlance," he explained. "I think you will find everything in order."

The document was in French legalese. As near as Alan could tell a magistrate of unknown power and authority had given the police the right to search his room. He noted the absence of an affidavit establishing probable cause. Even though this was France, some level of proof justifying the search should have been required, he thought. So he challenged the validity of the procedure.

Ignoring Alan's objection, the lieutenant said, "Now, if you would be so kind, please sign here." He pointed to a line at the bottom of another document entitled *Procès-Verbale de Perquisition* and told one of his storm troopers to uncuff him so he could do so.

Alan asked, "By signing this I'm saying what?"

"It is a simple acknowledgement of your presence during the execution of the judge's order and helps assure that our process is transparent."

"And what if I don't sign?"

"Signez-le!" screamed the cop who took the cuffs off. He was the one with the spastic left eye whom Alan had seen during his first encounter with Esnault in Villefranche. Obviously the guy needed anger management.

"Please excuse Monsieur Leroux," the lieutenant said evenly. "Unfortunately he has post-traumatic stress syndrome associated with his involvement in one of *your* country's wars and at times lacks civility." He yelled at his agitated sidekick to retreat as though he were speaking to a barking, overprotective dog.

After Leroux complied, Esnault redirected his attention to Alan. "If you do not wish to sign the form, I will simply mark it *refuse de signer.*" Receiving no response, that's exactly what the lieutenant did, while a scrawny clerical-appearing officer noted this on a clipboard.

The French police thereafter emptied the contents of the room's dresser and desk drawers on the floor, rifled through every item of clothing in the closet, and looked under the bed. They found what they wanted when they lifted the mattress off the box springs: the Moroccan semi-automatic pistol that Alan had purchased through Ludovic in the Moulins.

"You really should use more creative hiding places," Esnault said, while inspecting the gun.

"I bought it for self-defense, okay?"

"I assume you have a sport-shooting license?"

Alan shook his head.

"Ah, what a pity. The American lawyer has failed to cross his T's and dot his I's."

"Even if I don't have one, you can't charge me," Alan countered. "Your search is illegal."

"All provisions of *Le Code de Procédure de Pénale* have been observed," the lieutenant replied as he emptied the gun's bullets using plastic gloves. He then educated Alan on the requirements of a French search warrant: it had to be issued by a magistrate and executed between the hours of 6 a.m. and 9 p.m. by an Officer of the Police Judicaire (Esnault) in the presence of the owner or possessor of the residence searched, or in his or her absence, two independent witnesses.

"What about probable cause? I assume the woman on the bus observed me with the gun, but that occurred some time ago, so your information is not only stale, it's moldy and rotten."

"Probable cause is another one of your American inventions," the French cop declared with evident ennui.

"I don't care what standard you use," Alan said. "You had no basis for believing I had a gun in my hotel room on this particular day. A report from a busy-body bitch that has already turned yellow doesn't cut it!"

Angered at the crude reference to Miss Perfect, Monsieur Leroux suddenly poked the muzzle of his Uzi into Alan's forehead and pushed him back into his chair. His left eye twitched out of control, underscoring his rage.

"If I were you, I would not upset the good officer by speaking ill of a woman," Esnault advised. "He is quite sensitive, you see."

Once Leroux finally withdrew the Uzi, Alan resumed making his case with Esnault. "That gun will be thrown out as well as its fruits. You must have some version of the fruit-of-the-poison-tree doctrine here."

The particular body of law to which Alan had referred enabled an American defense attorney to get evidence suppressed that was derived from an earlier violation of a defendant's rights. If, for example, the police found drugs by illegal means, not only would they be disregarded, but also their testing, statements made by the defendant about them, and even the fruits of a later investigation based on such information.

Esnault smiled. "I can assure you, Monsieur Newberg, that no tree has been poisoned, since we have complied with all technicalities."

In way over his head, Alan became less legalistic. "Are you done yet?"

"No, in fact," the lieutenant responded while meticulously sealing the gun and its bullets in separately labeled plastic bags. "Since you have illegally possessed a firearm, I am afraid I must take you into custody."

"Whatever. A minor contravention."

"Au contraire," Esnault said. "Illegal possession of a Category B firearm in France is a *délit*, a serious offense that carries a maximum term of imprisonment of seven years."

Leroux snorted. *"L'Américain n'est pas si malin maintenant* —The American is not so clever now." He roughly lifted Alan to his feet at Esnault's direction, allowed him to dress the rest of the way, and escorted him out the door.

"Where are you taking me?"

"A cell."

"For what?"

"Une garde à vue."

* * *

The French cops drove Alan to the gendarmerie in Nice, handcuffed and seat-belted in the back of a transport van. Fortunately they took the time to do the latter, given Leroux's propensity to tailgate, swerve into the oncoming lane, squeeze traffic lights, and double the speed limit. Several near misses and the fact he would fly off the handle at the slightest provocation made the ride a harrowing experience.

Esnault, apparently accustomed to such antics, calmly rode shotgun and soothed his road-raging partner with small talk about the weather and mundane local sports events. Once they passed through the front gate of the gendarmerie with the assistance of the lieutenant's electronic card, Alan sighed relief and thanked the higher powers of all religions, past and present, for his safe arrival.

Inside Leroux impatiently marched Alan up two flights of stairs like a drill sergeant, then brought him to Esnault's office. There he dropped him into a chair in front of the cop's desk.

"The French version of your rights is as follows," the lieutenant announced. He read from a card and translated the words in monotone English. "You have been charged with Illegal Possession of a Class B firearm. You may see a doctor. You have the right to have a lawyer present during interrogation, and you may choose not to answer questions." Having finished this procedure, he asked Alan to sign a form entitled *Procès Verbale de Notifications des Droits*, which he did, acknowledging that his rights had been read.

"I suppose no one will hold it against me, if I remain silent," Alan said. His tone dripped with sarcasm.

"Our Constitution and the Human Rights Act say this," the lieutenant replied indifferently. "But people are people, of course." He smiled and signaled to Leroux, who hauled Alan to a cell with a seatless toilet and a steel bed.

During the early part of his detention, Alan stared at the wall, speculating naïvely about the outcome of the gun charge: a warning, a fine, a short jail sentence, or an order to leave the country, certainly nothing more. The latter might separate him from Jeannette and Chloé, but they'd reconnect somehow. He thought about whom to call for assistance, and Buck Treadway came to mind. Since Alan no longer had his iPhone, he yelled for Leroux, who came to his cell and told him in French to shut his mouth or he'd shut it for him.

After Alan explained what he wanted more clearly, Leroux growled and took him to Esnault's office. "*L'Américain veut télé-*

phoner á quelqu'un—The American wants to telephone someone," he said.

The lieutenant, who was in the process of reading a report, calmly put out a rolled cigarette and asked, somewhat annoyed, "Whom do you wish to call?"

"A person who can get me a lawyer."

Esnault put a land phone on the desk while Leroux removed the handcuffs.

"Don't I get some privacy?" Alan asked.

"*Non!*" screamed Leroux.

"Can't you chain that gorilla up?"

Apparently Leroux understood the simian reference, for he grabbed Alan by the shirt and slammed him up against the wall. Before the anger-challenged cop could do any real damage, Esnault backed him down, yelling, "*Calme-toi!*"

"You may have private conversations with a lawyer," the lieutenant indicated in polite contrast. "But if the person with whom you speak is not your lawyer, I must know the person's name and be able to listen to the conversation. I have to be assured that you are not communicating the fact of your detention to an accomplice and possibly telling him to hide evidence or warning him of an impending arrest."

Alan hesitated, not knowing what Esnault thought about Buck. Realizing he had little choice, he gave the cop his name. The lieutenant apparently knew the Texan, since he didn't bother to check him out on his computer. Instead he put the phone on speaker, and Alan dialed the number.

Buck answered luckily, whereupon Alan summarized his situation in panicked monologue. During this time, Esnault listened carefully, and Leroux cracked his knuckles just in case they became necessary.

"You got yourself another mega, mega problem, Al," Buck said. "Sounds like you need a French avocat."

"A name would help."

"Off the top of my head, I can't remember, but I'll find my man's card and get a hold of him."

"Does this hot shot know criminal law?"

"Well, he did get me out of a charge having to do with a whore-house in Nice once, though it was more in the nature of a contract dispute, if you know what I mean."

"This is a little different, Buck."

"Copy, pardner. Where ya at?"

"La Gendarmerie in Nice."

* * *

Four hours after the conversation with Buck, Leroux escorted an impeccably dressed dandy to a stark conference room where Alan waited. It had a table and two chairs. Leroux patted the man down, examined his belongings, and left. The visitor introduced himself to Alan as Richard Étienne and indicated that Buck had paid for his legal services. The fiftyish avocat had a closely trimmed goatee and wore a tan suede jacket, a crisp light-blue oxford-style shirt, and meticulously ironed blue jeans.

Étienne inspected the room with a nauseated look and re-trieved from an inner pocket of his jacket a piece of plastic. He unfolded it on the metal bed and exactly positioned his fancy attaché case on top of it, together with a notepad and pen. Still standing, he examined the wall carefully for grime before leaning against it. "It seems," he said, after clearing his throat, "you have a small problem with the French authorities."

"Uh, yeah."

"I must tell you that your case may take on an ugly dimension in the not-too-distant future."

"What do you mean?"

"The gun found in your hotel room is being compared to a bullet fragment extracted from Rolf Swenson's apartment."

"Rolf Swenson!"

"Yes, they think it may be the murder weapon."

Alan felt his body go clammy. "W-what makes them think that?"

"The fragment has the same caliber as your gun," Étienne said.

"Ludovic!" Alan screamed with sudden revelation.

"And what does he have to do with this?" Étienne asked.

Alan indicated that his French friend had arranged the sale of the gun to him. After going into the events that led to the purchase, he offered his theory on what had happened: the acrimonious taxi cab competition had spurred Christophe into thoughts of revenge, and since the drug lord was afraid of Buck, he decided to get the Texan back indirectly by targeting Alan. In addition, Alan had become involved with Christophe's ex-girlfriend and daughter, making the man extremely jealous.

"So Ludovic put the gun on you for Christophe?"

"Probably."

"What's Ludovic's connection to him?"

"He used to work for him. Now he fears him."

Sounding incredulous, Étienne said, "I suppose you will next claim that Christophe killed Rolf Swenson."

"Or had someone do it for him."

Étienne pursed his lips and turned his head away in disbelief. Apparently he had seen his share of defendants who claimed they were being framed. Alan was just another one of them.

"Look, I got the gun for self-defense, and I'm being played. Can't you see this?"

"Not really."

"Come on, man. You're supposed to be my lawyer."

"True. But I'm not your idiot."

"Whatever." Alan stood up and stormed to the other side of the cramped room.

"As to your claim of self-defense, such a position doesn't help you on a charge of illegal possession of a firearm," Étienne advised. "While you may be able to use a gun to defend yourself in response to a specific threat under very limited circumstances, it is nevertheless illegal to possess such a weapon in the first place without a sport-shooting permit."

"So what's going to happen to me?"

"You will be kept here under a *garde à vue* until it is determined whether you should be referred to court on a weapons offense, or worse, for Rolf's murder."

"So this bullshit gun rap is being used to hold me until they get their act together on the more serious charge?"

"Possibly."

"And what is a *garde à vue* exactly?"

The lawyer responded that the French police could hold a suspect for up to twenty-four hours, while they contacted the *procureur* or prosecutor about the case. By the end of that time frame, he or she could request a JI or judge of instruction to investigate and decide whether to charge formally. In that event, the case would be sent to correctional court or the Cour d'Assises, depending upon the seriousness of the accusation.

The procureur also had the authority to extend custody another twenty-four hours for a maximum of forty-eight, and in some cases, such as those involving terrorism, a judge could permit an even longer period of detention.

"Lieutenant Esnault will attempt to interrogate you and ask that you sign a *procès-verbale,* that is a confession,*"* Étienne cautioned. "You have the right to my presence during questioning. You may also speak to the police without me, but this is entirely up to you."

"Your advice is that I say nothing, I assume."

"I recommend you give a brief statement regarding your claim of *défense légitime* (self-defense) in mitigation of the gun charge, so the JI will have your side in writing. Nothing you say can be used in court for or against you, unless it is reduced to writing."

"And if they question me about the murder?"

"Say nothing. More importantly sign nothing."

* * *

Alan foolishly believed he could handle police questioning without the presence of Étienne, since he himself was a lawyer. For eight hours Esnault and Leroux took advantage of this stupidity by repeatedly interrogating him using every technique short of water-boarding.

This included: lying to the subject in a manner designed to make him think the case was airtight and that he might as well confess; floating alternative factual theories, one making the accused look bad and the other better, but the latter incriminating nevertheless; and the tried and true method of good cop bad cop.

The lie approach proved lame. Esnault claimed that someone had seen Alan hide the gun after the murder. Aside from the fact he did not have the weapon yet on the day in question, if such a person had truly seen this, the police would have recovered the gun immediately, making a perquisition months later unnecessary. Leroux took his turn and tried his best to convince Alan that a witness had heard an argument about money at Rolf's residence before the shooting and one of the participants spoke in American English.

When Alan asked Leroux to give him some examples, the cop interspersed the phrases heard with words like "chap, mate, and bloke." Leroux having failed miserably, Esnault tried again, stating that they had already obtained a ballistics comparison establishing that the Moroccan handgun had fired the fatal shot, but this could not possibly be true as the police had seized the weapon from Alan's hotel room just hours before.

The floating theories technique had more promise. A criminal suspect would be presented a version of the facts that would make him look reprehensible, which he would therefore deny. But a sympathetic cop, preferably a female, would then offer an alternative in which the accused could maintain the moral high ground. Unfortunately for the defendant, the police could easily disprove the alternative theory, once the more difficult issue of identity of the perpetrator had been established. In Alan's case, Esnault suggested that Rolf's shooting could have been accidental. Then he claimed it could have been accomplished in self-defense. Finally, he said that Rolf amounted to an inveterate scumbag, who ripped everyone off, and that Alan had actually done society a favor in killing him. Again the police strategy did not work.

In the good-cop-bad-cop drama, Leroux, having been destined for stardom as a bad cop, started off. He brought Alan to a separate room, where he sat him in a chair unhandcuffed. Thereafter he screamed in his face accusation after accusation concerning Rolf's killing. When his voice grew tired, he left the room, only to return later for more angry outbursts. Once Leroux had softened Alan up, the milder Esnault tagged off and presented another morally acceptable theory of inculpation. Alan saw through this as well, and the cops returned him to his cell, still unscathed.

At first, Alan tolerated being in custody well, but after ten hours of isolation he began to crack. His surroundings offered no books, magazines, television, exercise, or any form of diversion. Since the light burned the entire night, lack of sleep made the resulting sensory deprivation even worse. Like a turkey in an oven, he baked and baked until he was ready to be eaten. When the timer finally went off, Leroux brought him back to Esnault.

In front of the lieutenant on his desk, the Moroccan handgun lay motionless, still sealed in a plastic evidence bag. Esnault scrutinized the weapon's every detail in dead silence, while Alan, having no energy to question the curious inaction, did the same.

"Before us is an instrument of death," the lieutenant finally declared. "It is difficult to imagine that this device has such power, but it does."

Alan nodded slowly, hypnotized by the cop's voice in his current state of fatigue.

"This piece of iron and steel does not itself kill," Esnault continued, gesturing toward the gun. "Something more is required. The choice to kill, you see, does not reside in an inanimate object, but rather in the mind of a human being, an entity not nearly so perfectly designed." He slit open the evidence bag containing the gun with the blade of his pocketknife and donned some latex gloves. He withdrew the weapon and placed it on the desk for a clearer view.

Alan's eyes, stinging from lack of sleep, nearly bugged out of his head. He didn't know what was in store. Based on his experiences thus far, anything was possible.

"It is hard to believe that someone could be so callous," the lieutenant said. "Without thinking of Rolf or his family, he extinguished his life." He pointed the gun toward an imaginary target in the room and snapped its trigger so as to accentuate the point.

"The person who committed this dastardly act is you, Alan," Esnault stressed, shifting his eyes toward him. Thus far the detective had not used his first name, but now things had become considerably more personal.

"Soon the judge of instruction will charge you with murder," he went on, "and you will face a jury in the Cour d'Assises, a frightening prospect for a native of my own country and an even more daunting one for a foreigner such as yourself. The jury will be told that you possessed the murder weapon. In the absence of a compelling explanation for this, it will find you guilty and sentence you without the benefit of any contrition on your behalf." The lieutenant paused for dramatic effect, then mouthed in a barely perceptible voice, "none whatsoever."

Alan cowered, remembering the Palais de Justice in Old Nice and the Nuremburg-like courtroom there. His eyes welled up, signaling to his captor to go in for the kill.

"I believe you are a good person," Esnault said. "Beneath your confused veneer is someone wanting to flower."

"I've always tried to do the right thing."

"I know that," Esnault said softly. "But if you don't do 'the right thing' now, you will suffer. While in prison, your only associates will be scum, who will likely take advantage of you in a very personal way, *à la perpétuité.*"

Alan swallowed hard.

"But there is a choice, one that will show the jury the kind of a man you really are—a person who is strong, courageous, and forthright." Esnault slipped a document in front of Alan.

"What's this?"

"A *procès-verbale,*" the lieutenant replied with all the sincerity he could muster. "I would say it is a confession, but truly it is more than that. I believe it is proof that you are a man."

The relentless and prolonged questioning and manipulation had finally proven too much. *Nobody will believe Chloé,* Alan thought. *She isn't even considered a witness in France. They can put the murder weapon on me, and the jury will do whatever the cops want.*

Esnault must have read his face. "Are you now ready to speak the truth and show me and the jury the person you really are?"

Alan half-nodded, whereupon the French cop slid the *procès-verbale* closer to him.

"How much time will I get?"

"No more than twenty years reclusion," Esnault promised. "With *sursis* (parole), you will be out in half that time. The judge may even arrange conjugal visitation and protective custody, given that you are an American."

Alan started to sign, but the phone rang. He could hear Étienne's voice coming through the receiver once it was picked up.

"Your lawyer is here and wishes to speak with you," Esnault said with great irritation. He opened the door and permitted Étienne to enter, then left, leaving the unsigned confession behind with the avocat in case Alan would change his mind.

"Why did you speak to them without my presence?" Étienne asked.

"I thought I could handle it, I guess," Alan replied in a tired, far-away voice.

"Have you signed anything?"

"No. But they say it'll be better if I do."

"Well, they're wrong."

"I just want some sleep, okay? Can you get me something that will help me sleep?"

Étienne switched tactics in light of Alan's apparent delirium. "I spoke to your friend Buck Treadway, and he asked me to read you something."

"What is it?"

The avocat took out a slip of paper from his sport jacket and stated Buck's words without any inflection: "Appeasement never works, Al."

Alan nodded and mumbled something unintelligible.

"I didn't get that. What?"

"Stand your ground."

Having now understood his client, Étienne opened the door to the office. Outside it, Esnault sat on a chair next to the key hole and thus must have been listening. The avocat handed him the unsigned confession.

"I guess you aren't the man I thought you were," the lieutenant said to Alan, who responded emphatically to the cop's cut by spitting hard on the procès-verbale.

"Well done, Monsieur Newberg, well done," Esnault said. "I am glad you have displayed such courage, but I have some news that will likely cause you concern."

"And what might that be?"

"Le Procureur de la République has issued a *requisitoire introductif.*

"A requi—what?"

"A request for the judge of instruction to take jurisdiction over the case."

"Meaning what?"

"Meaning he will interview everyone and recommend whether you should be charged with the murder of Rolf Swenson," Esnault explained.

"And where do I go in the meantime?"

"La Maison d'Arrêt!" snapped Leroux, who by now had joined them. Fortunately he had not been present during Alan's expulsion of bodily fluids.

"What Monsieur Leroux is saying is you will be taken to the Palais de Justice, where the detention judge will decide your custody status pending a period of instruction," Esnault said. "Likely that will result in your incarceration in a place considerably less commodious than the one you have experienced thus far."

9

After the sordid activities at La Gendarmerie, Monsieur Leroux took Alan to the Palais de Justice. His legs were shackled at the ankles, so he walked awkwardly, something the unhinged cop seemed to enjoy. In fact the sadistic son-of-a-bitch found any pain or difficulty his prisoner exhibited amusing and sought unusual ways to provoke it. For example, on the way down from Esnault's office, he thrice stopped the elevator by activating the emergency button. Needless to say Alan reacted fearfully to the curious delays, speculating at the prospect that things might get physical before the door opened. Leroux laughed uncontrollably each time the alarm went off and ended the current installment of terror.

While the crazy cop waited for more balanced officials at the courthouse to take charge, Alan noticed something in the transport van that he hadn't seen before: someone had etched the walls with names like Hassan, Farid, and Salim. None of the graffiti showed French names—perfect evidence, he thought, of the ethnic background of his future company. He smiled and carved his own initials, using the sharp edge of his handcuffs. Not having the time or dexterity to write his full first name, he used two letters instead: A and L. Buck Treadway would have been proud.

Once the necessary paperwork had been exchanged, a court gendarme, the equivalent of a bailiff, escorted Alan to a holding cell, where he awaited his first appearance before the detention judge and another chance to speak with Étienne. He considered complaining about the creative interrogation tactics of Esnault and Leroux, but concluded that in the absence of independent witnesses, any allegation of misconduct would amount to "he said-he said."

Étienne arrived soon after Alan. He did not protect his briefcase with a piece of plastic before setting it down, nor was he repulsed by the idea of leaning against the wall. Apparently the place met his sanitary requirements better than the conference room at the police station. Since the first appearance would not take place for another half hour, he gave Alan a crash course in French criminal justice that added to what he had already learned.

Contrary to the lawyer-based adversarial approach used in America and derived from England, France employed an inquisitorial one that traced itself to Napoleon. As a result lawyers played a secondary role in all stages of the proceedings. An investigating judge and not a prosecutor made the charging decision, and the trial judge had primary responsibility for presenting a case in court. In modern times, the influence of avocats had increased, effectively making the French system a hybrid of the two models. Still it was fundamentally inquisitorial.

The competition of polar forces of defense and prosecution in American criminal justice supposedly determined the truth, but in order for this sporting theory to work, the forces had to be equal. If the defendant had a lawyer that didn't care or provide spirited and competent advocacy, the prosecution would have an advantage. If an underpaid prosecutor had a burgeoning case load and was going up against a defendant with unlimited means or a crooked politician with a bottomless war chest of campaign contributions, the defense would own the day. And if either side cheated the other out of vital information, trial by surprise would occur, and the truth would be ascertained by chance and not competition.

The inquisitorial method, on the other hand, sought to address such deficits with a neutral judge. When a defendant was suspected of having committed a serious offense or in complicated cases of fraud or government corruption, the judge of instruction, or JI, would investigate the case for both sides. This process was called a *mise en examen* (literally, put to the test). Such a judge had at his or her disposal the police, *perquisitions* or search warrants, wiretaps, and experts, and could summons or arrest witnesses and put them under oath in a deposition-like proceeding recorded by a court reporter.

Interestingly enough, the JI could interrogate the accused, albeit with his lawyer present, something completely foreign in America in light of its Fifth Amendment that protected the decision to testify all the way through trial and even thereafter. Typically in that system a defendant would testify, if at all, after the rest of the evidence had been introduced in court, allowing him to mold his testimony to fit the proof. Like in the States, legally at least, the French protected a defendant's right to remain silent, so he could refuse to testify in pre-trial proceedings before the JI. Practically speaking, however, a greater expectation existed for him to cooperate and spill his guts.

At the end of this judicial inquiry, called the period of instruction, the JI had two basic choices: decline to charge or refer the case to one of two courts—the Cour d'Assises or the Tribunal de Correctionnel. France divided offenses into three categories: contraventions (traffic violations and misdemeanors), délits (charges carrying up to ten years), and crimes (offenses that exposed a defendant from ten years to life). With délits the Tribunal de Correctionnel had jurisdiction and offered only a bench trial before a panel of three judges. Crimes that carried ten to twenty years went to the Cour d'Assises, again for a bench trial. Only if the offense carried more than twenty years, would the accused be given a jury in that court. This sharply contrasted with the system in America, where the right to jury trial was assured for all offenses involving any amount of incarceration.

The French approach had several advantages over the American. First, no cat and mouse game of discovery occurred. Both sides had the instruction judge's dossier before going to trial, meaning the lawyers didn't control the information exchange as would be the case in the States. Second, in theory at least, the JI considered the evidence fairly and objectively, and his or her decision was not influenced by the relative resources, skills, and competence of the parties and lawyers, the political aspirations of the prosecutor, or the pressure of the public or press.

This system had its drawbacks, however: the instruction period could take a painstakingly long time; the assumption of neutrality of the JI rang hollow in some cases; and lawyer advocacy wasn't as critical to the process. Moreover, members of the judiciary wore conflicting hats: the JI was an investigator, prosecutor, and judge, and trial judges in the Cour d'Assises were also on the jury. Most significantly, as Alan had already learned to some extent, defendants had fewer rights.

"How long does the instruction period take?" Alan asked.

Étienne consulted his statute book. "Normally a maximum of one year with the possibility of a six-month extension, but for offenses carrying more than twenty years, the limit is two years."

"And where do I stay in the meantime?"

"That is a question we shall determine in a few minutes," Étienne replied.

"So I might be able to post bail?"

"Sometimes the judge grants *'caution'* and allows a defendant out under certain conditions—paying a sum of money, staying away from witnesses, or wearing an electronic monitoring bracelet to name a few." In this regard the system was no different than in the U.S.

"How often is sometimes?" Alan asked.

"Well, the potential charge is murder."

"Meaning most likely I will stay in jail?"

Étienne's silence provided the answer.

"So this wonderful system of yours allows a bureaucrat called a JI to take up to *two years* to decide whether to charge, while a guy like me rots in jail."

"'Rots' is a bit harsh, don't you think?"

"Doesn't the concept of a speedy trial mean a thing to you?"

"True justice cannot be meted out in haste, monsieur."

"And justice delayed is justice denied."

Étienne scoffed. "Do you have other questions?"

"Yes. If the instruction judge decides not to charge, do I get out?"

The avocat did not offer an automatic yes, amazingly enough. Instead he leaned back in his chair and carefully pondered the question as though it presented an enigma. "In most cases," he finally answered, measured.

"Most cases?"

"The prosecution or victim can appeal the JI's decision just like you."

"And this is also true with respect to a verdict at trial?"

Étienne tilted his head upward as though he were gloriously observing a lofty principle floating about the room. "The Cours d'Assises is merely a court of the first *instance,*" he said proudly.

"Oh, really. How many *instances* are there anyway?"

"Two. The second *instance* is before the Cours d'Appel, where both sides can have another jury trial."

Though inexperienced in criminal procedure in the States, Alan knew an appeal in his own country did not involve a *de novo* trial and only considered legal errors made by a trial judge. Appeal and trial were two entirely different concepts. But in France two trials could occur, meaning it was never over until it was over, and over could be a very long time. Thus, he dropped his head onto the desk and covered it with his arms, imagining himself caught in a spider web of procedure all the while isolated in a French jail cell.

"What's wrong?" asked Étienne.

"In our country we would call that double jeopardy."

"Double jeopardy? I have not heard such a term. What is that?"

"Never mind."

"Well, at least you get a jury here."

"Yeah, one having three judges."

"You seem bothered by this."

"The judge-jurors will likely tell the lay-jurors what to do."

"Some say that, but each citizen is entitled to his or her own opinion, and the judges are there primarily to relate the law and keep matters on task."

"And how do you know that? Have you ever been present for deliberations?"

"No, but—

"Come on, man. The judges are more knowledgeable of the system and are familiar with all the arguments, so they control the discussion and the result."

"Assuming they do, is this a disadvantage?"

"I would prefer fresh, open minds."

"Stupid people, you mean."

"No, regular people with common sense." Indeed Alan had hit the nail on the head. Trial by one's peers in the U.S was a time-honored populist institution premised on the notion that the fairest and truest judgment of facts would more likely be rendered by a person who walked in the defendant's shoes. France, on the other hand, with its participation of judges on the jury and its two-tiered system involving a second jury trial, did not trust ordinary citizens to the same degree.

"How many jurors does it take to convict," Alan asked next.

"Six of nine in the Cours d'Assises and nine of twelve in the Cours d'Appel."

"You mean a verdict doesn't have to be unanimous?"

"A super majority is more than democratic, wouldn't you agree? What could possibly be your complaint?"

"Unanimity affords confidence in the outcome of a case and prevents innocent people from being convicted." Alan paused. "Most of the time, at least."

"It could also cause compromised verdicts that are not con-sistent with the truth," Étienne observed.

"I suppose," Alan replied. "But such verdicts are a small price to pay for protecting the innocent. Speaking of that, what about the burden of proof? I assume jurors must be convinced beyond a reasonable doubt or a similar high standard to find someone guilty."

"We have the presumption of innocence," Étienne insisted. "We are a civilized country."

"But that presumption means little without defining when it is overcome."

"So long as a juror believes in good conscience—"

"Good conscience?" Alan shook his head. The only thing he could think of was Buck Treadway standing at attention with his hand on his heart while the National Anthem blared from Ville-franche Harbor. At the time, he believed the Texan's display to be overly patriotic, if not melodramatic. Alan would never take his country for granted again—that is if he ever saw it again.

* * *

Before he was taken to the JI, Alan did what many criminal defendants in America often try to do: cop a plea. In exchange for admission of guilt to the gun offense and a short stay in jail, the murder charge would be dropped, he proposed. "Face it, they have no case," he told Étienne.

The avocat's reaction to the suggestion of a "plea bargain" was one of complete confusion, as though the very idea of it had come from Mars. Such a process did not exist in France. First and foremost, the prosecution did not decide if a case went to trial—the instruction judge did. So a prosecutor lacked the power to forego charges or reduce them, and hence to negotiate.

Second, plea negotiation would not save time, as a trial occurred regardless of a plea of guilty, if nothing else, to determine the appropriate sentence. The time necessary to conduct such a contested proceeding was far greater than a perfunctory ten or fifteen-minute plea and sentencing that took place in the States after a deal was struck. Thus, there was neither the authority nor the motivation to engage in plea bargaining in France, and Alan's proposal was roundly rejected.

At the end of his discussion with Étienne, the gendarmes took Alan to a small courtroom and sat him down in a partitioned-off area next to three other defendants. These bailiffs hooked him up with translator headphones, despite the fact his French was up to speed. Outside the prisoner area, Étienne and the other avocats milled about dressed in their customary black robes and white fur striping. Strangely enough the prosecutor sat on a chair next to one designated for the judge.

Without much fanfare the detention judge ambled in, also dressed in black robes with white fur stripes as well as a few red ones. One at a time he called defendants before him and coldly posed the same initial question: *"Nom—prénom?"* His voice reminded Alan of the principal in Charlie Brown cartoons—robotic and monotone.

When he offered his first and last name, his American accent became readily apparent. So the judge asked him about his legal status in the country. "You are a tourist?"

"I-I think so."

"How long have you been here?"

Alan was forced to admit he had exceeded the three-month-maximum stay permitted by his passport, since it was now July 20.

"So you are an illegal alien."

Alan's jaw dropped. In his own country, many undocumented immigrants existed, but he never thought of himself that way. "I am here because the authorities have required me to stay," he countered.

The judge grunted.

"Look, I have been a suspect in this case for months and remained here despite the possibility of criminal charges," Alan continued. "I have signed in at the police department every single day. If they thought I was a threat to flee or a danger, they wouldn't have allowed this."

His assertiveness was met by the steel eyes of an alligator about to clamp down on its prey. "The subject of this instruction is a charge of murder where the potential penalty is perpetual reclusion," the French jurist sternly noted. "Further there is a risk of flight."

"Oui, Monsieur le Juge," the procureur chimed in. "In addition, the defendant is charged with illegally possessing a firearm."

The judge turned back to Alan. "Your address?"

"Chez Betty, Villefranche-sur-Mer." The response prompted a stir of giggling among the other defendants.

"A hotel?"

"Yes, and a very nice one indeed," Alan said, causing still more laughs.

"Do you have a job?"

Alan considered mentioning his employment with Buck Treadway, but decided that saying he was involved in a clandestine enterprise run by another American would ruin his chances further. So he stood mute.

The judge ordered without argument from anyone *"la detention provisoire"* or preventive detention, essentially denying bail altogether. He then waved his hand cavalierly at the court gendarme, who put Alan back with the rest of the defendants, whereupon the next man's case was called.

"Nom-prénom..."

* * *

Rain made the ride to jail from the Palais de Justice more dreary than anticipated. As the transport van slowly passed through the streets, Alan grabbed its metal-grated windows with his fingers and watched apartment buildings, restaurants, and an infinite number of stores pass by in "eerie" silence. He was no longer a tourist on a bus.

Soon the van reached a nineteenth century embattlement with two black metal doors. Atop the doors, a rain-soaked French flag drooped over a sign that read Maison d'Arrêt de Nice. Dingy concrete walls with dark, depressing streaks of mildew extended from either side of the doorway. Alan surmised that this was the public entrance to the jail, for the van did not stop until it got to a large grey door, made of solid steel on the bottom and wire mesh on top. It swung open electronically, then closed and locked behind the van, causing a feeling of dread inside him.

A few minutes later a couple of guards hustled him through an empty exercise yard, abandoned that day due to the heavy downpour. The yard ran next to a complex of stark three-story buildings that had windows covered by more steel grates. The buildings stretched out from a central hub like spokes on a bike wheel. A twenty-foot-high chain-link fence, and beyond it, a concrete wall, surrounded the series of structures.

As the guards led him through the jail yard, he heard a chorus of whistles and hisses. Alan figured the inmates had already marked him for initiation. While he and his escorts waited for another door to buzz open, a piss-filled condom splashed on the ground in front of them. A prisoner must have tossed it through one of the grated windows. "*Bienvenue á la Maison d'Arrêt,*" one of the guards said, eyeing the condom.

Inside, a jail official assigned Alan a *numéro d'écrou* (a booking number) and took two photos of his face, one straight on and the other profile. When he finished this, he conducted a thorough search of his person that included all body cavities. Next the guards took him to an office, where the assistant commandant of the facility stood behind a metal desk and lectured about the place's rules and regulations.

He started with the permissible clothing, rattling off a memorized list he had no doubt repeated a thousand times: ten t-shirts, two regular shirts, ten pairs of socks, two *"gants de toilette"* or washcloths, four towels, a hooded sweatshirt, a non-hooded sweatshirt, seven sets of underpants, several long pants, a belt without a buckle, and one pair of shoes. Alan felt as though he had arrived at Boy Scout camp, but only for a split second.

The official also noted clothing that was *"interdit"*—prohibited. Anything blue, black, or khaki. Assuming Alan could get someone to bring him his clothes from Chez Betty, their color scheme would be prohibited. So he asked what would be available until he could have someone purchase conforming attire. The assistant commandant provided two white jail jumpsuits, one of which Alan put on.

Next the official recited a list of prohibited behavior and property: Internet access, sexual activity, drugs, cellphones, cellphone chargers, weapons, and any food items not purchased at the canteen. Exercise, access to library books, and visits were privileges to be earned, he said.

"Earned?"

"*Sauf des visites avec votre avocat*—except visits with your lawyer," the official said. He handed Alan a list of requirements for in-person visitors. So exacting were the requirements that poor and disadvantaged family members of an inmate would likely give up and not come, further isolating him or her from the outside world.

The list, translated into English, read as follows:

1. A handwritten letter, dated, signed and addressed to Monsieur le Directeur de la Maison d'Arrêt, requesting visitation and indicating the relationship of the family member to the inmate;

2. Two photos of the visitor in administrative format;

3. Photo identification in the form of a national identification card,

4. Passport, or driver's license;

5. A copy of a document establishing proof of domicile for at least three months such as a lease or telephone bill;

6. A booklet containing the name and date of birth of each family member or concubine seeking visitation. All documents establishing *concubinage* must be provided;

7. A stamped self-addressed envelope.

"Vous avez des questions?" the assistant commandant snapped.

Alan asked if *concubinage* included a girlfriend and her child with whom he did not yet live.

The jailer indicated it did not, and Alan sank into a gloomy funk. Under such rules he wouldn't be able to see Jeannette, Chloé, Buck, or any of his friends from Chez Betty. Prior to this time he had honestly thought he would be cleared, that someone would tell him it was all an April Fools' joke, or that the man from *Candid Camera* would jump out. Now the prospect of isolation from friends and family, forever perhaps, finally convinced him that his situation was very real and that his predicament had flourished into unfathomable dimension.

"Avez-vous d'autres questions, petit bébé?" the official asked, offering not a word of sympathy or understanding.

Stuffing his emotions, Alan asked about the physical surroundings. The assistant commandant gave him a brief description—the rest he would have to experience for himself. The Maison d'Arrêt had been constructed in 1887 and had a capacity of 339. Its current population was over 500, meaning the place was vastly overcrowded, and often its six-by-ten cells had multiple prisoners. The jail had three male *"bâtiments,"* or buildings, one *quartier* for women, ten disciplinary or isolation cells, and a half-dozen others in an area called *semi-liberté.* Like its equivalent in the States the facility held prisoners awaiting local court proceedings or those doing short sentences. Even though the Maison was not a prison, in a large city it amounted to such, and its population contained everyone from small-time thieves to violent terrorists.

At the end of the meeting, the jailer took Alan to an iron-bar-covered guard station that connected three long corridors that went out in various directions, one for each male bâtiment. Outside the station various officers hollered instructions accented by French profanity at numerous inmates who filed past. Most prisoners had tattoos and displayed an angry, hateful countenance, something which Alan knew he would need to mimic in order to survive. While waiting for a guard to deliver his paperwork, he peered upward at the second and third floors through a network of more iron bars and saw throngs of inmates milling about like rats in an overcrowded maze. He had become one of the rats, and the rats were not very friendly.

A guard opened an iron door that had a large letter A painted above it, which Alan assumed meant Bâtiment A, and escorted him down a long catwalk. Most of the cells along the way had bars, but some were made of concrete and had solid metal portals painted pastel-green, the same color as the shutters on the Villefranche train terminal, but not nearly so quaint. Above him a vast expanse extended to a ceiling with skylights that afforded a pitiful cameo of the clouds outside. As they reached his new home, the guard said, *"Vous avez de la chance, monsieur. Votre cellule ne comporte que deux personnes—*You are lucky, sir. Your cell only has two persons."

Alan waited nervously outside while his handcuffs were removed, wondering about the guard's definition of "luck" and what his new roommate would be like. He could see the cell had a very limited ambience: posters of soccer teams and naked women covered the walls; plastic Orangina bottles, candy bars, and an armada of single cigarettes occupied a small shelf above the toilet;

and a grated window provided a small amount of light and a glimpse of freedom. The final feature was a brown-skinned North African, who indifferently lounged on the lower bunk while reading a girly magazine.

"Matoub, vous avez un nouveau compagnon de cellule—you have a new cellmate,*"* announced the guard.

Alan reached out to shake the man's hand, but he rebuffed the gesture. The guard did not respond, presumably because impoliteness was not an infraction in the Maison d'Arrêt, but rather an assumption. He locked the cell door and left Alan to his own devices, and for the moment, they were few.

"Si vous touchez mes trucs, je vous tue—If you touch my items, I kill you," Matoub warned with his first attempt at conversation. From then on he spoke half in French, half in broken English, and all in jail vernacular.

Alan did not respond to Matoub's declaration, hopped up on the unspoken-for top bunk and focused on the ceiling to avoid him. After about a half hour, Matoub broke the silence. "What charge you catch?" he asked. The reference made Alan's legal situation seem like a disease. It was, in fact, but hardly the common cold.

"Murder,*"* he replied sharply, hoping the seriousness of the charge and tone would shield him from possible abuse.

"First time *Maison?"* Matoub asked.

"Well, yes, but—"

"Yes, no. First time?"

Alan looked down from his bunk pensively and conceded the fact.

"You soft," Matoub said, lightly pawing Alan's not-so-muscular body. "You not last long."

Alan didn't react to the macho gesture, for in sizing Matoub up he realized the guy was not much older than a teenager. Instead he asked him about his background, whereupon the young man related a story considerably more sorrowful than his own.

The police had first arrested Matoub when he was eighteen, though he had a long juvenile history. He and some North African friends had stolen a car and taken it for a joy ride. For that he spent two months in the Maison. His second stint in jail was for burglary and lasted six months, his third for safecracking, which resulted in nine months, and his fourth for armed robbery, which got him three years. On the last charge he was released on *sursis,* or parole, after a year. The French authorities later revoked him for drug dealing and dished out two more years, his current sentence. The rap sheet seemed no different than that of a run-of-the-mill criminal in America.

So too did Matoub's family upbringing, which he readily disclosed—perhaps because everyone else in the jail had long since stop listening or caring. He had grown up fast in a housing project in a Marseille *banlieu*, where he and his six brothers and sisters crammed into a small apartment ruled by his mother, a Tunisian immigrant. His father never materialized for reasons unknown. Raised on Arabic and surrounded by people who only spoke that language, he was forced to play catch-up in school due to being unfamiliar with French. Eventually he fell by the wayside, barely making it to the *lycée.*

At sixteen, he dropped out of school and never got his *Bac.* Instead he roamed the streets with his delinquent friends, having left home to make room for his younger brothers and sisters. He could not secure employment due to discrimination against the Maghrébins, or so he claimed. Since he hadn't contributed to the French social welfare system via employment, he could not receive public assistance. Crime became his default profession, not so much because he was intrinsically evil, but rather out of a desperate need to survive. Like many young North Africans, he had never assimilated into French society and found himself in a death spiral of jail and prison.

Now that the ice had been broken, Alan asked Matoub about the ropes of the Maison, since the inmate's jail age was far greater than his own. Matoub began with the toilet and instructed him on how to hang a sheet in front of it so he could take a dump without someone looking. Privacy otherwise did not exist, Matoub told him, pointing to a surveillance camera in the corridor that enabled the guards, or *matons* as he called them, to monitor inmate activity twenty-four hours a day.

"No discuss case at visits," he warned. "Matons listen, tell flics—maybe you admit something. Maybe you talk to snitch, and he tell flics. No discuss."

When Alan asked about the jail economy, Matoub told him that jobs were hard to come by. Unless Alan had access to money, which at the moment he most assuredly did not, the only way to obtain funds would be to secure menial employment, officially for the institution or unofficially for richer, more powerful inmates. What the latter might entail, he shuddered to imagine.

Matoub himself worked in the library. Other inmates had kitchen jobs, distributed meals at cells, manned canteen carts, and mopped jail floors. Matoub's library employment enabled him to escape the cell and avoid being stuck there twenty-three hours a day, the lone other hour being yard time. Another advantage of the job had to do with missing "the touch of woman," he said. In the library, several non-surveilled areas existed where he could masturbate.

"Uh," was Alan's only response.

The final reason the cellmate gave for getting a job had more to do with physical survival. *"Il faut cantiner,"* Matoub insisted.

"Cantiner" did not appear in any French-English dictionary Alan had studied, and he had not otherwise heard the term in his dealings in Villefranche. Matoub pointed to the shelf above the toilet and explained that "items" purchased from the canteen constituted the jail's medium of exchange: cigarettes, Orangina, Chocapic (chocolate cereal), Snickers, stamps, and newspapers were examples. Whether a prisoner himself smoked or consumed junk food did not matter, for he used "items" to pay for services he did in fact need. One of them was protection, and without it, life in the Maison would become an unforgiving experience.

Alan told his cellmate that he had few outside contacts who could put money on his canteen account. He mentioned his girlfriend, but noted the assistant commandant had said she couldn't visit him, as technically she wasn't a concubine.

"No tell anyone about *copine*," Matoub warned. He explained that the unscrupulous captains of cantiner in the jail would have their friends find her and extort money while holding Alan hostage.

"Okay, but how do I talk to her, if the jail won't let her come?"

"Call collect on pay phone in yard. Man's rules only apply to in-person visits."

Man's rules? Alan needed to learn them and learn them fast.

10

The day after Alan's arrival at the Maison d'Arrêt, Matoub took him to the yard. The asphalt triangular-shaped area appeared more like a parking lot than a field of grass. Bátiments A and B formed two of its sides, and the third consisted of a line of narrow cages for prisoners with "special" needs. Various activities entertained the current shift of inmates: le foot, played on a painted terrain; a weightlifting zone commandeered by hefty bodybuilders; a makeshift running track on which prisoners neurotically ran back and forth like animals in a zoo; and a gambling area where inmates bet canteen items on unknown games of chance.

At first the outdoor facility seemed very accommodating—plenty of room for exercise, sporting equipment, and a great opportunity for social interaction. Alan became quickly disabused of this naïve notion when he observed two inmates nearly beat a weaker one to death at the other end of the yard. Needless to say he did not feel very comfortable, having seen in living color the need to "cantiner."

After observing this disturbing spectacle, Matoub and he meandered through the rest of the yard amongst a background of yells, whistles, and French and Arabic chatter that echoed off the walls and buildings. Their most notable stop was the weightlifting area. It had several shirtless men with muscular bodies and crude tattoos. A particularly large and menacing inmate yelled in agony at each rep at the bench press. Another man with huge biceps did curls, and a third dips. Easily the weights and bars could be turned into weapons, but no one seemed to care, so long as violence remained in the yard.

"Who is the monster pumping iron?" Alan whispered.

"Abdul."

"What's his story?"

Matoub described the strongman's function in Maison society. He ran its main protection racket, providing security for weak and defenseless prisoners. He did this for a price, of course, and sometimes a very steep one.

"How much does he charge for his services?"

"Vingt trucs la semaine normalement—twenty items a week normally," Matoub said. *"Mais ça dépend."*

"On what?"

"Vous êtes Americain, par exemple. Coûte plus—cost more."

Alan next asked what Abdul did with the money he received. Matoub told him that after clearing his overhead, which consisted of paying the thugs who surrounded him at the weightlifting area, and bribing the matons with small amounts of marijuana that they in turn sold on the outside, Abdul purchased booze, sex, drugs, and other entertainment that made passing time while in jail a little easier for him.

"Sounds like a pretty powerful guy," Alan said.

Matoub nodded and explained the economic inequalities of jail life. Those who had jobs or a sponsoring family member or girlfriend were the haves. The rest were the have nots, such as the man they had witnessed being beaten. In effect, the cellmate suggested, the disparities his people suffered on the outside existed on the inside as well.

"Who's that?" Alan pointed toward a slight man who obsequiously scurried back and forth between prisoners.

"Rasil, Abdul's assistant."

"How does he assist him?"

Matoub responded that the guy ran protection invoices and other messages around the yard and was otherwise at Abdul's beck and call. This included everything from being a scuzzy snitch to providing him oral sex.

"How nice," Alan replied sarcastically.

A siren abruptly went off, and Matoub immediately dropped to the ground. Alan joined him and eyed the yard cautiously. All inmates, including Abdul, lay on their stomachs, whereupon several guards patrolled.

"*Fausse alarme, fausse alarme,*" they yelled suddenly. "*Levez-vous.*"

"What was that all about?" Alan asked as he got up.

Matoub explained that when an escape attempt or an attack on a maton occurred, the siren would go off. Sometimes the guards would sound the alarm for no other purpose than to remind prisoners of their status relative to them. Sometimes it just went off.

With Alan's cellmate in the lead, they next travelled to an area where five inmates sat on the ground while intently listening to a sixth man preaching. The men wore nothing special and were clean shaven, and the inmate delivering the address had a long beard. All appeared North African or Middle Eastern.

"Who's he?" Alan asked, nodding in the direction of the one who preached.

"Imam."

"A what?"

"Islamic cleric," Matoub said. "Others converts."

"What's it take to be an imam?"

Matoub gave a blank look.

Alan associated proselyting with television evangelists and Mormon missionaries, who purveyed Christian principles, but he didn't know that radical Islamists did the same. "Whom do they try to convert?" he asked.

"Anyone ready."

"Ready?" The word seemed dangerously loaded.

"Person not ready unless teachable, and he not teachable unless humble," Matoub said as though he had the sequence of words memorized.

They walked away from the group and circled the yard during which Alan posited a logical question: "When does a person become humble?"

"When he has no family or friends and nothing on this earth."

"Like an inmate here?"

"Oui," Matoub said with sad eyes.

Alan reflected on his own feelings of isolation and wondered if he would end up like the converts. He grabbed his new cellmate by the shoulders to gain his undivided attention and asked how he knew so much about the subject of conversion.

Taken aback by the aggressive gesture, Matoub blurted, "Because they did to me!"

"Did what?" Alan asked, but Matoub wouldn't answer.

"Are you afraid of them?"

The cellmate glared directly into Alan's eyes and repeated his mantra: *"Il faut cantiner."*

Alan started to laugh, but stopped when Matoub did not follow suit.

"Listen or die," the young man said bluntly.

Alan changed the subject. "Why don't the converts wear beards?"

"Law of *Taqiyya*."

"Huh?"

"Taqiyya teaches to conceal one's identity and live by pretense and dissimulation," Matoub said, big words for a man who otherwise spoke English poorly.

"You mean blend?"

"C'est exact."

"So there are people here who have radical beliefs, and I won't know it?"

"Oui."

"What does 'the man' do about this situation?"

Matoub indicated that jail officials had decided some months back to employ a strategy of de-radicalization to stop the proliferation of Islamic extremists. Some had proposed separation of the radicals from the moderates, so that the former would not poison the latter. Others had argued that the two groups should be integrated, thinking the moderates would provide a pacifying influence.

"What did they decide?"

Matoub replied with a sardonic smile, "We one big happy family here."

"Yeah, it sure looks like that."

Along a chain-link fence near the entrance to the exercise area, Alan found a bank of four overused pay phones. Each was encompassed by a silver metal box that supposedly provided privacy. Several prisoners monopolized the booths, hunching around them and speaking in whispered voices. Others waited impatiently for their turn. A sign above the phones announced the rules, which included a time limit of five minutes.

He hadn't spoken to Jeannette since his arrest and wanted to apprise her of the latest in his epic saga of breaking bad. More importantly he needed her to put money on his account, so he could "cantiner." It was either that or suffer at the hands of the jail extortionists and/or the radicals. So he excused himself from Matoub's yard tour in order to contact her.

When a booth finally opened up, Alan became befuddled, since he hadn't used a pay phone in years, much less in France. He dialed the operator, and in his best French, asked her how to call collect. *"Téléphoner en PCV,"* she called it, and put him through to Jeannette's cell. The phone rang numerous times, but she did not answer. Instead a recording came on and announced, *"Laissez un message, et je vous rappellerai dès que possible."* Before he could leave a message, the operator cut the call off. At least he had heard Jeannette's voice.

After the aborted call, Alan nervously hung out in the yard with Matoub, watching the comings and goings of its occupants. Desperate to get through to Jeannette, he tried her again, crossing his fingers that she would answer. After five electronic tones, she picked up and accepted his call.

"Where have you been?" she asked, noticeably perturbed. "I haven't heard from you in a week."

"You're not going to believe this," Alan said, embarrassed. "I've been arrested for Rolf's murder, and I'm at the Maison d'Arrêt."

"What?"

"Look, I don't have much time to talk, and I need your help."

Jeannette didn't exactly respond sympathetically: "My help? What about me? What about Chloé? Do you think of anyone besides yourself?"

At that moment Alan did not. But he had good reason: he faced indefinite incarceration with criminally minded thugs and radical terrorists. The explanation of this stark reality would have taken the rest of his minutes, so he simply said, "I'd like nothing better than to be with you, but right now I'm indisposed." He turned around and eyed several other antsy prisoners behind him, who edged closer and closer, pressuring him to finish his call with glaring eyes.

"What do you want from me?" Jeannette demanded.

"First, some clothes." Alan listed what he could remember from the sheet the assistant commandment had provided him. "Second, money."

"Money! You know I barely get by."

"I need it to pay for protection," he whispered.

"Well, I don't have it!"

"What about Buck? He owes me for the last week I worked."

"Buck's gone."

"Gone?"

"He decided that since you disappeared and couldn't drive his truck, he would take a break and go Zebra hunting in a remote part of Madagascar," Jeannette said. "He too is indisposed, I'm afraid."

"When will he be back?"

"Betty says several months, maybe longer."

"Look, just get me some clothes, and try your best on the money front."

"Even if I can obtain this for you, I don't know where to..."

The line went dead. Alan's time was up, but only with respect to his phone call.

* * *

At his cell, Alan read a travel book about Corsica that Matoub had gotten him from the library. Until Jeannette put money on his canteen account or he found a prison job, remaining inside this cubicle and reading would be his best option. *Better well read, than dead*, he thought, half-smiling.

After finishing the interesting description of the French-island territory, he sat up and stretched his arms, then did some jumping jacks, pushups, and dips using the side of the bed, something Matoub had taught him to pass time. During his second set of dips, he heard a rattle outside his cell, where he discovered a plastic Orangina bottle attached to some ratty string. It jumped about, beckoning his attention like a pet dog. He didn't know what to make of it, so he squeezed his arm through the iron bars and pulled the vessel toward him. From inside it, he retrieved a message written on a crumpled-up piece of toilet paper. It asked: *"Nom, prénom?"*

Alan chuckled. Apparently the sender had seen the same detention judge and possessed a sense of humor. He searched the cell for a pen, wrote his name on the scrap of paper, and put it in the bottle, whereupon the purveyor of the message reeled the device back. After a few seconds, the bottle happily danced out front again and announced the sender's name—Omar.

Omar told him he didn't look Maghrébin. Alan wondered how the guy could possibly have seen his face, so he inspected the area outside his cell. Eventually he discovered a small, irregularly shaped piece of mirror that darted around on a selfie-stick made from an old radio antenna. He asked the mysterious inmate how he could get a message bottle for himself, and he answered that Matoub had a yo-yo inside his mattress, along with a mirror and stick.

"Yo-yo?" Alan wrote back, not understanding the term's meaning.

Omar responded that the word referred to the message bottle and its string. Strings were made from torn bedsheets, he said.

Alan searched the mattress of the lower bunk bed for Matoub's "communication equipment." Eager to put a face on the person with whom he conversed, he extended his cellmate's stick and mirror in the direction of Omar's cell. After having gotten the hang of manipulating the device, he saw in the reflection a young North African of about twenty years, who posed with a wink and a smile.

"Is a yo-yo *interdit?*" Alan asked in his next missive.

"No yo-yo when matons nearby," Omar replied. "They search cell."

Omar went on to mention another unconventional method of communication in the Maison: the knock system. With it, inmates could tap messages on the walls or pipes and talk to their neighbors adjacent, above, and below them. In the absence of a yo-yo, this alternative worked well, he said.

He provided the following knock code chart on another piece of toilet paper:

	1	2	3	4	5
1	A	B	C / K	D	E
2	F	G	H	I	J
3	L	M	N	O	P
4	Q	R	S	T	U
5	V	W	X	Y	Z

Using the letters on the chart, Omar explained, short sentences could be constructed. The letter A, for example, was a single knock, a pause, and another single knock. The letter B had one knock, a pause, then two knocks. Since words and sentences took a long time to construct, a short hand was employed: BS-*Bon Soir,* BJ-*Bonjour,* O-*Oui,* N-*Non,* et cetera. At the end of each sentence, four knocks constituted a period. Three hard successive ones meant a guard was around and to stop. The two prisoners practiced the system, until Alan had memorized the chart and achieved a marginal level of competence.

And so the days went by for him in the absence of being able to *cantiner*. To keep from going insane in what amounted to solitary confinement, he read and participated in the jail network of yo-yo and knock, feeling as though he lived at the Hanoi Hilton. Much to his delight, the system yielded useful information: inmate charges and criminal history, the quality of lawyers, and even the relative fairness of various JIs. Products and services were sometimes advertised, such as yard haircuts, tattoos, and jail-made booze. A quasi-newsfeed enabled prisoners to stay connected to sports scores, the ranking of soccer teams in League One, and the headlines of the day.

So long as there was a will, there was a way. Fortunately Alan still had a will.

* * *

A steady day-long downpour caused the matons to announce that the indoor gym would substitute for the yard. Thinking he needed to take a break from yo-yo, Alan broke down and responded to the invitation. He hadn't gotten a hold of Jeannette to bug her about the money, nor had any materialized on his canteen account. So he went there at considerable risk. By now his days at the Maison numbered thirteen, an unlucky number.

The gym turned out to be slightly larger than a basketball court and afforded little opportunity to stay away from dangerous inmates. The walls and ceiling had been painted with a fake sky and clouds. The artwork included a simulated soccer goal, complete with metal posts. A strip of grass, drawn in front of the net, created the illusion of depth. Though well intended, the background constituted a cruel reminder of what inmates lacked, making them all the more edgy.

As Alan began to run in place in order to blow off steam, someone spewed some hateful words in his direction. Not since he had been chased from Chez Betty had he heard them: *"putain triche."* He knew the phrase's meaning as well as its import—Christophe, had infiltrated the Maison and would now exact revenge, unfettered by Buck.

Alan checked the make-shift yard for guards, but as usual they remained outside. Unlike the false door at the hotel, no quick exit-stage-right presented itself. So he moved to the other end of the gym, where more minions of the drug lord mouthed the same ugly phrase under their breath. Eventually the men surrounded him, and he fully expected that his next view would be from a jail infirmary bed, if he got one at all.

Then, with the magic of a cherub from heaven, a large, muscular man moved between Alan and the thugs. While brandishing a shank, he issued a threat: *"Le premier homme qui le touche est mort*—the first man who touches him is dead." So blood-curdling was his tone that Christophe's thugs quickly dissolved into a pickup game of le foot.

Alan effusively thanked Abdul for saving his life. Unfortunately the expression of gratitude went unrecognized, and the strong man demanded twenty items as payment for his menacing display of prowess. When Alan told him he didn't have any money on his account, Abdul happily extended him credit, but at an interest rate of five items per week. As to future protection, he told him he would add ten items to the normal weekly charge of twenty for the extra effort necessary to protect him from Christophe. Though Alan had no money, he reluctantly agreed. What else could he do?

"I will pay you as soon as possible," he told Abdul. "Just give me some time."

"You have family? Girlfriend?"

* * *

The day after his confrontation with Christophe's thugs, the matons fetched Alan, put him in a transport van, and escorted him to a large office in the Palais de Justice. *Anything to get out of jail,* he thought. He was wrong, for nothing good happened at the courthouse.

On a maroon leather chair behind a cherry antique desk, a balding man in his sixties, whom Alan concluded was the instruction judge, perched ready. That day the grand inquisitor wore a regal black robe with scarlet sleeves and a frilly triangular-shaped white scarf. Framing his face on one side was a stack of three-inch-thick dossiers, and on the other, multiple bound volumes of the latest edition of *Le Code de Procedure Pénale*.

A yellow-stained-glass lamp on his desk provided little light against the dark floor-to-ceiling woodwork. The resulting gloom, together with the annoying tick-tock of a grandfather clock in the corner of the office, created a macabre Star Chamber-like atmosphere. Arrayed to Alan's left and right were Esnault, a *greffier* or court reporter, a translator, Étienne, and of course, two matons.

Since no one had instructed Alan on the exact purpose of the proceeding, he waited in confused silence, nervously pondering what would take place next. The old judge, on the other hand, fixed his baggy eyes upon an unidentified document while pinching his temples for all available brain matter.

As the grandfather clock struck 9 a.m., the judge suddenly popped up from the document he had been reading and signaled to the greffier, who began feverishly tapping on a stenographic machine. The JI identified the parties, time, place, and purpose of the inquiry, and explained to Alan his rights, which didn't take long. He then narrowed his eyes, and in a gravelly voice that could barely be heard above the typing, asked, "When did you arrive in Paris on the day in question?"

Alan gave him the information, but before he had finished speaking the JI stepped on his response with yet another question: "On what airline?" He wrote Alan's answer on a small notepad in front of him and posed more questions: "When did you leave Chicago? What did you do with your boarding pass? What did you eat on the plane? What did you do in Nice-Ville? How did you know Rolf Swenson? When did you first contact him?" The inquisition went on for perhaps an hour. Since the JI likely already had this information, the strategy seemed purposely designed to provoke inconsistencies.

Apparently frustrated that he had not succeeded in this regard, the JI abruptly changed the subject to Jeannette, still continuing in his staccato-like cadence: "How long have you known her? Where did you meet her? What did you do on dates with her? Did you have sex with her? How many times? Where? How often did you talk to her about the case? Did you spend time with Chloé? What did you do with her? Did you talk to this child about your alibi? How did you bring this subject up? How were your questions phrased?"

With each effort, the crusty jurist twisted Alan's response so as to suggest he had improperly influenced mother and child and victimized them for his own selfish purposes. This attitude did not surprise Alan, for he had been introduced to it by Esnault on the Ferris wheel in Nice.

"You spoke to Jeannette on the phone from the Maison d'Arrêt. Did you discuss your alibi with her at that time?"

Alan had no clue how the JI knew about the contact, so he answered guardedly. "We only spoke about her getting some money on my jail account and not my case."

"So, in addition to soliciting your defense from this woman, you have demanded funds from her?"

"My alibi has not been solicited—it exists because it is the true," Alan replied. "And Jeannette gave me no money."

The JI leaned toward him and said, "I will not tolerate your attempts to cast a spell upon this woman."

"A spell?"

"Yes, a spell."

"You speak as though I were a sorcerer."

The judge grunted. "Perhaps in your sick mind you imagine yourself as such," he said, gritting his teeth. "You may think you are very smart, very cunning in fact, but you should know that you are not the only party in this manipulative dance. This woman has her own motives and views you as an investment of sorts, a potential financial provider who will permit her escape from an otherwise menial existence."

Outraged at the cynical cut, Alan started to jump out of his chair, but Étienne grabbed his knee and pinched it hard to remind him of his place. Meanwhile Esnault smiled wryly.

While wagging a gnarly, decrepit finger at Alan, the JI continued his condescending lecture: "And then there is this sweet young girl, an innocent victim of conniving adults who cruelly offer her the false carrot of fatherhood. I ought to have her taken away from both of you!"

Alan turned to Étienne, but got no help.

"Because I fear you may attempt to influence my quest for the truth, I am forbidding you from having contact with Jeannette Brouillet or her daughter, save through your avocat. The Maison d'Arrêt is instructed to prohibit communication by phone, in person, in writing, or via the Internet. I will not have you *ply* this woman or her daughter any longer."

Alan's world had gone to shit. Already thwarted by jail rules about in-person visits, he now couldn't contact Jeannette even by phone, and without being able to speak with her, it would be difficult to obtain money for protection, not to mention carry on a relationship with her.

"Ply?" he asked the judge incredulously. "Look, the person you need to worry about plying people is Christophe!"

A hush descended upon the office at this insolence. Then the JI suddenly barked, "Who is this man Christophe?"

"A drug-dealer who is framing me for Rolf's murder."

"Why? Why would he do this?" the judge asked, laughing scornfully.

Alan told him about the territorial dispute between Buck's company and Christophe's and recited the violence that had been visited upon him at Chez Betty and in jail at the mobster's hands. He described Christophe's physical abuse of Jeannette that might be used as leverage against her testimony. Lastly, he mentioned that Christophe was the father of her child, further complicating an already complicated morass.

"So you think this man doesn't like you," the JI responded. "I don't particularly care for you myself, but that doesn't mean I would frame you for murder."

At this remark everyone in the office except Alan joined the judge in mocking laughter, as though he had cracked a joke among friends on a private yacht. It appeared they did this in a sycophantic attempt to gain his graces. When the laughter subsided, the JI resumed the questioning, still slightly smirking: "And how has Christophe accomplished this evil artifice?"

"He tricked me into buying a gun that your detective thinks is the murder weapon."

Now treating Alan like a deranged mental patient, the judge squinted and asked, "Christophe, or one of his flying monkeys?"

"One of his associates," Alan replied.

"And who might this associate be?"

"Why should I tell you? You won't believe me anyway." Based on what Alan had seen so far, he was right. He chose to wait and mix Ludovic in the soup later, assuming it would do him any good.

The JI rocked back in his leather swivel chair, perhaps contemplating how to deal with such contempt. Then, for some unknown reason, he changed his tune, seeming to realize that the record had thus far proven him biased. "In order to maintain the integrity and objectivity of this inquiry—"

Alan cleared his throat, a bold move under the circumstances.

"For which I have a sworn duty to uphold," the JI said, raising his voice to override his subject, "I will also order that Christophe Chevalier not have contact with Jeannette Brouillet, nor her daughter. Now sir, are you satisfied I have been fair to you?"

Alan did not offer an opinion, since he didn't want to provoke the old fart further. Instead he asked, "Does it matter if Christophe has visitation rights?"

"I will speak to *La Juge aux Affaires Familiales* about this *examen*," the JI responded. "It takes precedence over all other matters." He seemed offended by the suggestion that his authority might be considered subordinate to that of another judge.

The matons got Alan up to leave.

"And one more thing, sir" the magistrate said. "If you so much as whisper another word about your case to this woman or her daughter, you'll not see—"

"I know, I know," Alan interrupted. "The light of day." Nor the light of truth, he feared.

11

The trouble with life at the Maison was the smallest things mattered. On the outside, people worried about their homes, jobs, and family, but in jail, though far bigger problems loomed on the horizon—perpetual reclusion, death by shank, and complete isolation—inmates focused on "items" and "yo-yos." This had to do with feelings of lack of control necessarily occasioned by incarceration, or so a psychologist would maintain. Sometimes such inner turmoil led to depression, anxiety, and conflict, even violent conflict under the right circumstances. Alan's cell and the swelter of late August constituted the right circumstances.

The subject of the dispute between him and Matoub had to do with the latter's yo-yo, which had been moved slightly from its original position inside his mattress. Someone had also taken three cigarettes from his cantiner stash above the toilet. Alan had been responsible for the former transgression, since he had used the yo-yo when Matoub went to his library job, but he had nothing to do with the missing cigarettes.

At first, the two went at each other in a highly erudite verbal argument, the most salient points of which were, "You messed with my shit," and "No, I didn't." As their rather immature exchange became more vocal, the other inmates in the cellblock began to whistle, which served to escalate the quarrel into a physical fight.

They relished the possibility of an honest-to-god bloody brawl that would add excitement to their otherwise dismal routine.

Matoub initiated the violence by grabbing Alan from his bunk and throwing him onto the cell floor, where the two wrestled about harmlessly in a stalemate. Neither person had access to any form of jail weaponry, so injuries were kept to a minimum. Had this occurred in the yard, another inmate might have changed the dynamic by tossing a shank into the fray.

As the fight progressed, the whistling of the other inmates evolved into a tumult of yelling, screaming, and clanging of hard objects against the cell bars. Most rooted for Matoub, since he had been in jail longer and was North African. A few supported the underdog, Alan. All bet precious items on the outcome, while a self-appointed ring leader/accountant kept track.

Just as the younger and stronger cellmate had begun to get the better of the altercation, several matons arrived and spoiled all the fun. After prying the two apart, they dragged the combatants to the disciplinary quarter, where canteen items, personal property such as yo-yos, and other objects of controversy didn't exist.

That night, Alan did not sleep, for like the cell at La Gendarmerie, the light never went out in isolation, and a steel bed didn't exactly provide Posturepedic comfort. In addition, the discipline area offered a different din than that to which he had grown accustomed in Bátiment A. This included maniacal laughing, terrified screams, entreaties to Allah, jungle-animal-like cackling, impassioned protests against imaginary enemies, and other disarming noises that could not be readily identified. The cell also had the distinct odor of disinfectant that had been used to sanitize it after the last occupant. The inmate had likely smeared excrement on the walls, Alan surmised, this being a common means of protest in jail.

At 7 a.m. the next day, the matons took Alan to the Assistant Commandant, the same person with whom he had had the depressing conversation about visitation rules at the beginning of his stay. The official conducted a perfunctory disciplinary hearing regarding the rule violation, very perfunctory in fact.

"*J'ai regardé la vidéo de l'affrontement*—I looked at the video of the fight," he said. "*Avez-vous des choses àjouter*—Do you have anything to add?"

Not knowing what mitigation might be relevant or the punishment alternatives, Alan stood mute.

"*Alors, sept jours de mitard, crédit un jour,*" the Assistant Commandant said with a high-and-mighty wave of his hand.

"Mee-what?"

"*Quartier disciplinaire.*"

One night there had nearly done Alan in, and now he had six more. He protested the decision, but his complaint was ignored, and the hearing, such that it was, ended.

By the time he got back to the isolation cell, mid-morning had arrived, and the cacophony of the night before had ceased. Perhaps the crazies here are nocturnal, and I can get some sleep, he thought. As he shut his eyes, he heard a tapping sound on the wall in knock code. "How much mitard you catch?" the sender asked.

Alan rapped back, "Seven days."

"Infraction?"

"Fight."

"You lucky."

"Why?"

"Me, twenty-one."

The neighbor provided his history, which, using the knock system, took until lunch. Originally he had received five days mitard for possessing jail-made hooch that the matons had found in his cell on a random search. With one day left on his disciplinary sentence, they conducted a second search of his isolation cell. This time they found a cellphone charger. He maintained someone else had left it there, but the officials didn't believe him and ordered fourteen more days. After he finished that sentence, he got the twenty-one for possessing a yo-yo, mirror, and radio antenna back at his original cell. At the mention of the term yo-yo, Alan knew who it was.

"Omar?"

"O (Oui)."

"Alan here. No talk in weeks."

"Been in mitard."

"How many days left for you?"

"Neuf."

"Can you handle it?"

"N (Non)."

After an awkward period of silence, Alan received another knock-code message: "JI charge you?"

"N."

"Murder, right?"

"O."

"How man die?"

"Shot."

"He deserve?"

"How should I know?"

"You kill him."

"N."

"What they have on you?"

"Gun mine."

"How you get?"

"Bought it."

"Where man shot?"

"Villefranche, apartment by old church."

"What kind gun?"

"Morrocan."

"You know dead man?"

"O."

"How?"

"He ripped me off."

"So he deserve, right?"

"N."

"How many times you shoot man?"

"I no shoot."

Finally, remembering Matoub's warning not to discuss his case with other inmates, he changed the subject and asked Omar for advice on how to take it in mitard.

"Have blade?"

"Blade?"

"Me want to die. Need blade. No sheet to hang self."

"What about clothes?"

"Matons take."

Alan imagined the suicidal Omar splayed naked on the cell floor. The creepy conversation ended when a maton walked by, and the yo-yo freak knocked three times hard to warn of his presence. The guard's boots slapped the floor one foot after another, slowly marking time like the annoying tick-tock of the grandfather clock in the JI's chambers.

* * *

The morning of the seventh day of mitard, the matons released Alan. He retained his sanity only because Omar had been a good knock partner. They talked about every subject imaginable—travel, women, sports, and whatever topic got them through the days and nights—except, of course, the murder case. In a strange sort of way, Omar reminded Alan of Ludovic, a pathetic victim of circumstance. But what was Alan? What was anyone at the Maison? What was anyone period?

The assistant commandant assigned him a new cell, which Alan assumed had to do with Matoub. Even though he had fought with him, the guy had taught him the art of cantiner and the ropes of the jail. For this reason, he missed him, not to mention Omar, who had been a yo-yo's toss away in the old cellblock and had gotten him through his disciplinary sentence. Now Alan prepared himself for a different roommate, and once again didn't know what to expect.

The escorting maton did an obligatory pat-down before opening the cell, again a six-by-ten nightmare. Inside Alan found another North African, who wore a white knit cap with a light blue stripe. The man quietly knelt on a small rug, facing the probable direction of Mecca.

*"Habituez-vous à lui. Il le fait cinq fois par jour—*Get used to it. He does it five times a day," the maton said.

After the prayer concluded, Alan introduced himself.

"Fakih," the man replied, then went back to his lower bunk and opened his Koran.

"Do those prayers help?"

"By remembering Allah, I will be rewarded in heaven."

"What if there is no heaven?"

"You speak like an infidel."

A radical, Alan thought. *Maybe he's a terrorist. Maybe he'll try to convert me, and when I refuse, kill me in my sleep. Even cantiner can't protect me.* But out loud, he stood his ground: "I'm not an infidel just because I don't share your beliefs."

"You worry only about life on Earth, something that is a small part of eternity," Fakih said. "That makes you an infidel."

"The only eternity I have is the time I spend in this shithole." Needless to say Alan's spirit had become hardened by Maison life.

Fakih ignored the profane response, stating, "When there is no shoulder upon which to cry, the floor works well, for there you can plead to Allah, and he will take away your pain."

"I'm stuck here no matter whose shoulder I cry on."

"Physically, that is true," Fakih continued, "but the walls of your existence are but a state of mind." He continued his lecture using a parable about a fellow prisoner, accused of assisting in the bombing of a city bus. While this man didn't commit the offense, he knew who did, according to the story. Even so he refused to identify the perpetrator, and the JI had him arrested and brought to jail, where he spent months and months during an endless period of instruction.

One day the matons took the man to a courtroom, since the JI had thought that the ravages of time had sufficiently softened his spirit. Even so, he would not give up the name. Accordingly, the JI sent him back to jail, hoping more time would break him. When the matons brought him before the judge again, the man snapped, leaped behind the bench, and tried to open a window in order to jump out. Before the matons could snatch him down and take him to isolation for more reconditioning, he grabbed a letter opener and brandished it, screaming repeatedly, *"S'il vous plait, tuez-moi!"*

"Sounds like suicide by maton," Alan said coldly. "What happened to him? Did they kill him?"

"No, he humbled himself before Allah," Fakih replied. "He dropped the letter opener, and they took him away. In mitard, he got down on his knees and cried, and Allah, in his infinite mercy and forgiveness, told him that the infidels who controlled his plight would one day atone for their transgressions—maybe not on earth, but one day."

"So he found God, huh?"

"Allah," Fakih said.

"But how did this solve his problem?"

"It taught him that the key to freedom and peace lay in the recesses of one's mind, not in the trappings that surround him."

"Did he rat on the person who bombed the bus?"

"You mean, *craquer*?"

"Yeah. Did he crack?"

"No. Allah gave him the strength to resist."

"Or the hope."

"Hope is the beginning of faith," Fakih replied. "You must follow its direction and happiness will be yours in the world beyond."

Alan had hardly been successful in pursuing "happiness" outside the borders of the United States, much less in another world. "Can we move on to something else besides religion?" he asked.

"I will oblige you, but only temporarily."

"My JI wants me to crack by giving up the name of a man involved in my case."

"Are you going to do it?"

"Thinking about it."

"Why?"

"Because I'd no longer be facing this nightmare."

"The infidels will simply tell your friend about your lack of loyalty and encourage him to testify against you in retaliation," Fakih said matter-of-factly. "In the end you will both suffer perpetual reclusion."

"What if we cooperate together? Maybe the judge will give us a break, as the case will be stronger."

"Even the word of two will not satisfy the infidels," Fakih cautioned.

At that, a maton interrupted the discussion and yelled for everyone in the wing to prepare for shower time. While normally going to this area caused Alan anxiety, this would temporarily extricate him from Fakih's preaching. Thus, he felt relief.

The matons advanced the prisoners of the cellblock to an iron door stenciled in faded red lettering, *Douche*. As usual Alan carefully eyed the others, speculating about their intentions.

The shower area was hardly like a locker room at a health club. Green moss had grown near the ceiling and everywhere mildew ran down the walls. In a vestibule double the size of a cell, the inmates stripped naked en masse and waited their turn for a rusted metal stall that offered only the pretense of security.

As Alan stood with his towel wrapped around his waist and bided his time for the next available shower, he noticed Fakih had not undressed. Instead he entered a stall fully clothed. After a few minutes he returned with his jail garb soaking wet and toweled himself off the best he could. Alan assumed this procedure had to do with an Islamic modesty code, so he said to Fakih smiling, "You're making Allah proud."

The cellmate said nothing, but his eyes spoke loudly as he arched his brows so as to warn Alan of impending danger. Fakih was, in fact, on his side.

Alan considered forgetting about the shower entirely, but knew he had become rank and could no longer wait. Nervously he turned on the faucet and began soaping up. As he finished spraying himself off, he noticed a movement between the metal divider and the wall. He leaned over to inspect it and observed a vulture-like eyeball peering salaciously at his genitals.

He slammed the barrier with his fist, and the eye withdrew like a hand caught in a cookie jar. After racing out of the stall, he saw the culprit disappear into a sea of naked bodies in the dressing area. It was Rasil, Abdul's assistant.

* * *

Fakih's habits differed greatly from Matoub's. There was no discussion of masturbation in the library or obscenity-laced dialogue. Instead of posters of naked women, the cell was decorated with depictions of various mosques. The new cellmate only read the Koran and Islamic prayer manuals, in between ranting and raving about the life hereafter. The fact that Alan hadn't paid for protection made the problem worse, for it forced him to stay in his cell and experience this single-mindedness 24/7.

Even so, part of what the devout Muslim had told him made sense and helped him solve the riddle that had started his journey. By altering his appearance, changing his ways and coming to France, he had sought liberation, but the result was the same as looking for love in all the wrong places. True freedom, whether it had to do with being in prison or life in general, was only a state of mind. The philosophy gave him solace, though at times he remained cynical if not paranoid, not knowing whom to trust.

An example of this occurred the day the matons came by and took him to a visitation booth. Since he had no family or *"concubinage"* as defined by jail regulation, and the JI had prohibited contact with Jeannette, he had only seen Étienne lately. Moreover, such meetings normally took place in the Parloir d'Avocat. So he wondered what this was all about.

Suddenly, the door on the public side of the compartment swung open and two sights for sore eyes slipped in: Jeannette and

Chloé. The former wore the same outfit she had on the first day they met. The thought of being with her and Chloé at the park across from Chez Betty caused him to long for the day he would be released. He remembered the good times: Mont Boron, Èze, the dinners at Jeannette's, and roller skating with the little girl along the Promenade des Anglais.

Jeannette and Chloé, on the other hand, gawked at him in undisguised distress. He could only imagine how his deterioration must have looked, with his long hair, overgrown and scraggly beard, dark-circled eyes, and a body that had become fattened by physical inactivity. After a short glimpse at him, his visitors turned their faces away disgusted, perhaps even thinking he was the wrong inmate. But a second look convinced them otherwise, and they smiled at him.

After dabbing the tears from his eyes and blowing his nose on his jumpsuit, Alan picked up the phone receiver and whispered, "I've missed you."

Jeannette's eyes turned downward, while she comforted Chloé by smoothing her light brown locks with her hand. The situation was hardly for a child, though the young girl often acted like an adult and seemed at times to be more capable of withstanding pain than anyone.

"I would have called, but the JI ordered no contact," Alan said, his emotions now in check.

"I know," Jeannette responded. "He sent me the order."

"Then, if you don't mind my asking, why are you here?"

"Lieutenant Esnault said it would be okay. I think he feels sorry for you."

"He doesn't care about me," Alan replied with muted anger.

"Why can't you see the good in people?"

"Because sometimes there isn't any."

"Jail life has changed you, Alan."

This was true, in fact. Even so the remark caused him pause. "Did the JI's order help you with Christophe?"

Jeannette's eyes diverted. After a few seconds, she said, "Christophe doesn't understand why he can't see *his own daughter.*"

"How do you know what he feels? He's not supposed to have contact with you."

Jeannette did not respond and resumed caressing Chloé.

"So you're getting back together with that scumbag?"

Needless to say, Alan's presumptuousness did not go unchallenged. "I was just thinking of my child," Jeannette said, very much antagonized.

"What do you mean?"

"Just that you no longer *qualify* as a father for her."

"Qualify?"

"You are in jail, Alan. In case you didn't know your situation doesn't provide a whole lot of opportunity for love and affection."

The couple continued to bicker in this fashion for several minutes, turning a joyful reunion into a fight. Fortunately the conversation was in English, and Chloé couldn't understand. But she squirmed in her seat, gaping back and forth between them.

"I guess Christophe is better than nothing, and nothing happens to be me," Alan said.

"I didn't say that!"

"Arrêtes!" Chloé yelled without warning, putting her hands on her ears and starting to cry.

Jeannette got up to leave, trying to protect the child from more unpleasantness. "See what you've done?" she asked, not recognizing her own role in the dispute. She grabbed her daughter's arm, but the little girl twisted away in protest.

Alan took a breath and declared earnestly: "Someday I will be there for you both. You'll see. Just give me a chance."

Jeannette's voice miraculously softened. "While I sympathize with you, I cannot wait forever. Nor can my child."

Unable to deal with the touchy topic any longer, Alan went on to something else: "So how are things at Chez Betty?"

"The same. Marseille is in second place with the start of the new season, and Buck is back from his hunting trip," Jeannette said.

"Speaking of Buck, did you tell him to put my last week's earnings on my canteen account?"

"Yes, and he even added some for your trouble—he felt guilty, I guess."

"Perfect. Now I can *cantiner.*"

"*Cantiner?* Is that some kind of dance?"

"Yes, a very complicated one, as a matter of fact."

After some light conversation in which Alan queried his surrogate daughter about what she had learned in school lately, Jeannette became serious again. "Lieutenant Esnault promised me he would help you if you would just—"

"Give up the person who put the gun on me?"

"Don't you want to save yourself? Don't you care about Chloé?"

"Of course, I do."

"Then why don't you cooperate."

"That's not how it works, Jeannette."

"But he said he'd get the charge lowered."

Alan shook his head. "He has no control over the charge."

"Then why did he tell me that?"

"To win the sick game he is playing."

"Have you lost your mind?"

Alan looked up at the surveillance camera and began speaking to it. "Nice try, lieutenant. But your little ploy didn't work."

"Now you talk to imaginary people," Jeannette said.

Alan smiled with confidence. "The person with whom I'm talking is not imaginary, nor are my concerns."

"Please, give him what he wants," Jeannette insisted.

"And what? Trust the infidels?"

At this point, Chloé tapped her watch, coming to the rescue once again. *"Maman, nous n'avons plus qu'un minute*—Mom, we only have one more minute."

The three rose to leave and each said goodbye. Chloé put her hand on the hardened glass that separated them, and Alan matched his to hers. Jeannette followed her daughter's example. Despite the difficult exchange in which feelings went from love to paranoia and back again, their relationship had survived, at least for the time being. As the matons took Alan away, he mouthed to his visitors French words he had learned long before his travels had begun: *"Je t'aime."*

* * *

Now that Alan's canteen account had been replenished by Buck Treadway, it was time to start taking yard time. But before he dared do this, he had to pay off his cantiner charges. On October 15, he got the opportunity.

He found an unidentified object in the putrefied puree the Maison called *le dîner.* In and of itself finding something suspicious in the gruel meant little, for he had discovered many questionable ingredients there in the past: insects, fish eyes, rodent parts, and stringy entrails of unknown creatures. After poking the thing gingerly with his spoon to make sure it wasn't alive, he summoned the courage to investigate its makeup. With great relief he determined it was a small piece of paper, an overdue invoice from Rasil. "*Payez quatre cent,*" it said.

The bill had charged four hundred items for interest and protection during Alan's entire stay at the Maison. Alan felt he had been unjustly docked, since he had remained in his cell during most of this time. Really he only owed for the incident in the indoor yard in which Abdul had defended him, a debit of twenty items. With interest from that day to mid-October, the bill should have been a total of a hundred items, not four hundred.

Knowing that Rasil resided in the same corridor, Alan ripped up one of his sheets, made some string and wrapped it around his spoon. He attached to the spoon messages using a rubber band he had scrounged earlier, and with this newly concocted yo-yo, found out Rasil's location from the neighbors. As it turned out, he lived two doors down.

Rasil was surprisingly receptive to Alan's complaint and messaged back a corrected bill without protest. He told him that protection henceforth would cost twenty items a week.

"How do I pay the balance?" Alan asked.

"Give items to *homme de cantine.*"

"And he will get them to Abdul?"

"*Oui.*"

After a slight hiatus in the yo-yo exchange, Rasil messaged again: "You can reduce balance in future for special favors."

Alan's stomach sickened. "What do you mean?"

"We talk in *douche, mon chér.*"

"*Non merci.*"

"What wrong? You not like me?"

"I prefer to deal with Abdul directly."

"But he no do books."

"Maybe he should learn."

* * *

The next day Alan paid his balance to the cantine man, who had come by the cell as usual with a cart full of items. To accomplish this Alan bought out the man's cigarette supply using the line of credit Buck had set up at the Maison, then gave him back the cigarettes for transfer to Abdul. Alan paid only the amount that he and Rasil had agreed upon.

Emboldened, he later decided to take yard time. It would be a nice break from Fakih's prayer rituals and constant exhortations about Allah. His first stop was the weightlifting area, where he asked Abdul if they were all good.

After the muscleman had finished doing ten dips with his legs tethered to some iron discs, he unfolded a piece of paper delivered to him by Rasil and read it. Then he angrily stuffed the note in Alan's shirt pocket and snapped, *"Non, payez plus."*

Instead of running away or cowering, Alan accepted the challenge. He retrieved his copy of the invoice from his pocket, examined it quickly and determined that Rasil had not given his boss the revised accounting. Angered at the ploy, Alan put his copy of the new bill in Abdul's pocket, an action that took much courage, as it could be interpreted as an affront.

Shockingly, Abdul did not explode. Instead he gave Alan the respect he was due and read the corrected invoice. He turned to Rasil and asked, *"Les frais sont différents ici, pourquoi—*Why are the charges different here?"

Rasil grimaced. *"L'Américain te montre une fausse facture—*The American has shown you a false bill."

"Mais cette facture est comme les autres!" Abdul bellowed, evidently not buying Rasil's story.

Alan explained exactly what had happened, showing Abdul the yo-yo message in which his assistant had proposed to reduce the bill for "special" favors at shower time.

"C'est vrai?" Abdul asked his assistant. When no answer came forth, he slapped the little man across the face, dropping him to the ground on all fours. *"Alors, dégage!"*

After the now-fired assistant scurried off, Alan told Abdul about his background in accounting and asked him for a job. His last week's wages with Buck would only last so long, and he didn't want to go back to staying in his cell all day.

"Combien?" Abdul asked sharply.

Alan replied that the only payment he required was protection and forgiveness of his current invoice.

"Bon. Vous commencez demain."

* * *

The next several days at the Maison went smoothly for Alan, he having once again found clandestine employment. He marched confidently about the yard, feeling like a new man. But as time went on, he became disenchanted, in part because he still had a moral compass despite all that had occurred. While his employment usually involved basic bookkeeping and dispassionate delivery of bills to cantiner customers, sometimes it entailed being the bearer of bad tidings.

Abdul's least intrusive method of debt enforcement was cancellation of protection, which meant the debtor would have to fend for himself in the yard or stay in his cell, as Alan had done. If the non-paying inmate chose to brave the yard instead, and Allah help him if he did, uncivilized predators of the jail would rob, beat and possibly sodomize him, if for no other reason than the thrill of it. If Abdul selected a more direct form of retribution, the debtor would end up in the jail infirmary, or worse six feet under.

During his first week on the job, Alan became well acquainted with this guilt-inducing problem. While roaming around the yard delivering invoices, he noticed the tattoo man, who earned items by inking prisoners. He had already set up shop and was in the middle of a teardrop on another inmate's cheek, which he accomplished by using a makeshift tattoo gun. He wore plastic gloves and periodically sterilized the needle with a Bic lighter, something which seemed overly germ conscious, since prisoners' lives were so short.

Alan struck up a conversation with the artist and asked how he crafted his equipment. He explained that he had obtained the motor from a canteen-purchased CD player and rigged it to a pen barrel. For the needle he had extracted a spring from a stapler and straightened and sharpened it. The ink had come from boot polish a maton had given him in exchange for some weed. Though he readily discussed the construction of the gun, he declined to disclose how he converted the polish into ink. That was a trade secret, he said.

Fascinated by the man's creativity and resourcefulness, Alan contemplated getting a tattoo for himself, an act of rebellion similar to the earring purchase that had irritated Sara Elliot-Newberg. He considered his options: an eagle representing the USA, an iron fist symbolic of his revolutionary spirit, or possibly a coiled snake. The other issue was where to put it. He didn't want to have a tattoo on his neck, face, or hands that would be readily apparent to a jury in the Cour d'Assises. He wasn't that stupid.

Without much further thought, Alan received inspiration. His tattoo should honor the person who had gotten him out of so many jams in the past. A pair of longhorns wouldn't work, as the tattoo man had likely never seen them. He thought of Buck's note that he had received from Étienne at the garde à vue and asked how much it would cost for fifteen letters across his chest and stomach.

"Cinq la lettre," the tattoo man replied. *"Quels lettres?"*

"S-t-a-n-d."

The man wrote the letters down.

"Y-o-u-r."

"*Oui. Continuez.*"

"G-r-o-u-n-d."

The tattoo man finished the job in the three days that followed, whereupon Alan attempted to settle up. He put four packs of cigarettes in the man's pocket, more than enough for full payment, but the guy refused the cigarettes, stating, "*C'est gratuit pour vous.*"

"No, no. This is what I owe," Alan said, attempting to hand back the cigarettes.

"*Mais non, monsieur, c'est à vous.*"

"*Quoi?*"

The man explained that he had an overdue cantiner account, which Alan confirmed by checking his paperwork. He, in fact, owed Abdul five-hundred items and hadn't paid in several months. "So you want some play?" Alan asked.

The tattoo man's forehead wrinkled in confusion, so Alan restated himself, while pointing to the invoice, "You want me to fix?"

"*Oui.*"

Alan knew better than to play fast and loose, so he declined the proposal. He left his payment on the man's equipment table and turned in the unpaid invoice to Abdul. It was a mistake.

The next day the tattoo man was absent from the yard. Word went around quickly that he had suffered an unfortunate accident in which his hand, the one he had used to make tattoos, had been broken in so many places that he would have to retire from his jail profession.

During Alan's second week on the job, the drawbacks of his new accounting experience became apparent again. He saw Matoub in the yard, who had an overdue cantiner balance of eighty items. This had been caused by the loss of his job at the Maison library when he got fourteen days mitard for the fight. Needless to say he didn't meet Alan with open arms when the latter brought up the bill.

At first the former cellmate tried to change the subject by claiming Alan had stolen items from him, the same accusation that led to their confrontation. Alan offered Matoub the three cigarettes the former cellmate claimed were missing, but Matoub wouldn't take them and instead demanded a break of forty items on his overdue account, a considerable departure from what he owed. Alan did not agree with this change and concluded that he had no recourse but to turn the young man's unpaid invoice into Abdul. Within five days, Matoub received a severe beating and never came back to the yard.

The last straw came when Alan and Fakih went to the douche area for their weekly shower. They were at the front of the line, and hence the first to discover Rasil's body. He had been stabbed countless times with a shank, and his throat was cut. Luckily Alan wasn't alone. Otherwise he would have had another murder rap.

He considered directly telling Abdul he wanted to quit and why, but wisely chose a different course of action: simply not showing up for work. Instead of burning bridges, he gave the cart man the cantiner bookwork and a well-drafted thank-you note. In it he apologized to Abdul for not giving two weeks' notice.

* * *

On a crisp, early November morning, two court gendarmes arrived at Alan's cell, appearing more official than usual. Dressed in fancy French police hats and armed with a clipboard that contained a transport order, they brought him to the JI's office. Something was up.

Before Étienne could tell him what the proceeding was about, the crusty judge of instruction came in and took a seat behind his desk, which brought the place to dead silence. He slapped down before him three copies of a four-inch-thick document. After a few minutes of careful contemplation, he identified the parties present. "I now have received the ballistics report,"he announced.

La-di-da, Alan mumbled.

"It seems the report is not favorable to your position, Monsieur Newberg," the old judge said.

Not waiting for permission to speak, Alan replied: "I suppose it says the gun the police found at Chez Betty is the murder weapon."

Appearing shocked at this casual attitude, the judge curtly read the report's conclusion. Essentially, a firearms examiner had compared under a microscope a bullet fragment extracted from a wall in Rolf's apartment to a known one fired from the Moroccan handgun. The questioned fragment matched the latter perfectly, of course.

"Since the weapon was found in your room sometime after the murder, the only way for you to be innocent is for another person to have shot the victim and for him or one of his associates to have put the gun in your possession without your knowledge of its involvement in the crime," the JI correctly noted.

"That much we can agree on," Alan said.

"Since you have refused to tell me the name of the person who supposedly gave you the gun, I must conclude that he does not exist and that you are the one who killed Rolf Swenson."

"But I'm innocent!"

The JI handed one of the thick documents on his desk to Étienne, together with two sheets of paper.

"Wait a minute. What did you just give him?" Alan asked.

"A copy of the dossier, an order transferring jurisdiction in this matter to the Cours d'Assises, and a legal instrument that charges you with the murder of Rolf Swenson," the JI said, smiling.

"Bonne chance, monsieur. Or perhaps I should say, *Bon voyage."*

12

Étienne opened his briefcase in the Parloir des Avocats and placed in front of Alan a ten-page property settlement. "Fortunately your American lawyer has been working hard on your behalf," he said.

Alan read the agreement quickly. Essentially he and Sara would take their own pensions, he would quitclaim the house in Schaumburg to her, and she would sign over their investment portfolio. Neither party would get any alimony or maintenance. Though he had received the short end of the stick, he was hardly in a position to complain.

"Your lawyer requests that you execute this as soon as possible," Étienne said. "I will certify your signature on the document and send it back to him, and he will arrange a stipulated divorce proceeding in which you will be appear by Skype. The prison authorities have approved this procedure."

"How long will it take to get my accounts unfrozen?"

"Several months."

Finally, Alan could untie the knot that should never have been tied in the first place. With any luck, he would receive enough money to pay back Buck for his legal bills and *maybe* start a new life with Jeannette and Chloé. But this depended on his beating the murder rap, and in that regard, Étienne produced another document that brought things back to reality.

"What's that?"

"An order from the Cour d'Assises setting your case for trial," the avocat said.

Alan grabbed the single sheet of paper and read it. "Trial right before Christmas?"

"Frankly I didn't think we would get a date until well into next year," Étienne said. "But your American lawyer has lobbied the U.S. State Department, and it has in turn lobbied the French Embassy. Justice for you will be swift."

Alan rolled his eyes.

"Unless, of course, you want to appeal the JI's decision."

"No, no, that's quite all right. But will six weeks be enough time for you to prepare?"

"Prepare? The case is already prepared by the JI."

"Try not to overwhelm me with your enthusiasm, okay."

"What do you mean?"

"As my lawyer, you should investigate the case independently and plan my defense."

"I suggest you not judge me until you have read the entire dossier," Étienne replied, handing him the long-awaited document. Alan skimmed it while Étienne read a book—ironically, a police detective novel.

The case for guilt focused on the murder weapon naturally. The JI noted it had been secreted beneath the mattress in Alan's hotel room. Estelle Beauchamp, pejoratively known as Miss Perfect, recounted with precision his handling of the gun in the pickup outside Chez Betty. At every opportunity she gratuitously described him as abrupt, insolent, and overbearing, emphasizing that she wasn't surprised he had become involved in antisocial behavior.

Monsieur Leroux corroborated Miss Perfect's character assassination by pointing out that Alan had called her "a busy-body bitch." Leroux left out the fact that he himself had displayed bad manners in sticking an Uzi in his prisoner's face in response to the disparaging reference.

With the exception of the spin, Alan did not dispute his possession of the gun. He did take issue, however, with whether it proved his involvement in Rolf's murder, since such possession took place months after the man's demise.

Much to Alan's chagrin, Esnault had freshened up the connection. The detective had miraculously found a cab driver, who claimed he had picked Alan up from Nice-Côte-d'Azur airport just after noon on the day in question and dropped him off in the Moulins. This would have given Alan plenty of time to obtain a gun in advance of Rolf's shooting. The idea that an American would be familiar with such a crime-ridden area and its many shopping opportunities was, of course, absurd. But absurd had become the norm.

After Alan got the gun, according to the JI, he arrived at the real estate office in Villefranche at 2:50 p.m. There he learned once and for all that he had been ripped off and left for Rolf Swenson's apartment determined to get his money back "hell or high water." The shot rang out when the church bell chimed three times just as the blind lady had said. The exact circumstances of the killing left many options open for the Cour d'Assises in terms of a mitigated sentence, said the JI. This hint conceded the weakness of the case, Alan thought.

The dossier provided a timeline of the events. Converted to a twelve-hour clock, it was as follows:

7:05—Newberg arrives in Paris on overnight flight from Chicago.
9:48—Newberg's flight for Nice departs.
11:08—Newberg's flight arrives in Nice.
12:00—A cab takes Newberg to the Moulins.

12:30 to 2:30—Newberg purchases gun.

2:30—Newberg arrives in Villefranche by unknown means of transport.

2:50—Newberg appears at real estate office.

2:55—Newberg leaves the real estate office and goes to victim's apartment.

3:00—Newberg shoots Rolf.

3:05—Police are dispatched.

3:15—Police arrive at murder scene.

4:00—Newberg returns to crime scene to observe police investigation.

Alan wrote down his own sequence:

7:05—Arrive in Paris from Chicago.

9:18—Leave Gare de Lyon in Paris by train.

2:55—Arrive at Nice-Ville.

3:00—The murder occurs, when I'm still in Nice.

3:15—Arrive in Villefranche by local train.

3:50—Arrive at real estate office.

3:55—Leave the real estate office for Rolf's.

4:00—I find Rolf dead, an hour after the murder.

Plainly the real estate agent and the cab driver were the lynchpins of the République's case in terms of timing of events. The former witness had Alan arriving at his office one hour too early, which made no sense. The latter had simply lied, which also made no sense. Perhaps Christophe was behind the cabbie's last-minute statement.

The dossier mentioned something even more worrisome. Alan had omitted his connecting flight to Nice in his description of his travel itinerary to the JI. Although he had purchased the ticket originally with his transatlantic flight, his budding spontaneity had gotten the better of him in Paris, and out-of-the-blue he had decided to take the train to Nice and forsake the flight. He had never been on a train and wanted to avail himself of this opportunity. In his prior life he wouldn't have dreamed of such dalliance, nor would any rational person. And this was precisely the point: the jurors in the Cour d'Assises would assume him to be rational and wouldn't understand that he was a man caught in transition.

Alan had failed to mention the flight to the authorities, because he was embarrassed about being so impractical and spending unnecessary funds on a train ticket. On the one hand, he had wanted to escape the persona of Mr. Organized, but on the other, he could not. In any other situation this inner turmoil would have been understandable or perhaps laughed off, but this was no ordinary situation by any stretch of the imagination, and no one was laughing.

"Surely a person in the defendant's position would not have been so quixotic," the JI argued in the dossier, suggesting Alan must have taken the connecting flight after all and deliberately omitted it from his itinerary to cover his tracks. As to the train ticket, the records showed he had in fact made such a purchase. The JI said that this was nothing more than a feeble attempt to create a false alibi. This further evidenced consciousness of guilt, according to him.

Alan checked the appendix of the dossier for the flight manifest from Paris to Nice figuring this would prove he wasn't on the plane. He couldn't find it. He looked up at Étienne, who was still reading, and asked why it was absent.

"The JI issued a perquisition demanding the airline produce records confirming or denying your presence on the flight," Étienne replied.

"And?"

"An accurate manifest does not exist."

"What?"

"It indicates you were not on the plane, but it also shows that no other passengers were on it. Needless to say this is at odds with the head flight attendant's recollection."

"How can this be?" Alan asked, now convinced that the conspiracy against him had grown to include an airline company.

"An investigation revealed the boarding-pass scanner from which the manifest would normally be prepared was malfunctioning that day."

"You've got to be kidding me."

"I wish I were."

"How did this happen?"

"Any number of possibilities: user error, mechanical or electrical problems, bar code issues—"

"Or some fucker rigged the scanner!"

"Perhaps, but I rather doubt it."

Alan went back to reading the dossier despite his obvious disappointment. He came across another document, obtained in response to a perquisition served on the company that was in charge of the location function of his iPhone. The JI had left no stone unturned apparently. According to an explanation from that company, this function could track where a possessor of the phone had been. This was recorded on it and at the company's electronic repository when the device connected to a Wi-Fi hotspot. While normally such a revelation would put a chill down a person's spine, it did not with Alan, for such records might put him at a place and time that would re-establish his alibi.

Yet once again his own personality had defied him. He had turned off his iPhone on the train except to make phone calls. He had purchased a data plan before his trip to France that had limited units. Thus, he wanted to avoid depletion of them as a result of roaming charges. His practical inner self had gotten the better of him, for if his phone were off or in airplane mode, it would not connect to a hotspot. If it did not connect to a hot spot, he could not prove where he was, a fact noted by the JI in all too gleeful a fashion.

In another section of the appendix, Alan found Rolf's phone records as well as his own. They indicated an originating number, time, date, and length of conversation for all calls leading up to the murder. Alan had phoned the Norwegian five times, each lasting several minutes, and four of those calls occurred the morning of the shooting. The volume of such communication suggested that something had gone wrong between lessor and lessee, the JI claimed, and buttressed the idea that the apartment agreement had fallen through in time to motivate "the American" to purchase the gun in the Moulins.

Truthfully, in making such calls, Alan was simply being conscientious to a fault, for he wanted nothing left to chance. But this cut against the notion that he would change travel plans so suddenly. Either he was spontaneous, or careful and responsible—A or B, said the JI. A person couldn't possibly be both.

All of the calls except the last took place before Alan left Paris. That call occurred at 10:28 a.m., when his train would have been in Lyon according to its schedule. Another document in the phone record part of the dossier, entitled La Cartographie du Téléphone Cellulaire, corroborated such timing. It had a circle around a point in Lyon. *Must be cellphone mapping*, Alan told himself.

Indeed he was correct. By a series of cell towers that a defendant's phone had used, each represented by a circle, the police could map the route a suspected criminal had travelled. If the accused had moved around during his or her calls in a city, for example, an overlapping series of Venn diagrams, called a cell tower map, could sometimes pinpoint his or her presence at a crime scene or travels to or from it. In this case there was no series of calls, as only one had been made. But that single call proved Alan was at or near Lyon in mid-morning, meaning he had to have been on the train.

"How do they explain this?" he asked Étienne, while showing him the records and feeling triumphant.

"Ah, La Tour Métallique de Fourvière, you mean."

"You are familiar with this particular cell tower?"

"But of course. It is very famous, for it represents Lyon's version of La Tour Eiffel."

"Well it gives me an alibi."

"No, it proves your phone contacted that tower."

"But I would have to be within five to ten kilometers of it at 10:28 a.m. for my phone to do that."

"True enough."

"I don't get it. What's your point?"

"The JI insists you made the call from the plane."

"Oh, come on!"

"Maybe you should read this part of the dossier, before continuing your stridence." Étienne turned to an appendix containing the lab reports and showed it to Alan.

Esnault had the tan jacket tested for gunshot residue, though he never bothered to have Alan's hands checked, as Alan had washed them at the fountain at Place du Conseil. The residue test on the jacket was negative. Another report, however, established that the victim's DNA was on there. On the chance that Rolf's bodily fluids had exploded upon it during a close-range shooting, the JI had requested the analysis, and he hit pay dirt.

Alan writhed in his seat over the revelation. "I never met the guy. How could his DNA be on my jacket? It has to be a plant," he told himself. While it was quite incredible that Alan would have called Rolf from a jet airplane at the exact moment it was near the Lyon cell tower, it now seemed probable in the context of this scientific evidence that put him at the scene at such a time as he would have to have taken the flight. In insolation the Lyon call might have exonerated him, but evidence was never viewed in isolation, not in any courtroom, whether in France or America.

The DNA report concluded one thing in Alan's favor, however. Besides his own biological fluids being found on the gun, two errant alleles were noted on its grips, one for French descent and the other for blue eyes. Ludovic had both such characteristics. *Bingo*, Alan said aloud, causing Étienne to startle.

While Alan knew better than to rat out his former friend directly, given what Fakih had told him, he could live with the authorities stumbling across the man's involvement based on an independent source. In a moment of epiphany, he remembered that Ludovic had said that he had once been arrested for assault involving a lug wrench in connection with his cab job. Perhaps his DNA was in the French database and could be matched with the alleles found on the murder weapon.

Before consulting further with Étienne on the issue, Alan read the other salient points in the dossier. Jeannette and Chloé dutifully told the JI that Alan had been on the regional train until 3:15 p.m. To undermine this account, the judge spoke to witnesses who had seen Alan and Jeannette on dates at Èze (the perfume factory tour guide), Monte Carlo (the ticket man), and La Grignotière (the waitress). He recounted the time they admitted they had sex, something that seemed to interest the old jurist greatly.

Such testimony militated against the alibi to the extent it proved a strong relationship between the two lovers, giving Jeannette a motive to lie and even manipulate her own daughter for

Alan's benefit. The JI concluded that the *"accusé"* had "plied" Jeannette, a woman in difficult economic circumstances and in desperate search for a man.

In conjunction with the alibi testimony, the JI emphasized a five-year-old's susceptibility to suggestion. Alan remembered that he had recorded Chloé on his iPhone when the subject had first come up at Jeannette's apartment, something that proved no suggestion had been employed. Perhaps his iPhone had been returned to his belongings by the authorities, and Étienne could get it.

The last part of the dossier revealed another untoward development. A jail snitch claimed Alan had told him that Rolf, in being shot, had gotten what he deserved. It was not a complete confession, but it certainly didn't help. The snitch's name was none other than Omar, a fact that evoked more feelings of betrayal.

Alan stopped reading and exploded with a litany of objections to Étienne. "Ludovic put that gun on me for Christophe. Omar was suicidal and would do anything to get out of mitard. That DNA on the jacket is a plant, and the airport cab driver is lying. I was on the train just like that cell tower says. I'm being framed!"

"Oui, monsieur. Je comprends," the French lawyer replied in a tired voice.

"Don't you believe me?"

"Yes, of course, but you must admit the conspiracy has become quite broad," Étienne replied. "The gun was foisted upon you, the DNA on the jacket was concocted, the cab driver is on the take, and the snitch wanted a time cut. Do you really expect the jury to ignore everything?"

"Okay, I admit we have our work cut out, but you got to believe me. This is a frame, pure and simple."

"Tell me something," Étienne said calmly in response. "Where did you and Ludovic get the gun?"

"The Moulins."

Étienne's jaw dropped.

"What's the matter?"

"You actually obtained it in the same place that the airport cabbie says he drove you," the French lawyer noted. "What are the chances you would have gone there on a different occasion? The jury will not excuse this as mere coincidence."

"The cabbie probably works for the company that is owned by Christophe," Alan insisted. "Records of his employment and the company's organizational structure must exist somewhere in this bureaucratic country."

"Suppose I am able to persuade Monsieur le Président (the main trial judge) to obtain them," Étienne said. "What if they establish nothing? It would be yet another arrow in the quiver of the *procureur.*"

"Can't you get them without involving him?"

"It would be better to go through Monsieur le Président."

"Fine. Obtain the documents anyway. As far as the snitch is concerned," Alan continued, "we need his jail records. Maybe they'll show that he was released once he gave the statement."

Étienne pursed his lips as though Alan were wasting his time. "Any other special requests?" he asked, "keeping in mind I'm not a short-order cook."

"There are two."

"I don't have time to play twenty questions. What's the first one?"

"The JI says I suggested my alibi to Chloé," Alan said. "I recorded the conversation on my iPhone when we brought it up with her.

You need to get that recording from my property, as it proves the absence of such suggestion."

Étienne wrote down the request, then looked at Alan askance. "Are you okay?"

"No, as a matter of fact I'm not."

"It's just that you say that so many people are conspiring against you. I am beginning to wonder if an insanity defense would be more appropriate."

"The JI has overlooked critical facts and has been manipulated."

"Now why would he do that? He is a career professional."

"Because he didn't examine the evidence in the spirit of advocacy—something absent from your fucked-up system!"

Étienne ignored the crude indictment, perhaps not wanting to set Alan off further. "So what is your second request?"

"It concerns the DNA on the gun."

"What about it?"

"Haven't you read the report thoroughly? The gun has unidentified alleles on it that came from a male of French descent with blue eyes."

"And what good does that do?"

"It needs to be cross-checked."

"Cross-checked against whom?"

"I should say Ludovic, but you can't mention his name. Esnault would find out and tell him, and Ludovic would make up more lies to get me back."

Visibly frustrated, Étienne asked, "How am I supposed to cross-check the DNA on the gun without a name?"

"Have it compared by computer against the entire French DNA database. Don't you have such a thing here?"

Étienne stuck out his chest with pride. *"Oui. Le Fichier National Automatisé des Empreintes Génétiques."*

"And whose DNA does that contain?"

"Everyone who has been arrested for a serious délit or crime."

"Like assault?"

"Yes. But what difference does that make?"

"Ludovic told me he was arrested for that."

Étienne shifted in his seat and leaned forward toward Alan, but not too close in order to avoid his germs. His interest had finally been piqued. "All right, suppose independent of you, we can prove Ludovic handled the gun. How does that help your case?"

"If it can be shown that he works for Christophe, and that the airport cab driver does also, we can prove a connection between all three men and the murder weapon, provided the DNA on it turns out to be Ludovic's," Alan responded. "The case for the République would have its own set of coincidences to explain."

"Yes, and the jury could easily infer that both such persons were influenced by Christophe and thus his motive to frame you."

"Exactly."

"And who can establish your acrimonious relationship with Christophe?" asked Étienne.

"Buck Treadway."

"I am familiar with him as a former client and your benefactor. Isn't he listed as a character witness?"

"A character as well as a character witness," Alan said, smiling.

"And you want to pin your hopes on him?"

"Some of them, and the rest on the shoulders of a five-year-old girl and her mother."

Étienne frowned incredulously.

"Look, I know that in France the system is quasi-adversarial," Alan said. "But can't you take it to the next level, just for me?"

"I always imagined myself as an aggressive courtroom lawyer," Étienne said softly, genuinely moved by this request.

"Then do it now," Alan said firmly. "Fight for my life as though it were your own!"

* * *

Exactly seven days before the opening bell, Étienne came by one last time to report back on Alan's requests.

"I have some good news," the avocat announced.

"I could use some. What is it?"

"First, you were right about the snitch," Étienne said. "Omar Hussan got twenty-one days mitard. He did half of them, and the JI released him from the Maison. This came after he gave a statement to Esnault indicating you had said Rolf deserved to die. Curiously enough the records also show he did his mitard in an isolation cell next to yours."

"I forgot to tell you about my time in the disciplinary quarter, but I do recall a conversation with him about the subject."

"Well, did you say that Rolf had it coming?"

"No way."

"How did you communicate with each other in the first place?"

"You don't even want to know."

Étienne next removed another report from his briefcase and handed it to Alan. "Monsieur le Président agreed to have an expert cross check the DNA left on the gun with the French database. I was quite surprised by the results."

"What were they?"

"The unidentified DNA closely resembles that of a man arrested for assault with a lug wrench," Étienne said. "He is one of three persons in ten thousand who could have left such DNA on the murder weapon. It is not an exact match, but—"

"What is the arrested person's name?" Alan felt sure it would be Ludovic.

"Jean-Paul Sartre," Étienne responded, unable to stifle a laugh.

"Seriously?"

"Personally I would have used the name Albert Camus," Étienne said, still chuckling.

After more discussion about the literary subterfuge, Alan went on to a different topic. "Have you been able to link the cabbie at the airport to Ludovic and Christophe," he asked.

"They worked for a company that has the same name," replied Étienne. "And it is owned by Christophe."

"What's the name?"

"Côte d'Azur Taxi."

"My case has that name in another place—"

"—Côte d'Azur Immoblier," Étienne exclaimed with sudden revelation. "It is a common business designation here, but the fact that two aspects of this case have that same mark will sow doubt in the mind of Monsieur le Président and the rest of the jurors," he touted. "And doubt can add up."

"Even in France?" Alan asked.

Étienne paused. "Even in France."

13

According to a front-page article in *Nice-Matin,* no one could remember the last time an American had been tried for a crime in a French court, much less the Cour d'Assises. The article, copied for Alan by Étienne, quoted loose-lipped witnesses such as Miss Perfect, court officials who spoke in guarded generalities, and local avocats amused by the fact that a fellow lawyer was being put to the test. For background purposes the reporter interviewed Sara Elliot-Newberg, soon to be Sara Elliot, and she scornfully described her husband's sudden departure from reality. An unflattering mugshot of Alan, taken at the Maison d'Arrêt, indented the first paragraph. The headline read: *La Justice Française Montrée au Monde*—French Justice Shown to the World.

Though the pronouncement created unrealistic expectations, it did have one saving grace: it would force Monsieur le Président and his two assisting judges to behave themselves. While the electronic press would be excluded from the courtroom, print-media watchdogs would take copious notes and scrutinize their every move. Unlike the Star Chamber approach Alan had previously experienced with the instruction judge or the shenanigans pulled by Esnault and Leroux, the trial would need to have the appearance of fairness and impartiality, lest the French court system might, heaven forbid, compare unfavorably.

In keeping with this spirit, the assistant commandant had a hairstylist trim Alan's long locks back to his cool-guy messy look.

He also gave him a dapper black French sport jacket and some sexy tight pants that a previous Maison inmate had abandoned. A red shirt, a narrow dark tie, and pointy shoes completed the look, one of a well-traveled *bon vivant*, not exactly the image Alan wanted to project, but better than his jail clothes.

Despite the fact that he was dressed for a night on the town, a limo didn't transport him to court. The jail van took him instead, and after he exited it, a couple of photographers snapped some shots. He wondered if they were members of the paparazzi, but quickly discarded the notion, since he was neither rich nor famous.

Outside the *box d'accusé*, Alan met Étienne and breathed a nervous sigh. "The day has finally come," he said, shaking his avocat's hand. "Maybe I'll get an early Christmas present."

"You seem optimistic. What has brought this on?"

"You finally have enthusiasm about my case."

"I took to heart what you said about fighting for your life."

"You're going to stand your ground then?"

Étienne laughed and shook his head. "As best as I can, monsieur, but Buck Treadway I am not."

Alan patted his lawyer on the back. "Richard Étienne, avocat *extradonaire*, will be enough for me."

"Now that I can manage."

"Good. So what's on the agenda for today?"

"The jury has already been chosen, so we will start with the proof."

"What? No *voir dire?*"

In America the phrase referred to a process in which lawyers questioned prospective jurors in person at the beginning of a trial. If an attorney discovered a bias or prejudice through this inquiry, he or she could challenge a juror for cause and ask that this person be removed from the panel. Failing that, each side received a set number of preemptory challenges or strikes that required no justification. Those not eliminated constituted the jury.

Ironically, while "*voir dire*" was a French phrase, it did not exist as a procedure in France. Instead, the prosecutor could strike four persons and the defense five from a list of citizens without the benefit of in-person questioning. After that, the jury was randomly drawn.

"That makes the jury composition potluck," Alan said with a worried look.

"Potluck?"

"Okay, I'll stop."

"You'd better. Your penchant for American slang has gotten you in enough trouble already."

Alan nodded reluctant agreement. "So, does anything happen before the judge starts calling witnesses? An introduction or an opening statement from the two sides?"

"Monsieur le Président will address you in the *box d'accusé*, where you and I will remain the entire proceeding."

"What will he say?"

"He will read the charges to you and ask whether you admit or deny them."

"And after that?"

"The match begins."

Alan laughed, causing the attending court gendarme to become anxious. He had been present during the JI's mocking interrogation of him and likely believed he had a screw loose. This was not far from the truth, for the Maison experience had given Alan more than a few of such screws.

"As you know, Monsieur le Président will question the witnesses," Étienne continued. "Followed by the procureur, the victim's family attorney, and me."

"So the head guy acts as judge, juror, and prosecutor all at the same time?"

"I'm not sure about the prosecutor part, but he does present the evidence."

"Who will be called today?"

Étienne opened his briefcase and removed an official list. "It looks like the police officers who found the body, and the pathologist."

"Will you be able to ask them what you want?"

"Pretty much."

"Pretty much?"

Étienne shifted in his seat and cleared his throat. "Very well. I will demand to be heard."

* * *

Monsieur le Président and the other two magistrates had the appearance of royalty. For this special occasion, they dressed in velvety red robes banded in white fur with black polka dots. The regal fashion show and the rest of the pomp and circumstance would intimidate the six lay jurors, Alan believed, and they would likely not ask or say a thing during the trial, much less challenge the judges in any way.

After the introduction of everyone, the chief judge read the charges. Everything was in French, of course, though Alan got a real-time English translation via headphones provided by the court.

"Do you admit or deny the charge of murder?" the judge asked sternly.

"I deny it," Alan said.

"As to the charge of illegal possession of a firearm?"

"That I admit."

The judge noted Alan's responses on a legal pad. "Very well, on the latter charge we will take proof for sentencing purposes at the same time as the evidence on the murder case."

And so the proceeding began. From the outset it seemed more like an intellectual debate or discussion with the assistance of witnesses than a trial. Instead of the prosecutor orderly presenting his or her case, followed by the defense evidence, rebuttal proof, instructions, and closing arguments, the judges did the lion's share of questioning.

There was no prosecution or defense case per se and witnesses were not divided accordingly. Further, the judges, avocats, and parties interspersed testimony with their opinions and assessed and weighed the evidence as the trial progressed rather than at the end. Few rules of evidence governed the proof as well. Instead the court heard everything from character evidence to hearsay, sorting out on its own what was credible and relevant. Make no mistake about it, things weren't haphazard, and Monsieur le Président kept everyone on task, but he never did so at the expense of the truth, often calling back witnesses two and three times and requesting opinions and arguments from the parties on issues before proceeding further.

At first, Alan struggled with this flexible approach given his frame of reference. As time went on, however, he realized that too much structure sometimes impeded the truth. Black and white rules of relevancy and hearsay, exacting foundational requirements for the admission of evidence, and labyrinthine dictates of search and seizure, while having their purpose, more often than not prevented jurors from hearing pertinent facts in America. Then too, unless a judge permitted jurors to ask questions, lawyers there could not adapt their presentation to what the trier of fact needed to hear and often proceeded blindly, not even knowing who the jury foreperson was. In France this did not occur, as the search for the truth was an evolving process in which all parties actively participated as the case progressed. While some rights were lacking in the country, a fair trial didn't seem to be one of them.

The contrast between the American and French systems in this regard constituted a metaphor for Alan's life. He too had been fixed on rules, norms and structure, thereby narrowing his world. By living a more balanced existence and opening himself up, he had broadened his horizons so that he could see things more clearly. It remained to be seen whether the Cour d'Assises would do the same.

"I thought we would begin with the crime scene," Monsieur le Président said. The other judges and jurors nodded approval.

The responding cops testified that they were dispatched to Rolf's apartment at 3:05 p.m. They didn't make it to the scene until 3:15 p.m. for reasons unknown. By then their sirens had ceased, which was why Alan never heard them after arriving in Villefranche.

With the assistance of an overhead screen projecting a diagram of the apartment as well as photographs, police criminalists described their collection of evidence, being careful to note their strict compliance with all protocol. They gave the position of everything, including a beeline of blood drops of three meters from the entrance, where Rolf was found, to the rear wall of the front room.

After being shot, the victim must have stumbled directly from this wall to the stoop, the cops surmised, where he collapsed. Around the body and along his path, no identifiable footprints marred the blood line, though there were some smudges. Significantly nothing evidenced a struggle anywhere in the apartment, and no signs of forced entry were noted. Whoever did it must have known Rolf.

The criminalists also testified to the recovery of a bullet fragment from the front room back wall. The bullet hole measured about fifty-six inches off the floor. After extracting the projectile with tweezers and cutting out the drywall around it, they preserved the evidence in a sealed plastic bag.

This dry testimony took most of the day. With each witness, the head judge asked his fellow jurors if they had questions after he had finished. He informed them that they would have to write their questions down first, so he could determine their appropriateness. Obviously he did not do this for his fellow judges, who were free to interject whatever they wanted and whenever they felt like it. Since the other jurors had nothing to ask, the judge turned to the avocats almost as an afterthought.

With one of the evidence-gathering cops Étienne went on the attack. His protest: their slow response to the scene after the blind lady's call. "This was an emergency, where someone's life was in the balance," he vehemently contended. "Apparently you didn't take her seriously."

"What difference does it make?" Monsieur le Président interjected. "The question is whether *we* take her seriously."

An argument ensued among the avocats and the three judges over the larger question of whether the police officers were biased against the woman and other witnesses sympathetic to the defense. This in turn led to a discussion of whether Esnault and the JI had been guilty of a narrow-minded investigation. While this did not prove such an allegation, Étienne had used good trial strategy in sensitizing the triers of fact to the issue.

The chief judge ended the dispute by stating that Esnault's possible bias could be explored when the lieutenant testified. "In the meantime I am told the pathologist has arrived," he indicated.

"Lest we deprive him of the opportunity to tend to the dead, I suggest we continue with him."

The rest of the jurors smiled at the judge's off-color humor, and the print reporters present feverishly wrote down the remark, perhaps to add levity to their story.

Dr. Jean-Pierre Didier was sworn in after the crime-scene cops, a balding man in his early fifties who wore semi-circular reading glasses. After Monsieur le Président detailed the good doctor's illustrious qualifications ad nauseum, Didier testified that he first examined the body at 5 p.m., an hour and forty-five minutes after the police found it. Later he performed a full autopsy.

When asked about time of death, the doctor hesitated. Based on body temperature and the extent of rigor and livor mortis, he guardedly estimated that Rolf had been killed a short time before the police dispatch to the scene, but refused to offer anything more specific. He concluded that a single bullet had entered the center of the victim's chest at the level of his nipples, penetrated his heart, and exited his back between the first and second rib. "Death occurred rapidly," he declared.

Apparently thinking his services were no longer required, the French death doctor got up to leave. But Monsieur le Président gently stopped him and questioned him for another hour, much to the expert's obvious annoyance.

Slowly more details emerged: Rolf stood six-feet-one or seventy -three inches; the entry wound in the center of the chest measured fifty-four inches from the ground and nineteen from the top of his head; and significantly the larger exit wound on Rolf's back was an inch or so above the entrance one, meaning the bullet traversed the body upward at a five-degree angle and continued at that trajectory before it finally lodged in the wall. The latter revelation caused Alan to rustle in his seat.

"What does such an angle indicate to you?" asked the chief judge.

The doctor used a Styrofoam torso to illustrate his response that the court gendarmes hustled to the parquet. The torso had a straight dowel stuck into it at the precise angle and location of the wound described. "It suggests the muzzle of the gun upon discharge might have been slightly lower than the entrance wound," replied Dr. Didier, drawing the dowel downward and backward from the model's chest.

The judge pondered his next question with his hand on his chin. "And could this be caused by the barrel being pointed slightly upward?"

"Possibly. Then too, it might have been level, and the bullet itself deflected off a hard object in the room or possibly the victim's sternum, thereby changing its angle after it exited the muzzle," explained the pathologist. He excluded both alternatives, since the police did not find any objects in the room damaged by a bullet, and the beveling of the sternum did not indicate this.

"What else would cause the barrel's angle to be upward," the chief judge asked next.

"Any number of factors—the position of the shooter's body or his hand, the angle of his aim, or the movement of the muzzle during a possible struggle," the expert delineated. "Only the killer knows for sure," he emphasized, staring at Alan. "The other witness to this tragedy is dead."

The judge doggedly went through each alternative. With respect to the position of the shooter, the doctor doubted he or she had been seated, as there were no chairs found near the presumed path of the bullet. Kneeling or lying down made no sense, since at most distances this would have caused a sharper angle of ascent. As to the perpetrator tilting the gun upward or shooting from the hip, the witness testified that in his opinion this would have created an awkward firing position, but was certainly possible in the heat of battle. The pathologist would not speculate on a struggle for the gun, suggesting this inquiry should be directed to the gunshot residue expert, who would testify later.

"There is one explanation for the angle that we have not yet discussed, and a simple one I might add," the expert piped up before finishing his testimony.

"Go ahead, *Monsieur le Docteur.*"

"The shooter crouched, thus lowering the position of the gun relative to the entrance wound." Didier left his chair and demonstrated several feet in front of the Styrofoam torso by holding an imaginary gun in his hands and aiming slightly upward as he bent his knees. "This would indicate a more deliberate act, of course."

Étienne immediately went on the offensive. "Do you know the height of the accused?" he asked.

"The same height as that of the victim."

"Well, you missed another possible explanation, didn't you?"

The pathologist leaned toward the glass box from which Étienne had posed the question. "And what would that be, sir?"

"That the shooter might have been much shorter than the victim," Étienne said. "And more importantly shorter than the accused."

Didier responded, "Unfortunately, that would be another possibility."

"Unfortunately?"

There was no reply.

After the doctor exited the courtroom, another furious exchange occurred among the parties. In light of the witness's last remark, Étienne again raised the issue of bias. "The pathologist is a court expert and shouldn't be rooting for one side or another," he argued.

"I am sensitive to your concerns," said Monsieur le Président. "But much of the man's testimony is not in dispute: cause of death, time of death, position of the victim relative to the wall during the shot, and the path of the bullet upward at five degrees. Do we have such agreement?" He looked at each juror, judge, and avocat, and they assented. "As to the cause of the shot's angle, without more evidence this is a matter of pure speculation."

* * *

Miss Perfect—that is, Estelle Beauchamp—took the stand the next morning, and she made a feeble attempt to steal the show. She described how she had first met Alan and her heroic efforts to assist him on the right bus going the wrong way. "My intervention was rewarded by Monsieur Newberg's disdainful mockery of our country," she said haughtily. "He suggested we should feel lucky to speak French rather than German—"

"—Madame," the chief judge interrupted, rolling his eyes. "I am more interested in your observations of Monsieur Newberg in reference to the firearm as opposed to his revisionist version of our history."

"Very well. Several months later I was on a similar bus in Villefranche," she said. "I saw him through the bus window, and he held a handgun while he was seated in a red truck."

"Can you describe the truck further?"

"It had on its hood the horns of a beast," she said. "I found it rather disturbing, but nevertheless entirely consistent with Monsieur Newberg's character."

"Please only describe what you saw, Madame."

"He had a handgun on his lap like this," she replied, demonstrating with her hands. "I could see it clearly, since I was well above him on the bus. He didn't simply hold the gun, either. I would rather say he *fondled* it."

"Fondled?" the chief judge asked. "You act as though he had amorous intent."

This time the gallery could not contain its laughter, causing Miss Perfect to turn purple. The two female judges remained stolid, however. Monsieur le Président quelled the levity with a few sharp raps of his gavel and permitted Étienne to proceed with the witness.

"Now, Madame Beauchamp, were you ever shown a gun by the police in this matter and asked to determine if it was the same one that you observed from the bus?"

"No."

"If you were shown the firearm today that killed Rolf Swenson, I trust you would not be able to identify it as the same one that you saw some six months ago."

"That is correct. It has been too long."

While Étienne did not dispute that the weapons were the same, especially given the firearm examiner's report, it was important to establish that the police had not bothered asking Miss Perfect this very basic question. Indeed the more he could show the existence of errors or omissions in the investigation, the more it would appear the police might have missed or even corrupted the rest of the evidence. And that was how the avocat proceeded throughout the trial: line upon line, here a little and there a little. It was a dink and dunk approach, but nevertheless an effective one.

"Madame Beauchamp," Étienne continued, "you first saw Monsieur Newberg in late March, correct?"

"That would have been my encounter with him on the bus in Nice, yes."

"You didn't see him with a gun at that time."

"Of course not."

"And you didn't see him at all after this until July."

"I made it a point to stay away from him," Miss Perfect responded with a prissy smile.

"It would be true, would it not, that you have no idea when Monsieur Newberg *first* came into possession of the weapon that you observed him with in July?"

"True, but I rather imagine it occurred through contact with undesirable elements."

"Could he have acquired the gun *after* you first met him on the bus and hence after the murder?"

"Do you want my opinion?"

"No," Étienne said. "I think we already know that."

"You're good," Alan whispered to the avocat as he sat back down.

Esnault followed Miss Perfect. He testified he had searched Alan's belongings at the identity check and found no gun. Monsieur le Président did not permit him to recount the statements Alan had made at the gendarmerie office in Villefranche that inferred his knowledge of the manner and timing of the shooting. Nor did he admit any statements made during other police interrogations, since they had not been reduced to a *procès-verbale*.

But Esnault did testify about Alan's spontaneous remark at the scene that Rolf had ripped him off for 6,000 euros. Alan's problematic statements to the JI about his travel itinerary were also allowed, since they occurred under oath. They did not have to be repeated, as the jurors each had a copy of the dossier that contained them.

In what seemed completely out of order, the chief judge suddenly sought permission to query Alan about the events that led up to his outburst in front of Rolf's apartment. In America this would have been unheard of, for the defense absolutely controlled when and if a defendant testified, given the Fifth Amendment. Merely asking to follow such procedure in front of a jury would have been reversible error, for if a defendant declined, it would suggest to the trier of fact he or she was hiding something.

Feeling he could not avoid the issue, Alan agreed to speak and responded that he had intended to take the connecting flight to Nice, but changed his mind at the last minute. Yes, had he gone by air, his alibi would mean nothing, but he had taken the train and arrived much later.

Monsieur le Président asked Alan about his background, in particular his exacting occupation as a title-company lawyer. He raised the issue of whether such an organized person would deviate from a planned course of action, similar to what the JI had done in the dossier. To be fair, the chief judge also brought out the details of his abrupt departure to France in the middle of his divorce. Such a precipitous decision suggested he was thoroughly capable of spontaneously changing his itinerary, the judge said.

While some present may have thought Alan to be unstable, the judge charitably characterized him as "complicated." He seemed to get that people in general were not black or white in their thinking process, possessing instead a considerable amount of gray and even contradictory traits.

Monsieur Leroux testified about the recovery of the Moroccan handgun underneath the mattress at Chez Betty. He presented himself as the perfect gentleman and remained calm until the chief judge started grilling him about his sloppy methods.

"The dossier indicates that you assisted with collection of evidence from the body."

"Yes."

"I assume you wore latex gloves."

"Of course."

"And you changed them often during your participation in this process."

"I believe so."

"You did this to avoid cross-contamination of evidence, that is an inadvertent transfer of DNA or other trace substances from one item to another."

Leroux became defensive. "I-I'm not sure what you are getting at."

"I am not required to inform you of what I am getting at," the judge said. "Now the reports also state that you were involved in the transport of the deceased."

"Yes, I tagged his corpse for identification purposes, helped put it in a body bag, and remained with it until securing it in a cooler at the morgue."

"When you did this, did you wear gloves?"

"I believe so."

"How many gloves did you wear on each hand?"

"I don't recall."

"Did there come a time when you removed the gloves once and for all?"

"Before I left the morgue."

"How did you remove them?"

"Inside out."

"You were careful then not to touch the outside of the gloves with your bare fingers when doing this?"

"That would be our protocol."

"Perhaps I should have been more clear. Did you or did you not remove the gloves in this manner?"

"I believe so."

"Did you wash your hands after you removed the gloves?"

"I believe so."

"Officer, you have used that phrase four times now. Do you *know* that you followed these procedures?"

"As best as I can recall."

The chief judge sighed irritation, and Leroux's spastic eye began twitching out of control. He, after all, had taken Alan's tan jacket into evidence at the police station in Villefranche. If he had somehow gotten a smidgeon of Rolf's fluids on his hands in moving the body before this point, he could have transferred it to the jacket, which would explain the DNA. The question was whether "could have" would be enough for the jurors and judges to disregard such evidence.

After lunch, the firearms expert established that the Moroccan handgun was the same one that discharged the bullet found in the wall at Rolf's apartment. As he had indicated in his report, he test-fired a bullet from the suspect gun and microscopically compared the striations and rifling characteristics of that bullet to those on the fragment found at the scene. They were the same. In his opinion Alan's gun was the murder weapon.

The expert also testified about gunshot residue testing. He explained that when a gun discharges, its barrel emits gases, soot, lead, and barium. Such substances could sometimes be found on surfaces, such as the clothing of a victim. To determine this, he applied chemical reagents around the bullet hole in Rolf's shirt, but could not develop any of the tell-tale residue. Nor could he find any on his hands or sleeves.

"Does this mean the hole was not caused by a bullet?" Monsieur le Président asked playfully.

"Absolutely not. When the distance between muzzle and target is greater than fifteen inches, gunshot residue can no longer be detected on the victim of a shooting."

"So it is unlikely the shooter and the victim were grappling with the gun at the time of the shot?"

"All I can say is that when the gun went off, the muzzle was more than fifteen inches from the victim."

Monsieur le Président continued with an obvious line of questioning. "Is gunshot residue sometimes left on a shooter's hands or clothing?"

"Yes, of course. Some of the same substances I mentioned explode upward and backward from the weapon and onto the perpetrator."

"To your knowledge, were Monsieur Newberg's hands swabbed for this purpose?"

"No, they were not."

The gallery began to mutter, causing the head judge to rap his gavel once again.

"The explanation I received from Lieutenant Esnault was that Newberg had washed his hands at a local fountain thirty minutes prior to meeting with him."

"And what about possible gunshot residue on his clothing?"

"After the DNA analysts had finished with the jacket, I tested it and achieved negative results."

"Does this mean the owner of this jacket could not have fired a gun?"

"No. The DNA retrieval process made the use of reagents very tedious, and the presence of gunshot residue hit or miss," the expert said, smiling thinly at his play on words.

* * *

Monsieur le Président moved into the heart of the case on the third day: the taxi boys. For this, he heard from Ludovic, Christophe, Buck Treadway, and Pierre DeLeon, the mysterious cab driver who claimed he had driven Alan from the airport to the Moulins. In the middle of such witnesses, he sandwiched Omar, the jail informant.

Ludovic, who Monsieur le Président correctly suspected was Jean-Paul Sartre, acknowledged he had worked for Christophe as a cab driver and that bad blood existed between the drug lord and Buck. He said that Christophe had complained more than once about Buck stealing customers. Ludovic appeared to be helping Alan's case, but then the subject of the gun came up.

"Monsieur Renard, did you ever touch the murder weapon?" challenged the chief judge, who gestured to the Moroccan handgun that had been brought out from a back room for the jury to view.

"No, "Ludovic replied.

The judge fumed. "Have you ever used the alias Jean-Paul Sartre?"

"No.

"Well, have you been arrested for assaulting someone with a lug wrench?"

"Yes."

"Funny. Jean-Paul Sartre was arrested for the same thing," the judge said. "Perhaps you and he have much in common. When were you taken into custody?"

Ludovic gave a vague date.

The judge leaned toward him and said in a firm, quiet voice: "I will have your fingerprints and DNA compared to that of Jean-Paul Sartre. If you have lied, I will send you to the Maison. Are we clear?

Now I will ask you once again, have you ever used that name as an alias?"

Ludovic looked down. "Yes."

"So you are the Jean-Paul Sartre who was arrested for assault with a lug wrench?"

"Yes."

The judge waved the DNA report in the air. "This document says that Jean-Paul Sartre, that is you, is one of three people in ten thousand whose DNA is on the murder weapon."

Ludovic did not respond.

"Monsieur Renard, did you shoot Rolf Swenson?"

"No."

"Do you know who did?"

"No."

"Did you handle this weapon for any other reason?"

"No."

"How then was your DNA left on it? Do you have an identical twin?"

"No."

"Did you give that gun to Monsieur Newberg?"

Ludovic hesitated, and the judge repeated his question. Finally, Ludovic denied it. It was a lie, of course, a lie motivated by fear.

"Perhaps you shook the hand of Monsieur Newberg, and he later transferred your sweat to the gun by accident," suggested the chief judge.

"Ahh. *Ça oui*," Ludovic exclaimed.

Christophe testified after Ludovic. His diminutive appearance could not be ignored in light of the testimony of the pathologist regarding the angle of the shot. As a result, Monsieur le Président focused on his motive for killing Rolf. But Christophe was a cool customer. He admitted the victim had racked up considerable gambling debts with him, but emphatically denied he had shot him. The chief judge wasn't impressed.

"In addition to Rolf owing you a great deal of money, you didn't particularly like Alan Newberg, correct?"

"He and his employer were stealing my business."

"Not to mention the mother of your child," the judge said quietly.

"I don't care about her."

"The mother or your child."

"The mother."

"Did you order any of your employees to exact revenge upon the American by running him off the road in Villefranche?"

"No." Christophe answered with the innocence of a schoolboy. He had obviously been on the witness stand before.

"Did you tell them to assault him at Chez Betty on another occasion?"

"No, Monsieur le Président. I am a businessman, and violence is not good business."

"Did you tell Ludovic Renard to give Monsieur Newberg the murder weapon in order to frame him for Rolf Swenson's murder?"

"No."

"But you do admit Ludovic was your former employee."

"Yes."

"And your answer would be the same with respect to Pierre DeLeon, the airport cabbie?"

"Yes."

"Given your relationship to Monsieur DeLeon, I suspect you have considerable influence over him."

"He is his own man. I couldn't possibly get him to say he brought Newberg to the Moulins. So my answer is no."

"Did you have access to the dossier in this case?"

"No."

"Were you told of its contents by anyone?"

"No."

"How do you know then what DeLeon told the authorities?" The judge waited for an answer while he calmly poured himself a glass of water.

Christophe remained mute. He had slipped up and knew it.

Buck Treadway took the stand next, looking like a Texas Ranger. He wore a dark suit and a white shirt, accented by a pewter bolo tie in the shape of a steer's head. When he sat in the chair before the judges and citizen jurors, he had in his hands a Sunday go-to-meeting white cowboy hat, which he used to gesture. He declined a microphone—he didn't need one. He also spoke in French. While the judges knew about Buck's fluency, the lay jurors seemed measurably impressed that a Texas redneck would have such a talent.

Buck spoke highly of Alan as a friend and business associate, stating he had never missed work and always followed instructions. When asked of the ongoing feud with Christophe, he minced no words, looking the jurors in the eye and bluntly telling them that he and Christophe were involved in nothing short of a war. He said that Christophe's men committed many acts of violence during this conflict, including chasing Alan from Chez Betty on foot, attempting to run him off the road, and beating Ludovic after the soccer match. Some of this he observed, but most was based on hearsay. Even so, no one objected.

"How would you respond to the testimony of Christophe that the territorial dispute between your companies never resulted in violence?"

Buck asked if he could switch to English.

"But of course. We have a wonderful translator," said the chief judge.

"Christophe is full of shit!"

The jurors gaped at the profanity even though it was in English, and the head judge cleared his throat to fill the impasse. "I take it you have strong feelings about the man," he said, half-laughing.

"Not as strong as the ones he has for me," Buck said, switching back to French. "And that is exactly my point. If you are shocked by my characterization of Christophe's testimony before this solemn court, use it as a benchmark to measure the strength of his emotions. He will do anything, *anything*," the Texan emphasized, "to exact revenge upon me or someone I know."

While long on emotion and short on facts, Buck Treadway had been impressive. Sure he was loud, abrasive, and rude, the quintessential American in the jurors' eyes. But they loved him nevertheless, for he delivered a certain kind of realness that they respected.

Next came the jailhouse snitch, Omar Hussan. He recited Alan's alleged statement in the disciplinary quarter. Monsieur le Président did a balanced presentation of the pathetic man's testimony, bringing out the reward he had received for cooperating. Étienne's questioning further explored the inmate's desperation, pointing out that he was suicidal as a result being isolated in *mitard*. Simply put, Omar's testimony was a wash.

The judge followed the snitch with the Côte d'Azur Taxi records, which showed DeLeon had picked up Alan at the airport around noon the day of Rolf's murder. Of course, the records were not simultaneously copied to any other agency, and their authenticity could not be verified other than by DeLeon.

Without significant impeachment, the airport cabbie identified Alan as the customer he had driven from Nice Côte-d'Azur airport to the Moulins. Yet he refused to say that he had seen him with the gun. This hurt Alan's case as much as it helped, for if DeLeon had wanted to frame him at Christophe's orders, he could have done a better job. Alan's case had finally taken a significant hit.

Étienne did his best to neutralize DeLeon. He brought out that the cabbie had worked for the same company as Ludovic, which also had the same name as the real estate company. He accented his cross-examination with various official records that established this and queried the cabbie about every detail he logically would have remembered had he truly transported Alan. But the avocat could not make any headway with the man. So he switched topics.

"Monsieur DeLeon, you have testified that after twelve noon on the day in question, you drove Monsieur Newberg from the airport to the Moulins."

"Yes."

"Not from the train station."

"That is correct."

"From an airport where planes land, right?"

"Yes."

"Have you ever flown in a commercial plane?"

"Yes, many times."

"Then you would know that a passenger is not allowed to use a cellular phone on such a means of transportation."

"That is true."

At this point, Étienne pulled out the phone records, the ones evidencing Alan's incessant calls to Rolf Swenson. He pointed out to the jury that one of the calls had been made at 10:28 a.m. the day in question, and that the call had accessed the cell tower near Lyon. This connection was made at the precise time the TGV train for which Alan had purchased a ticket should have been in Lyon. Since the dossier documented this fact, it came as no surprise to the jury.

"You would agree, Monsieur DeLeon, that if my client were on that train, you could not have picked him up at the Nice airport at noon?"

"Yes, that's true."

"Are you saying he made the call from the plane?"

"All I know is I picked him up from the airport at noon."

The *procureur* responded by noting the mathematics of the situation. The distance from Paris to Nice, the time that the plane took off, and its average speed would put it over Lyon at 10:30.

Étienne turned to the jury and judges. "At this point the case against Monsieur Newberg comes down to whether you believe he made a call from the air over Nice or from the train," he said. "If he called from the train, he could not have killed Rolf Swenson, as it didn't arrive in Nice until 2:55 p.m."

"And if he made the call from the plane over Lyon, do you concede his guilt?" the chief judge asked.

"That would depend on the rest of the evidence."

"Which is precisely the point," the judge replied. "We are required to examine the entire proof. If it establishes guilt otherwise, then we must conclude he made the call from the plane, however unusual that may have been. If it does not, we must conclude he was on the train and could not have committed the murder."

"I submit a third possibility, Monsieur le Président," Étienne countered.

"And what is that?"

"That we simply do not know one way or another, and if that is the case, we must free this man, for he is *presumed innocent.*"

"You are right. In our system ties go to the defendant," the judge said. "And tomorrow we shall determine the final score."

14

The last day of trial started with the DNA expert, who testified that Alan's bodily fluids (probably sweat) were on the gun grips, as well as those of Jean-Paul Sartre, also known as Ludovic Renard. A fingerprint man put Alan's paws on the murder weapon as expected, and the rest of the documents referenced in the dossier were introduced: airline records showing his purchase of tickets from Chicago to Paris and Paris to Nice and the departure and arrival times of these flights; a credit card billing proving he had bought a TGV ticket for a train arriving in Nice at 2:55 p.m.; and an e-mail exchange between he and Rolf about the apartment deal. The factual testimony stood in great contrast to Buck's screed, the lies of Ludovic and DeLeon, and the argument with the chief judge about the impact of the cell tower evidence.

The rest of the Villefranche contingent came next. Betty supported Buck's testimony regarding Christophe's thugs rousting Alan at the hotel. She described how Alan had forked one of them in the eye and escaped through the front window. Both Betty and Thierry provided positive character-related testimony, stating that Alan was trustworthy, punctual with his hotel room rent, and non-violent with the exception of acting in self-defense with the fork. While the waitress from La Grignotiére Restaurant, the tour guide at the perfume factory, and the ticket man at Monte Carlo had all seen Alan on dates with Jeannette, they said they'd found him to be charming and polite, Miss Perfect's statements notwithstanding.

Madame le Juge Leblanc, one of the other judges, conducted the examination of the real estate agent, Henri Girac. His testimony was quite memorable.

"Monsieur Girac, did you know a man named Rolf Swenson in March of this year?"

"Yes."

"And how did you know him?"

"From my office's representation of him in real estate matters."

"Did this include managing apartments for him?"

"Yes."

"And what did this involve specifically?"

"Accepting rent money, providing keys to tenants, obtaining signatures on leases, checking clients out at the end of their stay, and other routine procedures."

"Did you collect all the rent?"

"No. Sometimes Monsieur Swenson would do that himself, especially with respect to large advance payments."

"Are you familiar with the day Rolf Swenson was killed?"

"How could I forget it? The police went door-to-door near my business looking for witnesses. I came forward and told them about an incident that occurred at my office in which an American had become upset over one of Rolf's rentals."

"Is that person in the courtroom?"

"Yes." Girac pointed to Alan.

"Now Monsieur Girac, if you would, please describe what was said in your conversation with this man."

"Monsieur Newberg told me he needed the keys to an apartment he had rented from Rolf Swenson, and I told him we had no paperwork on this and could not help him."

"When you informed Monsieur Newberg that you lacked such documentation, what was his reaction?"

"He was angry, stating he had paid 6,000 euros to Rolf for the apartment. He even pounded his fist on my desk, demanding satisfaction."

"And what was your response?"

"I told him to take the matter up with Rolf and gave him directions to his home near the church."

"Did he say what his intentions were when he left?"

"He said he wanted 'vengeance' against Rolf for stealing his money."

"And what time did he leave your business?"

"About five minutes before 3 p.m."

Monsieur le Président interrupted the questioning. Apparently he and Judge Leblanc did not get along well, so in a rather condescending and chauvinistic manner, he decided to take over. "Now Monsieur Girac, the defendant didn't really use the word 'vengeance,' did he?"

"No."

"Do you remember in English exactly what he said?"

This was Girac's opportunity to show off. He sat up straight in his chair and enunciated the words perfectly, even adding Alan's angry inflection. "Monsieur Newberg said that he would 'get to the bottom of it.'"

"Is that it?"

Girac smiled. "No, there's more."

"Please, grace us with his words."

"He said he would do this 'hell or high water.'"

The translator stopped and told the judges she could not interpret the phrase, "hell or high water."

The chief judge gave out an angry moan that could be heard all the way across the courtroom. "Monsieur Girac, my translator is one of the finest in this city, and even she doesn't understand this idiom. Are your credentials in English better than hers?"

"No."

"Yet despite this fact you are testifying today that this meant Monsieur Newberg sought 'vengeance?'"

"Yes."

Sighing, the judge turned to Madame le Juge Leblanc. "It seems to me your suggestion about the defendant's motive is inherently problematic," he said. "I thought the theory was that Newberg had learned of the problem with the apartment in a conversation with Rolf Swenson on his cellular phone the *morning* of the murder and that this in turn led him to the Moulins, where he purchased the murder weapon."

The female judge turned her face upward and away. Obviously she was not happy with the chief judge upstaging her.

"The real estate agent," Monsieur le Président went on, "describes a conversation with the defendant that took place in the middle of the *afternoon* in which the defendant apparently found out for the first time that he had been taken by Rolf. Thus, I believe your position and that of the République to be incongruent. Either he learned of the problem in the morning or the afternoon."

Visibly offended by the suggestion of lack of neutrality, Judge LeBlanc snapped, "I am not aligned with Monsieur le Procureur—I seek only the truth." She offered an explanation: Alan had learned of the problem with the rental in the morning and purchased the gun before he went to the real estate office. In going there, he simply wanted to confirm that the deal had not gone through before he took any action.

The chief judge went back to questioning Girac. "You mentioned that Alan Newberg left the real estate office at 2:55 p.m."

"Yes."

"How did you know the time?"

"I used my father's watch."

"Do you have it with you?"

Girac pulled out of his coat a silver pocket watch featuring an ornate outer casing. He proudly opened it up.

"That is a fine looking time piece, monsieur. May I see it?"

The real estate agent detached the watch's chain from the button of his coat, and handed the device to the judge, who carefully manipulated it in his fingers. Then he put it next to his ear and shook it several times to make sure it functioned. It did, but the discussion of its accuracy on the day in question was not over.

"I note the date of the alleged offense was March 27," the chief judge said. "That was a Sunday. Do you normally work on Sunday, Monsieur Girac?"

"No."

"What time did you come to the office that day, understanding that it was a Sunday?"

"Just before Monsieur Newberg arrived, I believe."

"Would it be fair to say that you had no other appointments that day?"

"Yes."

"So you had no particular reason to note the time or verify that your watch was accurate."

"I don't remember."

"You have heard, I assume, of the phenomenon called Daylight Savings time?"

Girac hesitated. "Y-yes?"

"When does that occur?"

"March?"

"I will give you a hint. It started at 12:01 a.m. on March 27 of this past year, the same day the victim was killed."

"Okay?"

"Did you change your watch to reflect Daylight Savings either the night before or at any time before Monsieur Newberg arrived at your office?"

"I-I must have."

"How did you adjust your watch, forward or backward?"

"The way you are supposed to."

"And what way was that?"

"I don't know right now."

"Do you have an independent memory of resetting your watch on or near March 27?"

"No."

The chief judge looked at the other jurors. "If he had changed his watch, he would have moved the time one hour forward," he noted. "But if he forgot to do so, it would have shown a time one hour earlier than it really was. When he told the police about the time of the conversation with the defendant, he could have been wrong."

Girac said nothing. The lone witness chair had suddenly become very lonely.

"2:55 p.m. would have really been 3:55 p.m., right?" Monsieur le Président asked him.

"Yes, but I think I changed my watch and it was 2:55."

"You *think*?"

"I-I guess."

* * *

The fifth and final day of testimony began with the blind lady, Madame Helène Picard. With the assistance of the court gendarme, she quietly made her way to the chair in front of the jury, the only noise being the tapping of her cane. She wore her usual church suit and pillbox hat. Her disability as well as her unique appearance made a strong impression.

She established a critical fact for Alan's defense: time of death. In dramatic fashion she described the coincidence of the shot and the church bell chime at 3 p.m. With all the excitement, however, she could not remember how long after the shot she first saw Alan. But she did testify about his reaction to the news of the victim's demise in such a way as to suggest his innocence. "Lying in front of the apartment was Rolf's dead body, but Monsieur Newberg didn't even know who it was," she said.

"What allows you such a conclusion?" asked Judge Leblanc snottily. "I am persuaded you have a strong sense of hearing, but mind-reading is another matter."

"The American had to ask the victim's name."

"Perhaps he was feigning ignorance," replied the female judge.

"I rather doubt it," Madame Picard said calmly, clasping her hands together on her lap. "He seemed genuinely shocked by the news."

"What did Monsieur Newberg say once you informed him that it was Rolf who had been shot?" Judge Leblanc next inquired.

"He said, 'He's the guy who ripped me off for 6,000 euros.'"

"Do you have anything else to add, madame?"

"Yes, I do," the blind lady said. "Why did Monsieur Newberg tell me Rolf had taken his money if he had killed him for that reason? Wouldn't he want to hide that fact?"

"This is a matter of argument and not proof," Judge LeBlanc replied quickly. "The former is the province of the court, and the latter that of a witness. You are a mere witness."

"I realize that, but it still bothers me," she said in a grandmotherly voice. "If I had killed someone, I wouldn't be babbling my motive to a complete stranger in a public courtyard. I would have kept that to myself."

"Unless of course, you were engaged in a theatrical performance," Madame le Juge Leblanc replied.

Monsieur le Président rolled his eyes. So too did the blind lady, though she had difficulty doing so.

Jeannette Brouillet came next. Alan hadn't seen her since their visit at the jail. She had on a dark business suit and a cream silk scarf. The second female judge, Madame le Juge Simon, took a turn at questioning, and she challenged Jeannette about Alan's train-ride alibi with some hard-hitting questions.

"Madame Brouillet, you are the defendant's lover, correct?"

"Yes."

"You've dated him numerous times."

"Yes."

"You've had sex with him."

"Yes."

"You love him."

"Of course."

"Prior to meeting Monsieur Newberg, your economic situation was very tenuous, right?"

"Yes, but he couldn't help me, as he had no access to funds," Jeannette said.

"Not until he got his divorce money, right?"

"I know nothing about such money."

"But you would agree that a father figure for your child, who might someday provide financial support, would be a good catch."

"Chloé already has a father."

The judge perused the dossier and consulted quietly with the other jurors, then turned back to Jeannette. "Christophe Chevalier is the father's name, correct?"

"Yes."

"According to our records, you and Christophe do not get along."

"I am not sure what your point is."

"Well, not only are you Monsieur Newberg's lover, you are also Christophe's enemy."

"You could say that, but what difference does that make?"

"I will ask the questions, Madame Brouillet," Judge Simon lectured. "You would rather see Christophe charged with this crime than Alan Newberg, is that not so?"

"Yes."

"And if Christophe were charged and better yet convicted, this would get him out of your life, wouldn't it?"

"Yes, but I wouldn't lie—"

"Not even for the man you love?"

"No," Jeannette said, her voice now cracking. "Alan was in Nice when the murder was committed. I say this regardless of his relationship to me."

"How often have you spoken to your daughter about your lover's alibi?"

"Many times since he went to jail."

"When did this occur last?"

"Yesterday evening, before I kissed her goodnight."

"Indeed, madam. Indeed."

* * *

After lunch, in light of the questioning by Madame le Juge Simon that implied Jeannette had influenced Chloé's alibi account, Étienne introduced into evidence the recording of the child that had been made on Alan's iPhone at Jeannette's apartment. The judges weren't impressed, however, suggesting, as had Esnault on the Ferris wheel, that the conversation had been scripted. Needless to say Alan was disappointed.

The judges then huddled in a private conversation. Alan assumed that since Chloé was next on the agenda, they were discussing the procedural nuances of handling a child witness. A surprise ensued instead: Alan was called out of order again. Perhaps the thinking was he would say something for which the child would be unprepared, thereby minimizing the impact of her statement.

Monsieur le Président addressed various topics with Alan: his alibi, his relationship to Jeannette and Chloé, and his conversations with the real estate agent and the blind lady. After the chief judge finished, Madame le Juge Leblanc chimed in arguing her case against Alan once again.

"I'll tell you what I think, Monsieur Newberg," she said. "Rolf Swenson told you the apartment was not available in a call you made from the airport in Paris. You got angry, as you had already paid him the money for it. Instead of contacting the authorities or dealing with him through the courts, you took the law into your own hands, bought a train ticket to cover your tracks, went to Nice in the morning by air, and purchased the murder weapon in the Moulins in time to commit the murder at three o'clock."

"That's not true. I didn't learn about the problem with the apartment until the real estate agent told me," Alan maintained.

"Have you been to the Moulins ever in your life, monsieur?"

Alan floundered for an answer. *How does she know this? Ludovic must have told Esnault, and he related it to her.* "Okay, I-I have been to the Moulins before," he stammered.

"Are the Moulins a tourist attraction, or did you have a legitimate reason for frequenting this location?"

"I bought the gun there for self-defense," Alan said sheepishly. "But long after the day Rolf was shot."

"So not only have you been to the Moulins, you've purchased in that area the precise instrument used to kill the victim."

The chief judge conducted more questioning in an apparent effort to rehabilitate Alan. "I trust you are conceding you had the murder weapon at your hotel room."

"Yes."

"And in the truck?"

"Yes."

"Now with respect to your purchase in the Moulins, did you accomplish this with Monsieur DeLeon or someone else?"

The moment of truth had come. The judge had given Alan his chance. Up until now, for various reasons he had not disclosed that Ludovic was the supplier of the murder weapon. Whether this had been out a lingering sense of loyalty or because he believed Ludovic would make up more lies in response, did not matter. Now Alan's life was on the line, and he could no longer hold back. "I went to the Moulins with someone besides DeLeon," he replied narrowly.

"With whom did you go?"

Alan paused, at which point Madame le Juge Leblanc eyed Monsieur Président and said, "See, DeLeon has not lied. Otherwise Monsieur Newberg would have a ready answer!"

"It was Ludovic!" Alan blurted. Finally he had cracked.

* * *

Before the judges questioned Chloé, they engaged in a heated debate on the impact of her statement. Mesdames le Juge LeBlanc and Simon, and Monsieur le Procureur, argued a child could not be relied upon to establish specific facts in court, including Alan's alibi. They cited the *Outreau Affaire* in which several people in France had been falsely convicted of sex offenses on the word of children. As a result the inquisitorial system had been shaken to its core, and the mere mention of the case caused a pall to hover over the courtroom.

"This catastrophe has taught us never to rely on the word of a child again," Judge Leblanc emphasized.

"What if it is offered in exculpation?" Étienne asked.

"Still, it is of no moment," declared the other female judge sharply. "A child is as unreliable for the defense as he or she is for the prosecution."

"But there is a higher duty to protect an innocent person from conviction," argued Étienne. "That was the point of *Outreau*—to protect the innocent. And yet you would turn this shield into an executioner's sword!" It was the French avocat's finest display of advocacy in the trial.

Monsieur le Président resolved the impasse by stating that Chloé would not be sworn in as a witness, since she was a "mineur." However, the judges and jurors could still listen to what she had to say and give her statement credence to the extent the other evidence supported it.

With that the gallery was cleared, and Chloé took the witness chair. Despite her mother having testified, the judges permitted her to sit next to the child, so long as she said nothing to her during her statement to the court.

Monsieur le Président gave young Chloé an avuncular smile, and she giggled and shyly hid her face. "There is no reason to be nervous, my dear," he told her.

"I'm not nervous," she said through the translator. "I just think your red dress looks funny."

Those still in attendance, and especially Madame le Juge Le-Blanc, erupted in laughter at the child's naïve rebellion.

The chief judge cleared his throat. "I can see you are a very honest little girl," he said. "I'm sure you understand the difference between the truth and a lie."

Chloé nodded eagerly.

"Now, if I were to tell you that my robe is black, would that be a lie or the truth."

"A lie, because it's red," she replied, drawing still more laughs.

"And if I were to tell you I am a young man, would that be the truth or a lie?"

Chloé grinned. "A lie, because you're old."

"If I were to say that you are a smart young lady, what would that be?"

"The truth." Chloé had yet to master the art of humility.

"Well then, young lady, do you know a man named Alan Newberg?"

"He's my mom's boyfriend."

"And do you remember the day you first met him?"

"Yes. It was on a train from Nice to Villefranche. We were late for my dad's visit."

"And what time was that supposed to be?"

"Three in the afternoon, and we almost didn't get a chance to stop at the little yellow men."

"The little yellow men? This child obviously is mentally ill," said Monsieur le Procureur.

"She is talking about the *composteurs* at the *gare*," the chief judge said. "Now did Alan ask you and your mother the time on the train ride?"

"Yes."

"And who responded?"

"I did."

"What time did you tell him?"

Alan took off his translation headphones. He wanted to hear the glorious words directly in French.

"Quinze heures quinze."

"Chloé, do you remember the day Rolf Swenson was shot?" the judge next asked.

"Yes. My dad took me to my mom's apartment at eight o'clock after our visit. She lives near the man's house. There were lots of policemen around it."

"Was that the day you saw Alan on the train?"

"Yes."

The head judge asked the other jurors if they had any questions of the child. Madame le Juge Simon, the judge who had examined Jeannette, gladly volunteered and grilled the young girl.

"What did Monsieur Newberg wear on the train? What did your mother wear? Where did you sit? How long was the train ride? Was your mother carrying anything? What about Monsieur Newberg?" she rattled off. While the child did not have an answer for every question, it was very evident she was doing her best to tell the truth.

"Is the watch you have on today the same as the one you had on the train?"

"Yes. It's my Mickey Mouse watch," Chloé proudly declared.

"Did your mother buy you that watch?"

"Yes. For my birthday."

"And when was that?"

"September 15."

"Aha! That would have been well after the day of the murder in March!"

"My mother got me the watch on my *fifth* birthday, and that was the September before I saw Alan on the train. Now I'm *six*. My mother even put the date on my watch. See?" Little Chloé showed Judge Simon the back of her watch with the inscription.

"All right then, can you tell me what time it is now?"

The child looked at her watch. "It's five o'clock."

The judge didn't get into the issue of daylight savings, fortunately. Instead she questioned the girl about the excursions that she, Alan, and her mother had taken together. She narrowed in on their hike up Mont Boron. "What time that day did you and your mother meet Monsieur Newberg at Chez Betty?"

The poor child initially could not answer. Obviously the event wasn't particularly important, and she hadn't prepared herself for a detailed discussion of it, something the judge had probably counted on. But after some reflection, she said. "We met at eleven-fifteen. We were late, *again.*"

The lay jurors smiled, but Madame le Juge Simon did not—her attempt to undermine the child's credibility had failed. In a last-ditch effort to cross her up, she asked the current time yet again.

"5:05, and I'm hungry."

Everyone in the courtroom craned their heads toward a clock in the back. The child was right, of course.

"Very well, young lady, you may leave now," said the chief judge.

Chloé exited the courtroom with her mother. While her statement had helped, the judges could choose to disregard it in the absence of corroboration. And the other evidence—the possession of the murder weapon, the DNA on the jacket, and DeLeon's testi-mony—did not provide such corroboration. Thus, Alan's fate remained in precarious balance.

But there was something the girl had said that provided a ray of hope for Alan—the part about the little yellow men. He saw himself slipping his own ticket inside one of the yellow *composteurs* at Nice -Ville and heard the machine stamp the date and time. He felt the ticket go into the breast pocket of his tan jacket. In a dreamlike trance, he heard the chief judge say, "I believe we have concluded the evidence. We will now hear a summary from each party."

"No, wait!" Alan yelled. "I must speak with my avocat first."

Étienne conversed briefly with him in the box d'accusé, then demanded Monsieur le Président call Lieutenant Esnault back to the witness chair.

"This is highly irregular," declared Madame le Juge Leblanc. "The officer undoubtedly has gone home by now."

"It is a simple matter to check," said Monsieur le Président. He sent a gendarme out to the hallway, and he returned with Esnault.

"But the proof has been closed," the procureur protested.

"Our search for the truth has not," replied the chief judge. "Go ahead, Monsieur Étienne."

"Lieutenant Esnault, you mentioned in your testimony that Alan Newberg's jacket was taken into evidence in Villefranche. Did you search it?"

"I thoroughly patted down its pockets."

"Yes, but did you go inside them?"

"I had no need to, since I felt nothing."

"Monsieur le Président, I request that the jacket be given to the witness for his observation and inspection."

"Very well."

The court gendarme handed it to Esnault.

"Lieutenant, will you please search the pockets for us?"

"Certainly."

Esnault jammed his hands in the various pouches of the jacket, but found nothing.

"You forgot the left breast one," Étienne said.

The cop dug his hand inside it, and his face blanched.

"What is it?"

Esnault pulled out a tiny card from the pocket and examine it carefully. "A regional train ticket," he replied.

Pandemonium ripped through the courtroom. "I object to this procedure," said the procureur.

"As do I," repeated Madame le Juge LeBlanc.

"Well, I see we are about to have a very entertaining legal argument," Monsieur le Président replied. "My mouth waters."

"The ticket was not mentioned in the dossier," declared Judge Leblanc. "It cannot be considered."

"Forgive me, madame, but the jacket is mentioned in the document no less than six times," said the chief judge.

"But not the ticket itself," Judge LeBlanc replied.

"Must every item in a container be delineated as a separate exhibit?" Étienne asked.

"Yes," said the procureur. "Anyone could have put that ticket in there. With its specific reference in the dossier, we would have had the opportunity to examine it and argue whether it was genuine, and possibly offer testimony in rebuttal."

"But what if a tight chain of custody of the container, here the jacket, has been maintained by the authorities? Wouldn't that establish the ticket's integrity?" Monsieur le Président asked. He turned to Esnault. "As I recall your partner's evidence collection was somewhat sloppy. Can you assure us that La Gendarmerie strictly controlled this jacket from the moment it left Monsieur Newberg's hands to now?"

Esnault was not in a position to deny this, given how much his department's methods had already been called into question during the trial. "To the best of my knowledge, yes," he said.

"So no opportunity existed for someone to plant a ticket inside this jacket?"

"I am afraid not."

"I'm going to allow Monsieur Étienne to proceed," the judge ruled. "If Monsieur le Procureur wishes, he may appeal."

"Lieutenant, what is the destination on the ticket," Étienne asked.

"Villefranche-sur-Mer."

"What is the originating station?"

"Nice-Ville."

"Now, lieutenant, is it standard procedure for train passengers to have their tickets validated before entering the track area?"

"It is."

"How is that done?"

"A passenger puts his or her ticket in a composteur, and it stamps the date and time on the ticket."

With a dramatic rise in his voice, Étienne asked, "And what time does the stamp say on this particular ticket?"

"3:06 p.m. the day that Rolf was shot."

"Is it possible for Monsieur Newberg to be in Nice at 3:06 p.m. and for him to have committed a murder in Villefranche at 3 p.m.?"

"No, it is not."

15

"Y ou were like Perry Mason," Alan cheered.

Étienne had an "aw shucks" look on his face. "If it weren't for that train ticket, I wouldn't have been able to pull it off. The credit belongs to you."

"Don't forget Chloé," Alan added.

"Eight jurors said no to the question, *Did Newberg kill Swenson?*"

"Let me guess. Madame le Juge Leblanc was the lone holdout."

"Actually, she abstained."

"Yeah, well, screw her."

"Do I detect a note of bitterness?"

"Put it to you this way: she won't be getting a Christmas card from me."

"At least the French justice system worked in the end."

"And in between?"

Étienne shrugged, then led Alan into the dining room of his villa. "I thought we would have a bite of lunch before discussing the next step."

Alan slid himself into a chair in front of a place setting of fine china, real silverware, and smudgeless wine glasses, a far cry from his food tray at the Maison d'Arrêt. Holiday music played softly in the background, and the mood was festive. What appeared to be chicken, peeled potato chunks, and carrots soaked in a succulent brown sauce in a large bowl in the middle of the table. A basket of

French baguettes and a bottle of Beaujolais flanked the dish. "Hmm. Smells great," he said.

"It took me all morning," Étienne replied proudly. He ladled a large portion of the stew into his guest's bowl.

Alan waited for the French lawyer to serve himself before digging in. He noted his chicken portion had an unusually large thigh. At the same time, it was darker than any fowl he had seen. "My, that bird must've done a lot of hopping in its day," he observed. "Free range, right?"

"Non, non, monsieur. C'est du lapin."

Rabbit? Alan suppressed a major grimace. Growing up he had had several such varmints as pets, and Bugs Bunny had been one of his favorite cartoon characters. He couldn't imagine eating one of his furry friends for dinner. Even so he summoned the courage to eat the French delicacy, mostly out of intercultural courtesy. He picked up a tidbit of the meat with his fork and cautiously stuck it in his mouth. The stringy morsel had a gamey taste—though he had to admit it was superior to jail fare. "So is the République appealing?"

"I doubt it," Étienne said as he sopped up some gravy with a hunk of baguette. "While the victim or the prosecutor can do so, this would involve another embarrassing trial of the facts."

"So why is there a problem?"

Étienne aggressively chomped his food, while rabbit juices drooled down his chin and glistened in the light of the chandelier above the table. Between swallows, he slobbered, "Christophe wants 'vengeance.'"

"What will it be this time? Another frame?"

"More likely he will target Jeannette or Chloé."

"If he so much as touches either of them, I'll kill his ass," Alan yelled.

"Faites attention, monsieur," Étienne warned. "We have attorney-client privilege in France, but it doesn't cover neighbors

who overhear threats." He poured Alan another glass of wine, who downed it quickly in order to stifle himself. "Lieutenant Esnault wants your help in going after Christophe in the right way."

Alan choked. Up to this point, he managed to keep his food down, but now was having difficulty. After recovering, he asked, "The right way?"

"Your reticence in this regard is quite understandable, but you may not have a choice."

"Why do you say that?"

"If you are unwilling to cooperate, you'll have return to America."

"Huh?"

"The JI will get you deported otherwise."

"In that event I'll take Jeannette and Chloé with me."

"You can't do that—they are French citizens, not American souvenirs."

"So what do you propose?"

"Hear Esnault out. Maybe he has a plan that will work."

Having gobbled all his rabbit down, Étienne wiped his face off and dumped his napkin on his plate. "Dessert?"

"Nah, I've lost my appetite. Besides I need to get going."

"Got a hot date?"

"Yeah, in a way."

"Well, be careful. Bad things can happen out there."

"You're telling me?"

* * *

After the verdict and his post-trial lunch with Étienne, Alan wasted little time in getting out of town for a few days with Jeannette and Chloé. He wanted to avoid the ugly stares and gossip associated with the highly publicized trial, and especially the accusation that he had bought alibi testimony via false affection.

He and his new family decided to go to Italy—Ventimiglia to be specific—a small city thirty or forty kilometers beyond the border. They traveled there separately lest someone in Villefranche would recognize them and spread rumors that they had eloped. The train offered the most anonymous method of travel, since Buck's red pickup would draw too much attention. Despite his exoneration Alan felt the need to disguise himself, so he wore a broad-brimmed hat, a trench coat, and a scarf that covered his face.

On the train ride, Alan reflected on his situation. He couldn't believe he had been in France nine months. His voyage of self-discovery had definitely taken an extended detour, and he wondered whether in spite of everything, or perhaps because of it, he had achieved greater balance in his life. In his reflection in the train window, he removed the scarf from his face and flashed himself a satisfied and confident smile.

A mom-and-pop restaurant, inconspicuously hidden on a back street in Alta, the ancient, upper part of Ventimiglia, acted as a rendezvous point. Jeannette and Chloé were already there when Alan arrived. After some real cappuccino and thin-crust pizza, they decided to take a stroll across the Roya River. The river divided Alta from the lower, more modern part of town, and flowed into the Ligurian Sea. Eventually they made it to a park called Giardini Pubblici.

The park offered nothing special and was hardly a tourist trap, which was good, as they didn't want to do anything to draw attention, preferring instead to blend casually among the locals. They found a bench next to a jungle gym, which offered Chloé entertainment while the adults addressed the elephant in the room that they had thus far avoided: What now?

"Étienne and I had lunch together," Alan started off. He threw a pebble toward the jungle gym.

"Oh, really? What did you have to eat?"

"*Du lapin.*"

Jeannette whispered, "Don't tell Chloé."

Alan laughed, but then became more serious. "Étienne says our troubles aren't over."

"How so?"

"Christophe."

"So what's he up to now?"

"Étienne thinks he's a threat to you and your daughter, since the trial didn't go his way."

A long pause ensued as Alan worked up the courage to make his next point. "The JI is going to send me back to the States if I don't cooperate against Christophe."

Jeannette started to cry and blotted her tears with a Kleenex that she had retrieved from her purse. "What does that mean for us?"

"I-I don't know."

Chloé had just finished a crude sandcastle in front of the jungle gym. It had three stick figures next to it, made from twigs she must have found nearby.

"*Qui est-ce*—who is it?" Jeannette asked, pointing to the figures.

"*Toi plus moi plus Alan*—you, me, and Alan," Chloé said. Somehow she had understood their conversation. Her opinion on the subject of his departure was quite obvious, and Alan knew at that moment he would have to suck up his pride and cooperate with Esnault and the JI. He told Jeannette he would do whatever he could to stay in France, even if it meant knuckling under to the authorities.

They walked back to the old part of town, and as they crossed the Roya River again, they noticed something on the bridge that they had not seen earlier. Toward its middle, perhaps twenty padlocks had been attached to a light blue railing, some new, some old, and some rusted. Each had letters scrawled on them.

"What's this?" Alan asked.

"It is a tradition in this part of the world that couples purchase a lock, put their initials on it, and attach it to a bridge," Jeannette replied. "It's a sign of commitment."

"What do they do with the key?"

"Throw it into the water, of course."

They continued to the other side of the bridge. As fate would have it, they came upon a small hardware store and purchased a lock. Jeannette and Alan wrote their initials on it using an indelible marker at the counter. Not to be outdone, Chloé put hers on it as well. They returned to the bridge, fixed the lock to the railing, held the key aloft, and together tossed it into the Roya River.

* * *

A French squad car pulled up next to Alan as he did his morning walk along the Basse Corniche after returning from Ventimiglia. Though he wore the disguise he had donned on the train, Esnault immediately recognized him. Alan figured the cop would be licking his wounds a while longer, so he was surprised to see him so soon.

"Get in," the lieutenant instructed.

Alan obliged. He appreciated the fact Esnault was behind the wheel and Leroux rode shotgun, for the latter had even more fries missing from his Happy Meal in the wake of his humiliation in court over the possible DNA transfer on the jacket. Alan sat in the back with Ludovic. Under any other circumstances he would have avoided all three like the plague, but on this occasion, he resigned himself to the notion that the enemy of his enemy was his friend.

"Comment ça va?" Esnault opened pleasantly.

"Cut the crap," Alan said. "I'm only talking to you because I have to." He glared at Ludovic, who refused to look him in the eye.

"I trust you have spoken to your avocat."

"Yeah, he filled me in all right."

Esnault drove toward Nice. "Ludovic feels very guilty about the murder weapon in the Swenson *affaire*," he indicated, nodding toward the back seat. "He may have obstructed justice. Consequently he has chosen to cooperate."

"Cooperate?"

"Under our surveillance, we had him engage Christophe about his involvement in Rolf's murder," Esnault continued.

A bus stopped in front of them, blocking the road momentarily. Esnault turned to Alan and made direct eye contact while they waited. "The judge of instruction authorized a wire, and since the conversation involves you, we thought that maybe you would like to hear it."

Esnault pulled ahead of the bus and resumed driving.

"Okay, go for it," Alan said.

Esnault snapped his fingers twice at Leroux, who slipped a CD into the audio system of the squad.

A barely audible Ludovic could be heard discussing the trial with Christophe, who was expressing extreme dissatisfaction with the results. Ludovic suggested the police would now focus their attention on Christophe, which made the drug lord angry. He spewed several French profanities and bitched about Ludovic's incompetence in leaving his DNA on the murder weapon. Jean-Paul Sartre was a lame alias, he added.

In an attempt to get Christophe to confess to the murder, Ludovic replied that the frame-up was only necessary because Christophe had Rolf killed. Instead of admitting the deed, the French mob man yelled, *"Je veux l'Américain mort*—I want the American dead!"

Between the noise of traffic in Nice and the static on the tape, the next few minutes of conversation could not be heard. When Esnault turned down a quiet street, Ludovic indicated on the tape, *"Non. Sûrement pas*—Absolutely not,*"* in response to something inaudible Christophe had said. Then the drug lord suggested that for the right price Ludovic's mind would change. Further, he indicated that if such compensation were not acceptable, Ludovic might find himself at the bottom of Villefranche Harbor wearing concrete hip boots, or worse, barbecued. Thus, a meeting of the minds had been achieved in which Christophe would pay Ludovic 10,000 euros for a hit on Alan.

While stroking his mustache, the lieutenant continued: "Fortunately for you, Monsieur Newberg, Ludovic has declined this rather enticing proposal and agreed to continue to work with us."

"Okay, so what's the plan?"

"In another taped conversation Ludovic feigned agreement with Christophe's request and set up a meet tomorrow night at La Citadelle in Villefranche, where he will deliver proof of your demise in exchange for the money."

"Why can't you arrest Christophe for solicitation to commit murder right now?" Alan asked, somewhat shocked that the authorities would allow the man to remain free, given his statements.

"The JI insists that Christophe engage in an act that would prove beyond all doubt his participation in the conspiracy to kill you," Esnault replied.

They pulled through the gate at La Gendarmerie in Nice. "Why are we going here?" Alan asked. "The place gives me bad memories."

"The evidence that Ludovic will supply tomorrow night is a purported photograph of you dead."

Alan swallowed. "But I'm very much alive."

"An astute observation," Esnault said. "That is why we have come here. Inside we have someone who will make you appear, shall we say, not a part of this world."

"A makeup artist?"

"Oui. Normally he works for funeral homes," the lieutenant noted. "At first I doubted whether his experience in giving a dead man lifelike appearance would qualify him to make a live man look dead. But he convinced me otherwise."

"So your so-called makeup artist will do me up, you'll take a picture, and Ludovic will give it to Christophe as proof in exchange for the money."

"Under our surveillance, of course," Esnault qualified. "Once Christophe accepts the photo and/or delivers the money, we will arrest him, and you will be able to return to your pursuit of cathartic resolution in peace."

Alan reluctantly agreed to the plan, since it seemed like the only way to get Christophe out of his life and protect Jeannette and Chloé.

The makeup artist was a ghoulish-looking specimen in his own right. Rail thin, he had sallow, sunken cheeks and stringy black hair.

He had Alan lie down on a table and thoroughly scrubbed his face. Then he dabbed a thin layer of white powder on it to create a pale base. After brushing the powder just so, he drew dark bags under Alan's eyes, teased his hair with a comb, and wetted it with some type of animal blood. Finally, he dribbled still more of the blood down his chin from his mouth, which created the appearance that he had regurgitated it during the throes of death.

Alan examined himself in the mirror. The artist had done a good job—almost too good.

"After the blood dries and your hair mats, we will take a photograph," Esnault explained. He told Alan how to pose, emphasizing that he should relax his mouth open and show only the whites of his eyes.

Once the right look had been accomplished, Monsieur Leroux took several pictures with a cheap Polaroid camera. He laid them out on a nearby desk. One in particular delighted him. He picked it up and began cackling uncontrollably as he showed it to Esnault.

"What's the matter?" Alan asked.

"Nothing," the lieutenant replied. "Monsieur Leroux simply has a vivid imagination."

* * *

At 8 p.m. the next night, Alan met Esnault at Chez Betty. The detective had invited him to observe the meet between Ludovic and Christophe. Normally the police would not have involved a private citizen as a spectator, but Alan had insisted. He wore dark clothing as instructed, and Esnault had on swat-team black. They covered their faces with charcoal war paint once they left the bar. They decided to go early just in case Christophe had his minions case the fortress ahead of time.

On the way, Esnault explained the history of La Citadelle, a castle-like edifice on the edge of the water. In 1553 Emmanuel Philbert, a commander of Charles V, became the Duke of Savoy due to his success in various military campaigns, and his new position brought him great fame and fortune. As a result he had the finances and connections to build French defenses against the Spanish along the southern coast. Villefranche-Sur-Mer offered a harbor for the Duke's fleet, so he erected the large stone bastion to protect it, including a watchtower, surrounding moat, and drawbridge.

As they got closer, Esnault went through the drill. The meet would occur at 10 p.m. in the courtyard inside the walls of the fortress. This area had been chosen, as it offered limited avenues of escape that could be easily controlled. Three gates existed: one leading to a garden and the watchtower; another that crossed into an outdoor-theater area; and the main entrance, which connected to a former drawbridge that traversed a dry moat.

Though normally the caretaker closed all entrances by 6 p.m., Esnault had arranged for the doors to be left open that night, giving Christophe and his goons ample opportunity to enter the trap. The police would cover the three exits, with Monsieur Leroux being in charge of the garden gate, and two more detectives manning the others. Esnault and Alan would oversee operations from a vantage point above the courtyard that could only be accessed through the second floor of a museum that abutted the fort. If the meet were successful and Christophe delivered the money, Ludovic would issue a signal, and the police would block the three entrances and converge upon the culprits.

"What's the signal?" Alan asked.

"Ludovic will remove his beret," replied Esnault, smiling broadly. "When he does that, I will announce the go-code."

"Go-code?"

"Yes, of course. We absolutely must have a go-code."

Alan shook his head.

After a pregnant pause, Étienne asked, "Don't you want to know what the go-code is?"

"All right. Whatever."

"Allez LO-M!"

"Come on, give me a break."

"Since Ludovic is risking his life, we decided to let him choose it."

They hurried down a side street that led behind La Citadelle and their observation area. The path went alongside La Pétanque de Villefranche, a small country-club-like venue featuring eight courts and a bar. Before they got too close, Esnault outfitted Alan with some earphones that would pick up Ludovic's conversation with Christophe. He also gave him a pair of military-issue infrared binoculars, though a full moon made such equipment complete overkill.

"Cool," Alan said.

"Ça oui, monsieur," Esnault whispered. "Nothing but the best in France."

At the observation point they waited for the appointed hour, shooting the shit about soccer and all the comings and goings in Villefranche that Alan had missed while at the Maison. A slight fog had descended upon the medieval fortress, creating a Jack-the-Ripper ambience. Across the bay, a lighthouse beacon blinked while the harbor foghorn droned. At 10 p.m. Alan could see Ludovic hanging out in the courtyard, smoking a cigarette that brightly lit up through the infra-red binos like an orange flare.

Christophe arrived at 10:15, fashionably late. His thugs flanked him, including the one with the patch over his eye. Ludovic bravely walked to the center of the courtyard to meet them. His sacrifice made Alan feel better about the frame that had forced him to run the gauntlet of French justice.

"Donnes-moi la photo," Christophe demanded.

Ludovic handed him the fake picture of Alan dead.

Christophe raised it up in the moonlight and inspected it.

"*Ça va?*" asked Ludovic quickly.

Christophe darted his eyes around. He must have noticed something unusual, perhaps the shimmer of an errant police flashlight, so he hesitated to give a response. "*Ça me dérange que La Citadelle soit ouverte à vingt-deux heures*—It bothers me that The Citadelle would be open at 10 p.m.," he said. "*Normalement, c'est fermée à dix-huit heures*—normally it is closed at six o'clock."

"*Alors, où est l'argent*—So, where's the money?" Ludovic asked.

"*Nique ta mère*—fuck your mother!" Christophe said, not two inches from Ludovic's face. The gig was up.

Ludovic backed away slowly, as one of Christophe's companions started to draw his gun. Luckily for the soccer nut, a police sharpshooter had a bead on the thug's head.

Christophe waved his man off, telling him, "*Ne tire pas! Ils nous ont entouré*—Don't shoot! They have us surrounded."

Without warning, Christophe and his thugs ran toward the garden gate, which was supposed to be supervised by Monsieur Leroux.

"*Allez LO-M!*" screamed Esnault into his body mike. "*Allez L-OM tout de suite!*"

Alan could hear an altercation through his earphones, presumably coming from the garden area. A few minutes later a disconcerted Leroux informed him and Esnault that Christophe had made it through the line of defense, though the man's bodyguards had been captured. Leroux admitted that at the moment of truth, he had been taking a piss and unprepared for the sudden getaway.

Whether a better result could have achieved was anyone's guess. Even so Esnault, embarrassed by the blunder, repeatedly cuffed Leroux about the crown of his head with the back of his SWAT-team stocking cap. "*Idiot!*" he screamed, a massive understatement indeed.

Alan had no time for more Keystone-Cop activity: Christophe had been provoked onto the warpath and his first stop would likely be Jeannette's. Alan tried to warn her on his phone but got no answer. Shifting into auto-pilot, he raced to her apartment without a moment's reflection or hesitation, leaving Esnault and his crew behind arguing with each other. There he found Jeannette in tears, and she screamed, "He's got Chloé!"

"What direction did he go?"

"Toward the harbor and his yacht," Jeannette replied. "He's taking her to La Corse."

Alan spun toward the door, but she grabbed his arm. "You can't take him on alone."

"Go get Buck!" he yelled as he set off for the harbor.

Alan ran down a cobblestone footpath and three flights of stairs. On the way he passed the Citadelle, but didn't stop to see if Esnault and crew were still around to assist him, since they would probably screw up Chloé's rescue. He was on his own, unless Buck made it in time.

As he rounded the dry moat next to the fortress, he could hear the poor child's screams echoing off its medieval walls. Her desperate protest sent Alan's adrenaline level through the roof. From the top of the stairwell above the harbor, he could see Christophe yanking the child onto his medium-size yacht that was being driven by none other than the woman from Oslo to whom Alan had given a ride months before. At the time he had determined she was Rolf's wife, but never in his wildest dreams did he believe she had a relationship with Christophe.

Alan took the stairs down to the harbor two at time and leaped onto the yacht right when it started to move from the dock. Chloé ran toward him, but before she reached him, Christophe dove for her and wrapped his arm around her neck. He had in his hand a gun.

Alan decided to bluff Christophe: "I'll have you know a police sharpshooter has you in his crosshairs." He wasn't very convincing. In all the excitement he had forgotten Christophe didn't understand English, and the French words for sharpshooter and crosshair eluded him.

Chloé's father threw the little girl aside and trained the gun on Alan. Eva Swenson continued to motor the yacht through the harbor toward the open sea.

"If you kill me, Chloé will never forgive you," Alan said.

"Ahh!"

Chloé, now loose from Christophe's grip, had bitten his leg with all her pre-molar might. This gave Alan his chance, and he went for the gun, grabbing Christophe's wrists and pushing them and the barrel upward. The two wrestled while the little girl screamed, *"Au secours! Au secours!"*

Christophe twisted Alan's hands and pulled the gun toward Alan's chest, but Alan would not give in. With all the strength his scrawny body could muster, he thrust the weapon downward and away from his chest, using his foe's momentum. Christophe snapped the trigger, but not before Alan had shifted the mouth of the barrel toward the drug lord's crotch.

Bang!

Christophe dropped to the deck of the yacht in a fetal position, shrieking in both pain and horror. Apparently he had been shot in the balls.

Alan lunged for the gun, but froze at Eva's command to "Halt!" She had stopped the boat and grabbed Chloé. Now she held a knife to the girl's throat. "I wouldn't do that if I were you," she warned.

Alan slowly raised his hands away from the gun and toward the moonlit sky.

"Everything was going well until this stinking little brat rescued you in court," Eva said. "Rolf was dead, and you were headed for prison."

"I figured you killed him once I saw you on the boat," Alan replied. "Christophe couldn't have shot Rolf, as he was at home expecting a visit from Chloé."

Eva laughed. "Kick that gun over to me."

Alan stalled for more time. "I have to admit you had me fooled," he said. "Tell me something, Eva: What was it like being married to a petroleum engineer who never had any money?"

"Shut up!"

"I imagine it was easy for you to shoot him."

"I should have poisoned him instead, so that he would die more slowly and suffer."

"The part I missed was your involvement with Christophe," Alan said. "I would have thought a woman of your stature could have done better."

"Shut your mouth, or I'll slit her throat!"

At this, the unmistakable sound of a rifle shot rang out. The bullet missed Eva and shattered a window on the cabin instead. With the blast still echoing off the hillside, Alan dove for the knife and wrenched it from Eva's grip. She fell to the deck, hysterically sobbing. He retrieved the gun and trained it on her, while driving the yacht back to the dock.

There he told Esnault about Eva's confession. Since Chloé confirmed it, the lieutenant arrested the woman for the murder of Rolf Swenson, thereby causing Alan's nightmare to end.

* * *

At a table adjacent to the floor-to-ceiling front windows of Chez Betty, all except Chloé thrust upward a glass of champagne poured by the establishment's matron and chimed, *"Santé."* Chloé raised an Orangina, not to be outdone.

"I shot the window out to give you a chance for the knife, Al," Buck said. "If I had aimed for Eva, I might have missed and hit Chloé."

"You're right about that," Alan replied.

"Rule numero uno," Buck proclaimed. "Never take a knife to a gun fight."

Everyone laughed.

"So Al, what's next for ya? Back to work driving my pickup?"

"Maybe someday, Buck, but right now we're leaving for Disney-World."

"Pa-ree, right?"

"Nope. Orlando, Florida."

"A nice touch, my friend."

"It's only a vacation."

"And after that?"

"Villefranche-sur-Mer, where else?"

"Figured you'd say that," Buck replied. "Remember, if you ever need a job—"

"Yeah, I know. Just look for the longhorns."

Chloé eyed her watch. *"Maman, le train départ dans vingt minutes."*

After saying *au revoir* to all, Alan and his new family left Chez Betty and hurried down to the station. As they waited for their train, he reflected on whether he had found what he had been looking for in coming to France, his own pink-banded Mickey

Mouse watch. He had been taught much: thinking out of the box by meringue at the bakery, standing his ground by Buck Treadway, overcoming fear by Nietzsche, the need for balance by the tour guide at Fragonard, passion by soccer nuts like Ludovic, what freedom truly was by Fakih, and yes, love and devotion by Jeannette and Chloé.

Many lessons existed, to be sure, but the most important one still eluded him. Then, as the train stopped at the Villefranche station, and he lifted everyone's suitcase aboard, it occurred to him: the meaning he sought was not in the destination but rather in the experience of the journey in which all such lessons were taught. "Enjoy the ride," he told his new life companions.

Epilogue

Christophe Chevalier received a *"condemnation en perpétuité"* for being an accessory to Rolf Swenson's murder, obstruction of French justice, and conspiracy to murder Alan. He spends his days managing his cab company and other nefarious operations remotely from a prison cell. Lately he has expanded his business interests to include a lucrative extortion racket with Abdul. Unfortunately Christophe's love life has taken a turn for the worse in light of his incarceration and Eva Swenson's own life sentence, not to mention his severely damaged genitalia.

Lieutenant Gustave Esnault continues as a dedicated civil servant and detective for La Gendarmerie. His crowning achievement was putting away Christophe. Esnault tried to work the mob lord for criminals higher up in the French connection, but his efforts in this regard were unsuccessful, since Christophe would not crack. Lately, the lieutenant has taken up writing detective novels as a side interest. His skills in English have made him popular in the United Kingdom.

Esnault's partner in fighting crime, Monsieur Leroux, died in a tragic auto accident instigated by a fit of road rage. While driving the transport van to the Maison d'Arrêt with a prisoner, another driver cut him off. During the ensuing exchange of rude gestures, Leroux failed to notice he was approaching a train crossing. The train that demolished his van and left him and his prisoner dead was the 3:09 p.m. local from Nice to Villefranche.

Ludovic Renard, due to his cooperation with Esnault and the JI, was never charged for obstruction of justice in connection with Alan's frame. He got a job with the undertaker who did the excellent makeup work on Alan before the Citadelle disaster. Now he uses his driving skills to transport the real dead. Ludovic is still a loyal fan of Marseille and Ligue Un. However, he has yet to return to Stade de Nice.

As to Miss Perfect, she got a job doing public relations for Lignes d'Azur, the bus company. She has taken upon herself the gargantuan task of translating bus schedules and informational materials into six languages, including French, English, and German. Her goal is to make sure that no one ever has the dreadful experience again of being on the right bus going the wrong way.

Matoub finished his sursis sentence. Unfortunately, in three months he went back to the Maison for his involvement in several burglaries of tourist rentals. Although he hasn't gotten a job in the jail yet, on the outside he managed to find a young woman, and she puts money on his account so that he can *cantiner.*

Fakih went to prison in connection with his refusal to crack and provide information to the JI on a terrorist network. Upon his release, he went to school to learn how to be an official imam and opened a prison ministry involving moderate Islam. He has had numerous converts, and they have had a positive influence on the radicals at the Maison.

Buck Treadway has expanded his operations and has six drivers, who lease longhorn hood adornments from him for their vehicles. Christophe's cab company has not been a problem, since the mob lord is very familiar with the Texan's penchant for incendiary reprisal. Buck has also opened a line-dancing club in Nice, where he met a girlfriend. She shares his interest in Western apparel and cowboy-related decorative accents. Though she is French and has yet to come to terms with his spirit of independence and unabashed American patriotism, she has pledged never to abandon him. Ironically, he has offered appeasement in return.

Sara Elliot, formerly Sara Elliot-Newberg, experienced a personality transformation of her own after the divorce. She quit working as an accountant and sold the marital home in Schaumberg. This occurred after she met a yoga instructor who encouraged her to be less of a fuddy-duddy. She and her new boyfriend plan to open up a "hot" yoga business in Costa Rica with the proceeds of the home sale and her voluminous 401K portfolio that she salvaged from the divorce.

The blind lady remains a loyal member of the parish at the bell-towered church, always wearing her pillbox hat and keeping tabs on everyone in Villefranche. Nothing matching the killing of Rolf Swenson has since drawn the attention of her well-trained ears.

As to the real estate agent, he has improved his knowledge of English idioms and slang by taking an advanced class in the language. He has retired his father's pocket watch to a desk drawer and replaced it with a multi-functional time piece similar to Alan's that automatically changes for Daylight Savings time. This has helped improve his real estate business, where time is often of the essence.

Betty, Thierry and Alexis still run Chez Betty, also known as La Regence. Olympic-Marseille remains the bar's soccer team. On match nights they and the rest of the patrons can be found, rooting their team to victory.

Alan, Jeannette, and Chloé took in Disney World in Orlando. They availed themselves of most of the attractions, and Alan bought Chloé a new Mickey Mouse watch having many of the upgrades of his own timepiece. After Disney World, at Alan's whimsical suggestion, they decided to take two weeks driving Route 66 to California.

Along the way, they went to several national parks that Jeannette never knew existed.

Once their travels concluded, they returned to Villefranche via Italy, where Alan had 90 days' eligibility on his passport and could cross the French border without being stopped. If he had come to France directly, he would have been rejected at passport control at the airport, given how much time he had already spent there. At present he is bogged down in the bureaucratic process of obtaining a visa. It seems the French authorities have been unwilling to accept his documentation of health insurance coverage and financial self-sufficiency without double notarization of everyone's signature.

All of this may become moot, however, since Alan recently proposed to marry Jeannette before the setting sun at Nid d'Aigle and adopt Chloé. The adoption is possible, as Christophe's rights were cut off once he got his life sentence. Alan has decided not to change his name to Al, by the way, he having learned that the substance of a person is not determined by a label.

As far as a job to help support his small family, Alan has no grand aspirations. He still helps Jeannette with bookwork at the flower shop and works for Buck here and there. Sometimes he tends bar at Chez Betty on Marseille-match nights, when extra help is needed. Regardless, he isn't really worried, for he now lives in the moment, life being far too precious to dwell on the past or obsess about the future.

About the Author

Kenneth Farmer began his 34-year legal career as a public defender in Louisville, Kentucky, before moving back to his native Wisconsin, where he served as a prosecutor until he retired in 2011. During this time, he defended or prosecuted thousands of cases, including everything from the mundane traffic matter to the not-so-routine capital murder charge.

Farmer has lived and traveled extensively in France, speaks French fluently, and has studied the French criminal justice system with the assistance of lawyers and prosecutors from that country.

To date, he has published two novels: *Real Lawyers*, the story of a newbie public defender who proves he is a real lawyer, and now *Chez Betty*.

www.ingramcontent.com/pod-product-compliance
Lightning Source LLC
Chambersburg PA
CBHW020554260626
47157CB00003B/703